WHERE HAVE
YOU GONE
WITHOUT
ME?

WHERE HAVE YOU GONE WITHOUT ME?

PETER BONVENTRE

KEYLIGHT BOOKS
an imprint fo Turner Publishing

TURNER PUBLISHING COMPANY
Nashville, Tennessee

www.turnerpublishing.com

Where Have You Gone Without Me?

Cover design: M.S.Corley
Book design: Erin Seaward-Hiatt

Library of Congress Cataloging-in-Publication Data
Names: Bonventre, Peter, author.
Title: Where have you gone without me? / Peter Bonventre.
Description: Nashville : Keylight Books, an imprint of Turner Publishing,
    2021. | Summary:
Provided by publisher.
Identifiers: LCCN 2020054715 (print) | LCCN 2020054716 (ebook) | ISBN
    9781684426195 (paperback) | ISBN 9781684426218 (epub)
Subjects: GSAFD: Suspense fiction.
Classification: LCC PS3602.O657435 W47 2021 (print) | LCC PS3602.O657435
    (ebook) | DDC 813/.6--dc23
LC record available at https://lccn.loc.gov/2020054715
LC ebook record available at https://lccn.loc.gov/2020054716

Printed in the United States of America
17 18 19 20 10 9 8 7 6 5 4 3 2 1

For my wife, Donna, and for my son, Martin,
who make every day an adventure—and a joy

Mary Hoffmann was the first to see the miracle.

Sitting in the front pew, she removed her glasses and wiped the lenses with a crumpled tissue she pulled from her coat pocket. She was a few months shy of eighty years old, and she often joked that she believed only half of what she saw these days. She'd lately been suffering from what the doctor called "recurrent corneal erosion." Each morning when she woke up, her left eye felt like someone had sprinkled sand in it. Hurt something awful. But she'd followed the doctor's orders—eye drops during the day, ointment at night before bed—and was better for it.

Mary Hoffmann took the plastic vial from her purse and squeezed two drops of soothing liquid into her left eye. She blinked, and blinked again, and then again. She put her glasses back on, now certain she could see clearly. She knelt, leaning forward to get a closer look, then sat back down. And as she did, Mary Hoffmann thought maybe her mind was going, not her eyes.

"It just can't be," she said to herself, just loud enough for Pete Malyvos, kneeling in the pew behind her, to hear.

Malyvos whispered in her right ear, "Something wrong, Mrs. Hoffmann?"

She sniffed. "You think because it's vodka, folks can't smell you, huh?"

She kept her voice as low and as firm as she possibly could without drawing attention, without embarrassing him. She liked the young man. He worked for his father at the coffee shop around the corner, and he always gave her an extra paper cup of coleslaw with her egg salad on white toast.

"Sorry," Malyvos said sheepishly.

"You come with me, tell me I'm not seeing things."

Mrs. Hoffmann sidestepped out of the pew and into the right aisle, followed by Malyvos.

Gina Mineo was walking toward the main entrance of the church. Wearing a maroon knit cap and a belted trench coat over her white nurse's uniform, she'd made a quick stop to light a candle in memory of her mother before going to work. She was halfway up the center aisle when Malyvos's voice shattered the silence.

"My God, yes! I see it! I see it!"

"I told you!" Mrs. Hoffmann said. "Oh, Jesus, Mary, and Joseph, and here I thought I was ready for the squirrel factory."

Mineo hurried over. So did Johnny Bello, one of the altar boys who had finished serving Mass minutes earlier and heard Malyvos's astonished words as he emerged from the sacristy; and Katie Boyle, a pretty freelance accountant; and a retired cop named Daniel Simpson; and several others who had lingered to say the rosary, or pray before the marble relief sculptures depicting scenes from the Stations of the Cross that lined the side walls of the church, or simply meditate in the presence of their God.

Floyd Walker was among the last to join the crowd. The church's aging handyman arrived carrying rags and a large tin of cleaning cream to polish the brass altar railing. "What's going on here?" he wanted to know.

"See for yourself," Mrs. Hoffmann said, pointing to the statue above a black metal bank of flickering votive candles on the other side of the altar railing. The statue stood about ten feet above the floor, perched in a niche carved into the wall to the right of the altar.

Walker fell to his knees and made the sign of the cross.

No doubt about it.

St. Joseph was crying.

CHAPTER 1

EDDIE WAS ABLE TO INTERVIEW Tisdale before the cops showed up, and he was confident he had the goods to ace a column they'd at least bill on the front page.

Some twenty minutes earlier, he'd had nothing for the next day's column. Oh, he had a story he could fall back on, but it was for shit. He needed to head for his office and work the phone. He'd dressed quickly in jeans, a striped shirt, and a brown tweed jacket, and carried his dark-blue overcoat as he closed the door behind him and walked down the hall. Turning a corner to get to the twelfth-floor elevator, he noticed a strapping middle-aged man slumped against a wall, his face in his hands.

As Eddie approached him, he realized the man was crying. "Excuse me, but are you okay?"

The man looked at Eddie with red-rimmed eyes and said nothing.

"I know I've seen you around," Eddie said, then gestured toward the door next to the man's left shoulder. "This your apartment?"

"Yes."

"You okay?" Eddie said, extending a hand. "I'm Eddie Sabella..."

"I know who you are. You're the writer."

"Yeah," Eddie said, pausing, and then: "Funny, isn't it? We live on the same floor, and we've never spoken. It's so New York. What's your name?"

"Jack Tisdale," he said, and tears came streaming down his face again.

"What's wrong? Anything I can do?"

Tisdale shook his head. "It's my wife. She's dead."

"I'm so sorry," Eddie said. "When did she die?"

"A few minutes ago," he said. "I killed her."

"You what?"

"She's in there," Tisdale said. "In my apartment."

Eddie's first instinct was to reach for the doorknob and see for himself.

"You can't go in there," Tisdale said, grabbing Eddie's hand.

"Okay, but we have to call the police."

"I called the lobby, and the doorman said he'd do it." Tisdale took a long, shuddering breath. "Mind staying with me till they come?"

"Sure." An awkward silence started to gather between them, and then Eddie said, "You want to talk about it?"

When the cops arrived on the scene, they found Eddie interviewing Tisdale and taking notes. He tried to follow the officers into Tisdale's apartment, but they stopped him from entering, citing standard operating procedure.

Eddie was pissed. They recognized his name and his picture from the paper, and they claimed to be regular readers of his column. They even agreed he'd covered more murders than most cops would see in an entire career, and they had to admit he was probably savvy enough not to compromise a crime scene. Still, rules were rules. Everything was locked down until the homicide detectives arrived.

"You know the drill, Sabella," one of the cops said in an exasperated voice. "Why're you busting our balls?"

"Because that's my job."

Before Eddie left, he managed to badger the cops into describing the crime scene: The wife was seated at the diningroom table, face-down in a plate of cottage cheese and syrupy canned peaches, brains oozing out the back of her head. There was a bloody golf club on the floor.

"An 8-iron, am I right?" Eddie said, raking his fingers through some strands of dark hair that had fallen over his forehead.

"Looked like it. He told you, huh?"

"He did," Eddie said, shutting his notepad. "Thanks, Officer."

Eddie decided to hustle to the paper and start writing rather than wait for the homicide detectives to arrive and check out Tisdale's apartment. He'd call the precinct later to see if they had anything substantive to add to what he'd already pumped from Tisdale. He doubted they would.

On the way out of his apartment building, Eddie threw a few questions at Jorge the doorman to fill in some holes in his reporting. Jorge provided him with more than enough to flesh out his column.

Tisdale was a lab technician who worked nights at Lenox Hill Hospital.

According to Jorge, Mrs. Tisdale—her name was Elaine—was sullen and curt and often critical of the building's staff. She wasn't much more than five feet tall, her hair dyed pitch-black and cropped around a perpetually pale face.

Tisdale was a little taller and a lot heavier than Eddie, who pegged him for around six feet and a solid two hundred pounds or so. He told Eddie he was fifty-eight years old, and his wife was fifty-five. They had married late in life, twelve years ago, and they were childless. They only had each other, and he'd done everything he could to make a go of their marriage.

Tisdale ate lunch in his apartment every day before reporting for the four-to-midnight shift, and every day Elaine would ask him what he wanted from the deli around the corner.

"She never got me what I wanted," he'd complained to Eddie in a soft voice. "If I asked for tuna on whole wheat, she might bring me roast beef on rye. Or if I was in the mood for turkey on white with mayo, I'd get liverwurst on a roll with mustard. Like today. I wanted a simple ham and Swiss on rye with mayo. And you know what she buys me? Tongue on rye with mayo. Who puts mayo on tongue? And besides, she knows I hate tongue." Tisdale sighed heavily. "I just couldn't take it anymore."

"When she did this, when she'd come home with something you didn't ask for, what did you do?"

Tisdale shrugged. "I said, 'Thank you.'"

"Thank you?" Eddie's eyes shot up from his notepad. "Every time, all those years?"

"Well, for about five years. She started getting me lunch when we moved into this building."

"And each time you said, 'Thank you'?"

"Yes, and then I ate the sandwich she bought me."

"Why didn't you go to the deli yourself and get what you wanted?"

"I often thought about doing that, but I left it alone."

Eddie pressed, "You must've had a reason."

"That's the just way our marriage worked. She bought the sandwich, and I ate it."

That afternoon their marriage didn't work that way anymore. That afternoon Tisdale didn't say, "Thank you." That afternoon he didn't eat the sandwich she had put on a plate in front of him. Instead, he quietly watched her eat her own lunch, then went into the closet in the foyer, grabbed a club from his golf bag, and swung it with all he had in him at the back of her head.

"How many times did you hit her?"

"Just once," he said.

"You sure she's dead?"

"Oh, yes. I hit her flush with my 8-iron."

"An 8-iron? You just happened to have one in your closet?"

"It was in my golf bag."

After jotting down Tisdale's reply, Eddie stared at his notepad, then said, "Okay, now you got me wondering: Did you pick the 8-iron at random, or did you pick it on purpose?"

Tisdale rubbed the nape of his neck with his left hand, his lips locked in a tight grimace. "You know something? I have a pretty good short game, so maybe subconsciously I picked an iron. Sounds crazy…"

"Maybe not."

As the cops were stepping off the elevator, Eddie threw one last question at Tisdale. "You asked the doorman to call the police. Why didn't you call them yourself?"

"I was too embarrassed," he said.

CHAPTER 2

A guy in my building—a big guy, looked to be two hundred–plus pounds—had a wife much smaller than him. They didn't have any kids, just each other. He worked the late shift at his job, so he ate lunch at home. Every day she'd buy him a sandwich at the deli around the corner. And get this: she never, ever bought him the sandwich he'd requested. Like yesterday. The guy wanted ham and Swiss on rye with mayo. When she returned to their apartment, she presented him with tongue on rye with mayo. Tongue with mayo offended his sensibilities. So did tongue without mayo. He hated tongue.

Finally, after many years, their marriage didn't work the way it was supposed to. The guy took the sandwich she gave him, but this time he didn't eat it quietly and thankfully. No, this time he snapped—and killed her with a golf club to the back of her head. An 8-iron, to be specific.

EDDIE SABELLA SAT AT THE DESK in his cramped, book-lined office, which had a glass wall that looked out onto the newsroom. He was staring at his computer screen, reading over the first two paragraphs of his column, and he liked what he had written so far.

Max Ahern walked into Eddie's office. "If it's not a wet daydream you're having, tell me why you've got that shit-eating grin on your face."

"Because I'm the luckiest guy on the planet. A few short hours ago, Max, all I had for a column was some lame-ass tip about the mayor cracking down on parking permits for city employees."

"Oooh, makes my dick stiff," Max said.

"Glad I could help," Eddie said. "But then, on the way to the elevator, I ran into a guy who just killed his wife."

"No shit?"

"Hand to God. This one practically writes itself."

Max sat down in one of the two faded-mahogany captain's chairs in front of Eddie's desk. "Listen, I've got some pleasant news for you. After you left Pecky's last night, that redheaded reporter from the *Times* slammed down another couple of tequilas and felt loosey-goosey enough to inquire about you. Wanted to know if you were married or seeing anyone."

"I liked her. Jill Sawyer, right?"

"Yeah. I told her you weren't, on both counts."

"That's it? That's all she said about me?"

"Don't be greedy."

"You mean she made no mention of my dark, bedroom eyes?" Eddie said, a wide, boyish grin riding on the question. "Or my finely sculpted Renaissance nose? And what about—"

"Spare me, hotshot. And you'd better be careful. She looked like she was barely old enough to sit at the bar, and you're pushing forty."

"Still got three years to go. And remember, Max—I'll always be younger than you."

Max's reluctant smile suggested that he'd heard that gibe many times before. A man of medium height and large appetites, he wore his thinning, brownish hair neatly combed and his beard neatly trimmed. His shirt, a billowy, polyester palette of pink-and-green flora, barely concealed the bulge of his belly.

"By the way, Max, that shirt…uh, exactly what float do you represent in the great parade that passes by my office every day?"

"I'm a harbinger of spring in all its blazing glory."

Max had become Eddie's favorite sportswriter when he first started reading newspapers. Eddie was nine years old then. At the time, Max was a former Yale halfback of twenty-five who covered the Mets the first half of the season, the Yankees the second half. It was a plum assignment for someone so young, and Max deserved it. His game stories were perceptive and evocative, and when he turned his talent to Sunday features—profiles of third-string catchers, semi-senile assistant locker-room attendants, and others who scratched out an existence on the margins of the game—he wrote in lean, hard-boiled prose that earned him a column by his thirty-fifth birthday.

Eddie once dreamed of being a sportswriter himself, but that was before a stint at NYU's student newspaper had changed his mind. Meeting Max for the first time was one of the highlights of Eddie's early days at the paper, and even now, if he had to choose the columnist he admired above all the rest in the city, he'd go with Max.

"By the way, could you get me two tickets to the Yankees, Opening Day?" Eddie asked. "Gotta take care of my doorman."

Max stood up. "They're yours."

"Thanks, Max."

A few minutes after Max had left Eddie's office, Jake "Basic" Green, the paper's city editor, walked in. "How's it going, Eddie?"

"You're gonna love it. I still got the front page?"

"So far, but I need to get that story up online."

"Don't worry, Basic. Who's gonna beat us? I'm typing an exclusive here."

CHAPTER 3

EDDIE WAS INSTANTLY WARMED as he entered Pecky's and unbuttoned his overcoat. The walls were sheathed in dark wood that had absorbed the smells of cigarette smoke and spilled beer, sizzling meat, and cheap aftershave lotion. It wasn't the kind of joint where they brewed their own bitters and concocted trendy artisanal cocktails that cost a half-day's pay.

The bar ran the length of one side of the front room, beyond which was a dining room of equal size where customers sat in brown, vinyl-covered booths. Familiar sports photographs hung everywhere—Ali jabbing Frazier, Rose belly-sliding into third, Jordan soaring toward the basket—signed by the photographer and in some cases by the athlete featured in the picture. Elton John was singing "Bennie and the Jets" on the jukebox, a restored 1946 Wurlitzer that was programmed to play old crooners, songs from the 1950s through the 1970s, and Bruce Springsteen. Nothing else.

Eddie once had a date who wisecracked that Pecky's reminded her of *Braveheart*, only louder and with more beer. To which Max responded, "Now you know why we like it, m'dear."

"Hey, Pecky," Eddie called to the joint's owner, who carried almost 250 pounds on a five-foot-nine-inch frame, but moved behind the bar like a ballroom dancer. "If you think I came here to quit drinking, you'd be wrong."

"That'll mean a lot to my landlord," Pecky said.

Eddie jerked his head toward the other end of the bar, where Max and

Basic were watching a basketball game. "What's our boy drinking tonight?"

Pecky said, "Max's marinating in Manhattans. Says it's a perfect evening for an amber-colored drink with a cherry in it."

———

Max only drank beer during the day, but he never ordered the same cocktail two nights in a row, preferring to sample the almost endless variety of adult beverages.

Tomorrow night, he might indulge a taste for rye and ginger, and the next, an amaretto sour. The only cocktail he refused to imbibe was a gin and tonic. He'd sworn off the drink one day many years ago, when he was visiting his father in the hospital. His father was sharing a room with an elderly man who looked to be massively overweight, and the man wasn't expected to make it through the night.

"I was told by a relative of his," Max's father said in a hushed voice, "that the gentleman is dying of some nasty complications from obesity. Apparently, he loved his gin, drank at least a quart of it a day for much of his life. But it isn't the gin that's killing him—it's the tonic. Seems if you have a taste for gin and tonic, and if you're drinking a quart of gin a day...well, imagine how much tonic you're drinking it with. And here's what happened: the quinine in the tonic destroyed his adrenal gland, and he couldn't lose weight. He just got fatter and fatter, and now he'll die. Let that be a lesson to you, son."

Though his father's doctor swore the story was medically ludicrous, Max was so spooked he hadn't taken even a sip of a gin and tonic since that day in the hospital. He observed only one other strict rule regarding his eclectic consumption of cocktails. He avoided the hard stuff until, as he put it, "the sun deserts the sky." And oh, how Max loved winter, when it got dark early.

———

Pecky poured Eddie his usual: Dewar's, rocks, splash of soda. He grabbed the drink and joined his colleagues.

"I'm dying here!" Max screamed.

"Who's playing?"

"Knicks and Raptors," Basic said, "and it's too painful to watch."

Max watched the last few seconds of the game in suspenseful agony, holding his breath, then slapping his forehead with the palm of his hand when the Knicks failed to score at the buzzer. "And now I'm completely dead!"

Max had bet $200 on the Knicks, a nine-point underdog against the Raptors in Toronto. They lost 104–94. Max had come up short by a single basket, and he was sputtering, "Fucking Knicks! Fucking Marbury! Fucking Curry! And fucking Isaiah Thomas most of all! What? He couldn't squeeze two more points out of those overpaid misfits? Is that too much to ask? Is it, Eddie?"

"The team's for shit, and you know it," Eddie said. "Why do you insist on punishing yourself?"

Max hung his head, and only half jokingly said, "I'm so ashamed of myself."

"Let me buy you a drink," Eddie said, lifting Max's empty glass in Pecky's direction. "You want a refill, Basic?"

"Sure you can afford it?"

Basic's drink of choice was a Diet Coke with two limes. He abhorred the taste of booze, thought beer was too bitter and filling, and had never found a wine that heightened the flavor of his steak. And few people in the newspaper game had eaten more steaks than Basic— which was one of the reasons he was nicknamed Basic.

Jake Greene wore only white or blue button-down shirts, striped ties, navy blazers, gray pants, and black penny loafers. His daily menu never varied: oatmeal, orange juice, and coffee for breakfast; tuna on whole wheat and milk for lunch; and steak, baked potato, and salad with Italian dressing for dinner. And as the evening wore on, he unfailingly drank the same beverage: Diet Coke with two limes. The only people Eddie ever saw Basic get really angry at were waiters who delivered his Diet Coke with lemon or one lime instead of the two he had specifically requested.

Basic wasn't the sort of editor who was plugged into a socket and all lit up. He ran on batteries, like the pink bunny in the television commercials, steady and reliable. When he ran down, he'd take a week or two off, spend it with the wife in a cabin he owned up around Lake George, and come back refreshed, his bloodlust reignited for the trench warfare that was tabloid journalism.

———

It was Basic who plucked Eddie from the newsroom's pool of general assignment reporters and gave him the column when he was just thirty-three years old. At the time, everyone knew that the paper's long-time city columnist, a short, portly curmudgeon with a lisp named Chandler Wilson, was on the verge of retiring, but Eddie hadn't allowed himself to imagine he had a shot at replacing him.

Then one afternoon Basic took Eddie to a coffee shop, and after they ordered lunch, he said, "You want Wilson's column and the office that goes with it?"

Eddie stared at Basic and said nothing for several long seconds.

"Not the reaction I expected," Basic said.

"Could you repeat the question?"

Basic smiled paternally. "Do you want Wilson's column and the—"

Eddie jumped up from his chair. "You're damn straight I want it!"

"Sit down, please. Would you like to know what I want in return?"

"Anything, Basic, anything. Just name it."

"I want you to take your best swing at each and every column and hit it out of the park."

Eddie sometimes wondered how he could ever repay Basic for his guidance and countless kindnesses. He gave Eddie the name for his column: "Write Now." Gave him a new byline: instead of Edmond Sabella, he became Eddie Sabella, the reader's trusted friend. Gave him his unflagging attention. Gave him ideas, advice, and the right words when he needed them. And when Eddie hit his stride, Basic gave him the freedom to dazzle or screw up.

———

"Here it is, hot off the presses."

The three men turned from the television to see Phoebe Morris, the assistant city editor, waving a couple of copies of the next day's paper. She handed a copy to Eddie, who scanned the front page where his column began under the headline: EXCLUSIVE: DEATH BY 8-IRON. Then he checked the layout inside.

"Are we good?" Phoebe said.

Eddie pulled a look she wasn't expecting.

"What?"

"You had a cigarette on your way over here, am I right?"

Phoebe rolled her yes.

"How many times do I have to tell you? If I can quit, anybody can."

"Yes, Daddy," Phoebe said in a semi-sarcastic, girlish voice.

Eddie sighed, shaking his head. "Enough said. Can I get you a cocktail?"

"Now that's what I like to hear."

Eddie ordered Phoebe vodka on the rocks with olives, and he was pretty sure she'd hang around for another. He'd buy that one too. He adored Phoebe, an unflappable newspaper veteran who was the last person to read and double-check his column for accuracy and clarity before it went to bed.

Eddie handed the paper to Max, teasing, "Read it and weep."

Glimpsing the front page, Max said, "Whoa! You didn't tell me he scrambled her brains with an 8-iron. Love the sports angle. Now that *really* makes my dick stiff."

"What's wrong with him?" Phoebe said, looking at Eddie with a lopsided smile.

CHAPTER 4

ON HIS WAY HOME, Eddie realized he'd left his copy of the paper at Pecky's, so he stopped to buy another one.

"Ay, Eddie, I already read your column," Al said, waving a cigar in one hand and taking Eddie's fifty cents with the other. "You gotta ask yourself what this world is coming to when a guy kills his wife like that."

"I've seen worse," Eddie said.

Eddie had featured Al in one of his first columns, profiling him as one of the last of a dying breed: a Jewish owner of a city newsstand, a business now dominated by Indian and Pakistani immigrants. At seventy-five, he was still spry and garrulous, and still smoked half a dozen cigars a day.

"Yeah, well, I've already sold a bunch of papers. You got good play, right there on the front page."

"Nothing like it, Al," Eddie said. "Nothing like seeing your name in lights."

As he uttered the words, Eddie felt a ripple of excitement in the pit of his stomach—the same feeling he always got whenever he glimpsed his byline, going all the way back to his days on the NYU student newspaper, *Washington Square News*.

Early in his junior year, he was assigned to cover the murder of a prominent English lit professor, and his follow-up story—which required two weeks of relentless digging and shadowing the detectives on the case—exposed a scandalous love triangle fueled by cocaine and weekends in the Bahamas, blown apart by blackmail and a bullet to the brain.

The *Washington Square News* played the story on its front page, and several days later, an interview with Eddie appeared in the *New York Times*. He even got a call from the celebrated columnist Jimmy Breslin, congratulating him for showing up "every fucking reporter in town. And that includes me, kid."

That sealed it. Eddie walked away from his adolescent dream of hanging out with Max Ahern in the Mets press box and stepped into another—one in which he envisioned himself haunting the city's streets and courts and halls of power, not its ballparks and arenas.

Eddie took a cue from Breslin when he joined the city-side staff: report, report, report. He vowed he'd be the first reporter at a fire or a crime scene or a courtroom, wherever, and he'd be the last to leave. He'd talk to everybody and anybody worth talking to. No detail would be too small or insignificant to escape his observation and detection. He'd knock on one more door, make one more phone call, work one more hour, whatever it took to nail the kind of story that would make his readers whistle in admiration.

Before long, he became a ferocious reporter and competitor. He was hard to beat when the gloves came off. He also developed an intuitive and visceral writing style. The rules of grammar had been pounded into his head by the good nuns, but he no longer worried about such things as split infinitives and ending a sentence with a preposition. He wrote like a piano player who plays by ear. If his sentences sounded right, they were right. And he always struck the right note with his ear for the rhythms of his subjects' speech patterns: their quotes crackled on the page.

———

When Eddie got to his apartment a couple of blocks from Al's newsstand, it was sliding past midnight. He poured himself a Dewar's and turned on his CD player. On came Sinatra singing "Only the Lonely," the first track on the album of the same name. He had played it several nights before, and thought, *Fuck it*. Instead of struggling to unwrap one of three new CDs on his coffee table—and having to choose at that moment between three women he admired: Diana Krall, Amy Winehouse, and Lucinda Williams—he left Sinatra on.

One of these days, he kept telling himself, he'd have to buy an iPod, and a docking station with speakers, and every other damn accessory you could buy for it. Just for the apartment. He'd never plug an iPod into his ears as he walked around the city or rode the subway. He loved listening to music as much as the next guy, but he didn't need to listen to it every minute of his waking life.

On a night like this, though, maybe he should switch *Only the Lonely* for another album. It was one heart-wrenching song after another, each reminding him how deep the misery cut when you came home to an empty apartment with your newspaper in hand and your column on the front page.

As the fifth track, "Willow Weep for Me," kicked in, Eddie poured himself another drink, this time skipping the ice. *Sinatra and Scotch*, he thought, shaking his head and murmuring, "Don't try this at home, kids."

Eddie's mother once asked him why he spent so much time at Pecky's. He told her because that was where his friends hung out, and that was true, as far as it went. He didn't want to tell her how much he hated the silence in his apartment. That was why he drank probably more than he should. As the night crept from one hour to the next, where the hell else was he supposed to find laughter and conversation but in a saloon? Neither was waiting for him in his apartment. Not tonight. Not in several months.

Eddie drifted inside himself, remembering Carlotta and her sleepy smile when he'd bring her coffee in his brass bed. She was a blue-eyed brunette, a science teacher at a Catholic high school in Manhattan, and her intelligence and warmth magnified her beauty.

On nights like this one, he wondered why he'd let Mimi slip away. Tall and sleek and generous, she was a financial analyst at Morgan Stanley who delighted in just about anything on or off Broadway. She had picked out the brandy-brown leather chair he was sitting on, and he went for the price, said the color matched the gleam in her eyes.

And then there was Susan, a ponytailed honey-blonde who was five-foot-nothing in her bare feet. She could drop a grown man to his knees with a smile—or with any one of a number of moves she'd learned in her taekwondo class.

But Carlotta, Mimi, and Susan hadn't stuck around. He blamed the paper and the hours that kept him from them. His job was a jealous mistress, he'd told Carlotta near the end, and she'd said the cliché wasn't worthy of him. There was a chasm too wide for her to get over, was how she put it, and she doubted the paper had anything to do with it.

Carlotta later married an art history professor from Princeton and moved to Paris with him. Mimi hooked up with a doctor, and Susan went back to the boyfriend she'd broken up with the year before, a guy she'd insisted was an asshole.

Eddie wasn't sure whether it was the memory of putting Susan in a cab for the last time or Sinatra singing "Guess I'll Hang My Tears Out to Dry" that made him reach for another Dewar's—his fourth or fifth of the long night. He'd stop after this one, he promised himself.

Four months had passed since Eddie had heard from Susan, and he wondered if she still managed that dance club downtown. Once in a while, he was tempted to call her there, like tonight, when he was drinking alone and remembering that first night with her.

How she settled on top of him and shook her hair loose before pinning his arms and kissing him and promising to give him the world until he begged for mercy.

Eddie's glass was nearly empty when the final track of the album snuck up on him. "One for My Baby (and One More for the Road)" was as sad a song as was legal, the boozy lament of a distraught lover that Sinatra had turned into a punch in the gut. No man in his condition, he thought, should be allowed to listen to Sinatra sing this song, listen to him inhabit the lyrics and milk every ounce of melancholy from this ode to the unhappy end of a love affair.

Eddie had once written a column about a guy who kept playing "One for My Baby" on Pecky's vintage jukebox. His name was Jerry Stiles, a carpet salesman known around town as Jerry the Rug. He was always smartly dressed and one of Pecky's more convivial customers. Not that night. His tie hung like a noose from an unbuttoned collar, and he was drinking Crown Royal neat, one after another.

Jerry and his fiancé had busted up, and he said it was all his fault, said he deserved the heartache and pain he felt each time he played the song. When he stumbled back to the bar after playing the song for the fifth time and held up his glass for a refill, Pecky poured Jerry another drink, warned him it would be his last, and said, "Next time you come in here with the intention of playing that song again, I want to see a prescription from your doctor."

Clutching his empty glass, Eddie knew how Jerry the Rug felt that night. He'd been there a few times himself. Hell, he was almost there again right now. He also knew it would be useless to pour himself another drink. One more Scotch might help him forget Carlotta and Mimi and even Susan. One more Scotch might make his head spin fast enough to blur all the pretty faces etched in his memory.

Except one. There wasn't enough Scotch in the gin mills along Second Avenue that could spin her out of his head. Nothing could. He had spent almost fifteen years without her, and once again he reeled from the smothering presence of an absence that could still haunt him so.

CHAPTER 5

EDDIE'S REGULAR COLUMN appeared on page three in the paper and ran two days a week— Wednesdays and Sundays. If a story broke that warranted his attention, and if Basic or Phoebe wanted his take on it, Eddie would swing into action. And Eddie loved the action. It wasn't uncommon for him to write three columns a week, and occasionally even four.

The Friday after the 8-iron murder, Eddie was at his desk, working the phone for his Sunday column. He had already considered and rejected a pitch to profile Timothy J. Rooney, the president of Yonkers Raceway, who was just named the grand marshal of the upcoming St. Patrick's Day Parade, and he told a source that he was shocked, *shocked* that two building inspectors were about to be arrested for taking bribes.

"Only two?" he said. "Bloomberg should throw a party."

Eddie told the source to stay tuned, that he might be calling him back because he had nothing else going. There were days when you had to take what you could get, and hope you didn't embarrass yourself.

"The worst thing is to choke and come up with nothing at all, and leave me with a hole on page three to fill with shit," Basic warned Eddie when he'd tapped him to write the column. "Don't ever do that to me, and more importantly, don't ever do that to the paper and your readers."

And so, when Eddie's desk phone rang, he jumped on it like a fumble. The caller identified himself as a reader of the paper. He said he'd attended the twelve-fifteen Mass at St. Joseph's Church on East Eighty-Seventh Street, and stayed after Mass along with about a dozen other worshippers to say a few extra prayers.

"That's when it happened," the caller said. "The statue started to cry."

"What statue?"

"The statue of St. Joseph. It's a miracle. The statue is crying real tears."

"Okay, let's back up," Eddie said, and started taking notes. The caller's name was Mike Loughlin, and he told Eddie he was calling from the church on his neighbor's cell phone.

"There's a twelve-fifteen Mass on a Friday at this church. Really?"

"Yes. That's why I'm here."

"And you're sure you saw the statue crying?"

"Yes, I'm looking at it right now."

"And it's crying?"

"Yes."

"Will you put your neighbor on the phone?"

"Why? You think I can't see with my own eyes?" Loughlin was clearly annoyed. "I'm not crazy, you know. And if I am, Sabella, it's 'cause I been reading your damn newspaper for fifty years."

Loughlin hung up, leaving Eddie to stare at his brief notes. "What the hell," Eddie whispered to himself, and then a little louder, "When you got nothing, you got nothing to lose."

In the taxi to the church, Eddie figured it like this: even if this crying statue was some kind of hoax, or even if the tears were caused by something like a leak in the ceiling that was dripping water onto the statue's face, it was the kind of chicken shit he could turn into chicken salad. Eddie would bet against the statue shedding real tears with both hands and everything he owned. Just imagine, though. A bona fide fucking miracle? Oh, man, he could write the hell out of that.

Eddie's phone rang. It was Phoebe. She said she'd seen Eddie dash through the newsroom and wondered what was up with his column.

"Got a tip on a statue of St. Joseph that's crying. A church uptown."

"If you run into St. Peter, tell him I look forward to meeting him at the pearly gates."

"Joke all you want, but I've got nothing else shaking."

"It's oh-six, Eddie. Who's going to fall for that hocus-pocus these days?"

"Please don't disrespect my readers, Pheebs," Eddie said, grinning.

Eddie used his BlackBerry to research St. Joseph's Church and dig into its website.

By the time he got to St. Joseph's, he'd learned the church was built in 1893 in the Romanesque style, a limestone gem of columns and arches and a large circular rose window above the main entrance, with a bell tower soaring over it all. And since the church was located in the Upper East Side neighborhood of Yorkville, Eddie didn't need a website to tell him that St. Joseph's had served waves of German immigrants who'd settled there.

Inside the church, Eddie was impressed with St. Joseph's recently reported renovation, rendering it lighter and fresher than the dim churches of his youth. The walls were scrubbed clean, the statues carved out of the whitest of white marble or limestone, and the wooden pews gleamed with vigorous polishing. Stained glass windows commemorating holy events from the life of Christ—from baptism to resurrection—dominated the long east and west walls of the church.

As Eddie walked down the center aisle, he marveled at the five stained glass windows, each depicting a saint, that were arranged in a semicircle in the half-dome of the apse, behind and high above the altar. He couldn't identify a single saint. Maybe they weren't majestic enough, he thought, and thus deemed unworthy of study by the Sisters of Mercy and the Holy Cross brothers who had taught him through twelve years of Catholic schooling. Or maybe he knew them once, but so many years away from the church had blurred his memory.

When he reached the altar railing, Eddie genuflected and crossed himself, an instinctive act the nuns had baked into his DNA. He may have quit attending Mass on Sundays, receiving Communion, and confessing his sins, and he may have forgotten the images of certain saints, but he had never stopped being a Catholic.

Eddie approached the small crowd that had gathered before the statue of St. Joseph, which stood maybe ten feet above the floor in a niche to the right of the altar. He counted sixteen people, all of them staring at a man on a ladder who wore a heavy gray sweatshirt over his white collar, black pants, and black wingtip shoes. He was peering inside the niche above the statue's head.

"Who's that on the ladder?" Eddie asked a husky, sweet-faced boy.

"That's Father Keller. He's the pastor here."

"What's his first name?"

"Arthur. Father Arthur Keller."

"And who's the guy holding the ladder?"

"That's Floyd Walker. He's the handyman."

Pen in hand, Eddie opened his notepad. "What's your name, and how old are you?"

"Johnny Bello, and I'm thirteen, almost fourteen."

"He's an altar boy, just served Mass," an elderly woman chimed in. "If you're a reporter, you better talk to me. I saw the miracle first. My name is Mary Hoffmann—with two *f*s and two *n*s. I'm a widow these past four years. Want me to tell you what happened?"

"In a minute, ma'am," Eddie said, and turned his attention back to the altar boy. "Tell me, Johnny, did you see the statue cry?"

"Yeah."

"And what was your reaction when you saw the tears?"

"I was surprised. I wasn't, like, creeped out or anything, just surprised. I'd never seen a miracle before. This was my first one."

"Kinda cool, huh?" Eddie said.

"Sure. It's something I'll tell my friends about, but I don't know if they'll believe me." Then: "Hey, you really a reporter?"

Eddie asked Johnny a few more questions before interviewing Mrs. Hoffmann and then seeking out Mike Loughlin to thank him for the tip, all the while keeping an eye on Father Keller and the statue.

A fine statue, Eddie thought, unlike any other in the church. About four feet tall, carved out of wood and delicately painted, the head looked slightly too big for the body—a minor flaw, in his estimation. St. Joseph had reddish-brown hair and a beard. His tunic was a light shade of purple, and the robe over it was a darker brown than his hair and beard. And those serene blue eyes seemed to hold Eddie in their gaze from almost any angle and distance.

St. Joseph cradled the Christ Child in his left arm, and in his right, he held a green branch of white lilies, three in all. The lily, Eddie knew, was the Catholic Church's traditional symbol of purity.

The priest finally stopped poking around the area of the niche above St. Joseph's head. Still standing on the stepladder, he pulled out a half-smoked, unlit cigar from between his teeth and addressed the crowd.

"Listen up, everybody," Father Keller said. "There's a water stain in the area above the statue's head, which means we have a leak of sorts. St. Joseph wasn't crying real tears."

A low groan from the crowd prompted Father Keller to say, "I know, I know, you're all disappointed you didn't witness a miracle. Sorry. But please stay and continue praying if you'd like."

Father Keller stepped down from the ladder, and Eddie heard him tell his handyman to check out the source of the leak and get it taken care of. As the priest started walking briskly up the right aisle, Eddie stepped next to him. "Father Keller, I'm Eddie Sabella. I'm with—"

"I know who you're with."

"I was hoping we could talk about the statue."

Without breaking stride, Father Keller said, "I needed a crying statue like I need the swine flu. And that's off the record."

"Can I talk you out of it?"

"Follow me," he said, and bit on the cigar he'd been holding.

Father Keller was older than Eddie had imagined when he was up on the ladder. He was a couple of inches taller than Eddie, and he seemed in robust shape for a man who looked to be on the far side of seventy. His hair was gray and sparse, and he had a long face, a florid nose, watery blue eyes, and a no-nonsense air about him.

Eddie followed the priest out of the church and across the street. When they arrived at the rectory, a four-story brownstone, the priest held the front door open for Eddie and said, "We'll go to my office. It's down the hall."

Father Keller sat at an immense, extravagantly carved partner's desk that dominated his office, and lit his cigar. "You don't mind, do you?" he said without a hint of concern if Eddie did.

"Not at all," Eddie said, smiling to himself and sitting opposite the priest, his legs crossed, notepad opened on his lap. "You know, I had a feeling the tears were caused by a leak in the ceiling."

"Doesn't take a genius."

Right then, Eddie knew he'd found what every reporter dreams of. The cantankerous old priest was just the sort of colorful character who could animate his column.

"Okay, Father, I'm curious: What did you mean when you said you needed a miracle like you needed the flu?"

"Honestly?" Father Keller said, running a hand over his head.

"Hey, Father, I gotta tell *you* to be honest?"

"We're still off the record, so close that pad there," the priest said, and Eddie did as he was told. "What I meant was, this crying-statue business would have surely ended up being one huge pain in the ass. People from all over the city, including a lot of wackos and loony tunes, would have mobbed my church. And so would the newspapers and magazines and TV crews. I would have had to call in the cops to maintain order, and have ambulances on alert. And even worse, I'd have to deal with the cardinal and his minions sticking their noses into how I run my church. I'm one lucky S.O.B. Trust me."

"What did you think when you saw the statue crying?" Eddie said, opening his notepad again.

Father Keller stared warily at Eddie for a few beats, then: "Look, occurrences of this sort are very rare. Extremely rare. I was inclined to believe there was a rational explanation. That's why I got up on the ladder and investigated it myself."

"Your parishioners were disappointed."

"They'll get over it. What about you? Were you disappointed?"

"It would've made a helluva column."

"A helluva lot better than the guy who killed his wife with a golf club."

Eddie was pleased Father Keller had read his column. "Did you like it?"

"Yes, God forgive me," he said. He took a deep drag on his cigar, blowing the smoke up at the ceiling, then leaned in toward Eddie. "Miracle or no miracle, that statue has the makings of a good column."

"I'm listening."

The priest leaned back in his chair. "It was carved by a master craftsman, that seems obvious. He was Sicilian, but nobody knows his name. Not even Nick Arena, who gave us the statue many years ago. Do you know who he is, by any chance?"

Eddie hesitated, trying to remember where he'd heard the name before. "Sounds familiar, but I'm drawing a blank."

"He's a restaurant owner. Nonna's and Filomena's. Two of my favorites."

Eddie nodded slowly. "Oh yeah. I've been to Nonna's. I think I may have even met the guy."

Father Keller snuffed out his cigar in a round, green-glass ashtray, cleared his throat, and launched into the story of Nick Arena and the statue of St. Joseph.

Arena had come to America from Alcamo, Sicily, as a young man, and quickly found work in a bakery. He returned to Alcamo several years later, in 1965, when summoned to his father's deathbed. Suffering from stomach cancer, Giuseppe Arena died in agony, cursing God that he was ever born, cursing all the saints in such foul and violent language that the priest who administered the last rites thought he might be possessed by the devil.

Arena spent the week after the burial trying to convince his mother to come to America. He'd done well in the bakery business, and there was plenty of room in his Brooklyn apartment. It was bigger than the house in which his mother still lived. She insisted she had to stay in Alcamo to pray to the statue of St. Joseph, her husband's patron saint, which resided in the local church. It was her sacred duty, she said, to plead with St. Joseph to intercede with God to have mercy on her husband's wretched soul.

"So you know what Nick does?" Father Keller says with a wide smile, revealing a stretch of cigar-stained teeth. "The day before he's supposed to return to America, Nick presents his mother with the statue, which he'd purchased with a donation of $1,500 to the church. He told his mother she'd have to choose: follow the statue to Brooklyn with him, or find another one in Alcamo to pray to."

According to Father Keller, the statue occupied a seat between Arena and his mother on the flight from Palermo to New York. Eventually, Arena raised enough money to open Nonna's, and after his mother died, he moved from Brooklyn to Manhattan.

"That's when he made me an offer I couldn't refuse," Father Keeler said. "And this part truly is off the record. He told me he would be an exceedingly generous benefactor if I provided a suitable home for the statue in my church. He wrote a very big check to the church, and that very night I switched a marble statue of St. Joseph with that beautiful old wooden one."

"When did this switch take place?"

"Early 1985. I had just become the pastor, and here I get this gift, like manna from heaven."

"How big was the check?"

"Don't be a wise guy. I told you that's off the record."

"I had to try."

"Tread very carefully, my son. I'm a fool for Italian food, and Nick picks up a lot of checks for men of the cloth. Don't get him pissed off at me." Father Keller winked at Eddie and smiled slyly. "Will you join me in a cigar?"

CHAPTER 6

BEFORE SENDING HIS COLUMN about Nick Arena's statue of St. Joseph and the miracle-that-almost-was to Basic and Phoebe, Eddie gave it a final read. A perfect fit for a Sunday column, he thought. He was particularly delighted with the last paragraph—maybe it was a *little* over-the-top, but a sappy kicker to a column, he knew, was like catnip to a tabloid reader. And he was grateful that it had swooped into his brain just when he needed it. God, how he loved it when that happened:

> "Your parishioners seemed disappointed they didn't get a miracle," I said.
>
> Father Keller shrugged. "They'll get over it."
>
> And they will, if they look upon the statue of St. Joseph as a reminder that there are miracles all around us. And I'm not only talking about the earth spinning on its axis, the sun rising each morning in the east, the flowers blooming in spring. To the homeless, a roof over one's head is a miracle. To the hungry, it's food. For too many people in too many corners of the world, it's freedom from oppression.
>
> Read Shakespeare's *Hamlet* and listen to Beethoven's *Fifth*, and then tell me a brilliant mind isn't a miracle too. Luciano Pavarotti's voice, Derek Jeter's grace, Toni Morrison's imagination—miracles all. And tonight, when those near and dear to you are gathered around the table for Sunday dinner, remember to give thanks for the miracle of your family.

After his interview with Father Keller, Eddie had returned to his office and searched the Internet and his own paper's files to see what had already been written about Nick Arena and his statue. He found only a few pieces, and none had the detail that Father Keller had provided him with.

As he had promised the priest, Eddie called Filomena's to talk with Arena and confirm for himself how the statue had come to reside in the church and how precious the statue was to him. The maître d' told him to please hold.

"Sorry to keep you waiting," Arena said.

"No problem, Mr. Arena, I just..."

"Before we continue, let us agree that you will call me Nick, and I will call you Eddie. *Va bene?*"

"Fine by me."

"Father Keller told me you would be calling."

Turned out, the priest's account was right on the money. Arena had only two concerns. "You will, of course, honor Father Keller's request—which is mine as well—and make no mention of money."

"Yes, but can't I at least note that you are a charitable man?"

"No. The money I give to charity is nobody's business but mine."

"I can respect that, Nick."

"One more thing. Father Keller tells me he may have been too explicit about my father's last days. I am sure you can understand how hurtful it would be to have one's father described as a blasphemer on his deathbed. I would be most grateful if you simply say he died in great pain, and that my mother prayed to the statue for the repose of his soul, as any devoted wife would."

"I can do that. Is your mother still alive, by any chance?"

"Unlike my father, she died a peaceful death."

"That's a blessing," Eddie said.

"Her name was Filomena," Arena said, "and before she died, I promised her that one day I would name a restaurant after her."

Eddie closed his notepad. "I think that's a wrap, Nick. Thanks for—"

"Ah, before I forget, I host a lunch at Nonna's every March 19th, which is the Feast Day of St. Joseph. I made a vow to my mother I would always honor my father on that day with a Mass at the church where everyone can pray to our precious statue. After Mass, we eat.

Only family and friends. I hope you will come as my guest."

"I thought you'd never ask," Eddie said.

———

With his Sunday column done on a Friday night, Eddie figured he had at least two days before he had to start thinking about his next column—unless, of course, a story broke that Basic wanted him to jump on.

On Saturday, he thought he'd see a movie, but the only film that even vaguely interested him was a horror movie titled *When a Stranger Calls*, which he quickly rejected when he checked out the director and the cast and didn't recognize a single name. Instead, Eddie grabbed a subway uptown to Barnes & Noble, and was glad he did.

He'd nearly forgotten how much he enjoyed roaming the stacks of a big bookstore and scanning the rows of titles until one caught his fancy, and he could pluck the book from its perch and actually hold it. It had been months since he'd purchased a book that wasn't mailed to him by Amazon, and when a young salesperson asked if he needed any help finding what he wanted, he said, "No, thanks. Right now I'm feeling like a kid in a candy store."

"Then eat up," she said with a radiant smile.

Eddie bought *The Lincoln Lawyer*. It was climbing the bestseller charts, and he liked Michael Connelly's whiplash style of crime writing. He also ended up buying a paperback edition of *The Stranger* by Albert Camus, a classic novel he was ashamed to admit he'd never read. He vowed to get to it before he cracked open Connelly's latest.

On the subway back to his apartment, Eddie noticed a heavy, middle-aged man devouring a heaping Styrofoam plate of linguini with clams, one of his all-time favorite dishes. And when he reached his stop, an Asian woman in a blue wool beanie pulled down over her ears brushed past him and entered the subway car clutching chopsticks and a container that emitted an aroma of…fried rice? Chicken chow mein?

While walking to his apartment, he recalled that just the other day, while riding on the 6 train, two teenaged boys in their private-school blazers had sat next to him, one eating a slice of pizza, the other a hot potato knish.

He realized that eating on the subway was something of a New York tradition. A bagel, a donut, a candy bar. Okay. But *linguini con vongole*? It was hard to dispute those who claimed that this ludicrous sort of subway dining had greatly contributed to the growing rat population beneath the city's streets.

Seemed to him like a worthy subject for a column. He made a mental note to call the chairman of the MTA on Monday.

CHAPTER 7

FIRST THING MONDAY MORNING when Eddie got to his office, he called the MTA publicity department and was quickly put through to the chairman. He was pleasantly surprised to learn that, in the past few months, the MTA had received numerous irate calls about the smell and the mess from food being eaten in the subway cars. The chairman said he had a team of investigators looking into it, and he was seriously considering banning certain types of food from the subway.

"I assume linguini and clams will be near the top of the list," Eddie said, a smile in his voice.

"Yes," the chairman said, "along with Moroccan lamb and couscous. Can you believe one of my investigators saw a guy eating that with his fingers?"

The interview over, Eddie was confident he'd scored a solid column for Wednesday's paper. Basic approved it, and Phoebe asked the picture editor to assign a photographer to roam the subways and "find some messy munchers."

No sooner had he started thinking about lunch than he got a call from Max, inviting Eddie to join him and a special guest at the Jockey Club at twelve thirty.

———

Max and Moe Vogel were sitting at a small round table in the back of the Jockey Club's wood-paneled dining room. Moe was Max's bookie, a transactional relationship that had bloomed into a thir-ty-year friendship.

"Moe 'Over the River,' be still my heart," Eddie said out loud as he approached the table.

"Eddie, my love." Moe stood to embrace Eddie in a hug that would make a bear swoon. "Look at you, a real upstanding gentleman in that jacket. Very sharp."

"You've just made my day," Eddie said, pleased that a man of Moe's sartorial reputation had complimented him on his black-and-white houndstooth blazer.

"Will you two either sit down or get a hotel room," Max said.

Moe was born and raised in Greenwich Village, though for many years he worked for crews in Brooklyn. He'd also married a Brooklyn girl, and most of his closest friends ended up being Brooklyn loyalists. He was the lone Manhattan native and resident in his crowd, and after drinks or dinners or late-night poker games, he'd drive over the East River via the Brooklyn Bridge to get home. Hence, Moe's nickname: Over the River.

Moe had recently slipped past seventy-three, but he could pass for sixty on a bet. He was a large, handsome man with a pencil-thin mustache and large ears, his graying hair parted in a razor-sharp line. Moe's wife, Connie, claimed she married him because he looked like a Jewish Clark Gable. He favored custom-tailored, luxuriously soft camel-hair sports jackets, punctuated with colorful polka-dot or pais-ley pocket squares, and open-necked, white silk shirts with his initials stitched in blue thread on the cuffs: *OTR*, for Over the River.

If Eddie hadn't known Moe was a bookie, he would've made him to be a movie producer or the owner of a Mercedes dealership, some kind of occupation that required the charm and dexterity of a natural-born raconteur.

"Have a glass of wine with me, Eddie," Moe said, filling Eddie's glass from a bottle of pinot noir.

"He looks good, huh?" Max said to Eddie, flicking his head at Moe.

Eddie nodded. "That's a helluva tan, Moe. Palm Beach?"

"Got back in town yesterday. The wife likes it down there. Takes her mind off things."

"And how is Connie?" Eddie asked.

Moe paused, his eyes shedding the joy Eddie had seen in them only moments before. "It's still so hard—the pain. Just terrible, and always with us," he finally said, his voice thickening with sadness. "Coming up on five years. Five miserable, fucking years without my son."

Albert Vogel was a successful bond trader with Cantor Fitzgerald, married, and the father of two sons and a daughter, all under the age of ten. He was only thirty-three years old when he died in the 9/11 attacks on the World Trade Center.

Eddie had drinks with Albert on several occasions at Pecky's, when he'd accompany his father who would drop by the bar to settle up Max's weekend bets. An All-Ivy tackle at Columbia, he was bigger than his father and just as sweet-tempered. Eddie profiled Albert in a lengthy feature that appeared in the paper the Sunday after his death. It was the only time he could remember writing a piece while choking back tears.

"Such a smart boy," Moe said. "I wanted him to be a doctor, you know, but he said he had a head for numbers, like his old man."

"I know, Moe," Eddie said, reaching out and gently squeezing Moe's hand. "It was a privilege to write about him."

"Connie reads your story a lot, and she always cries when she's done. She says it makes her feel close to Albert. You got some talent, Eddie, to make Connie feel like that."

"I'd like to write a column on the fifth anniversary in September," Eddie said. "Maybe interview the kids. How're they doing? And how's Cathy?"

"All doing good. Cathy just started dating. I don't blame her. She's a great mother, and she has a right to live a happy life." Moe took a deep, jagged breath. "Hey, Eddie, let's lighten things up, talk about something else. By the way, in your column yesterday, you wrote about two of my favorite people."

It was hardly surprising to Eddie that Moe would know Father Keller and Nick Arena. Few men were as well-connected as Moe, who became one of Eddie's prime sources years ago when Max introduced the green reporter and the dapper bookie to each other. Moe had betting customers in every borough of the city and in every line of work—politicians, investment bankers, doctors, lawyers, college professors, actors, bartenders, plumbers, hard hats, you name it. He had the best table in the best restaurants, and always scored the best seats to the hottest Broadway plays and the most crucial games in any sport anywhere in the city.

"In that case, I hope you liked the column," Eddie said.

"You can't write anything I don't like, *boychik,*" Moe said, pinching Eddie's cheek. "I loved it. I go way back with both those guys. That story about Nick's mother and the statue and bringing it to America, all true. How'd you like to hear what wasn't in your column?"

"I'm listening."

"Whatever I tell you, Eddie, you didn't hear it from me. Got that?"

Eddie leaned in. "As always. And besides, Moe, it's a long shot I'll ever write about them again."

"Maybe so. Anyway, Nick Arena owns two restaurants outright, and has pieces of others around town. Nonna's over on Fifty-Sixth and Broadway was his first."

"I like that place," Max said.

"Who doesn't?" Moe said. "I've been eating there since it opened."

"I know about his restaurants, Moe," Eddie said. "Tell me something I don't know."

Moe took a slow, deliberate sip of his wine. "He used to operate a few bakeries for John Vitale. *The* John Vitale. They were fronts for the family's numbers business, and other things."

"Like what?"

In a low voice, Moe said, "They sometimes baked more than bread in those ovens, if you get my drift."

"I get it, and I like it," Max said. "This is getting interesting."

"Nick didn't give a damn about the numbers, or anything else," Moe said. "All he really cared about was the bakery business, and he made the family good bread with them—literally and figuratively."

"Are you saying he's a member of the Vitale crime family?" Eddie asked.

"No," Moe said, shaking his head. "From what I understood, he could've been a made man, but he had bigger plans. Word was he thought he was too good for them."

"Couldn't that get you killed?" Eddie asked.

"Come on, Eddie. You think Nick turned up his nose at Vitale to his face? He's too smooth for that. Vitale loved the guy. They both came from the same town in Sicily, and Vitale had a rep for giving young Sicilian immigrants a helping hand. Like I said, Nick shined in the bakeries, and so when he asked Vitale to bankroll him in a restaurant, they became partners in Nonna's."

Moe paused to take another sip of wine. "Nick knew that Vitale's support also meant he wouldn't have any problem with the unions. He'd get his booze and his fresh fish at a fair price. He'd get his clean napkins and tablecloths delivered every morning, and the garbage carted away every night. And so on, and so on. This was a big advantage for somebody starting out in the restaurant business, which is one of the toughest games in town. When Vitale died, Nick took full control of Nonna's, and nobody questioned it."

"Bottom line, then: Arena's not mobbed-up?" Eddie said. "He's a legitimate citizen?"

"That's what I'm saying."

"What about Father Keller?" Eddie said. "How do you know him?"

"This is also strictly between us girls," Moe said with a smile, his voice taking a lighthearted turn. "Father Keller loves the Knicks, and it's cost him plenty. But he always settles up on time. He says that betting on the Knicks is his way of atoning for his sins."

"Good for him," Max said. "If more priests were practicing the fine art of wagering instead of diddling their altar boys, this'd be a much better world."

Moe raised his hands, palms out. "I don't know anything about that. I'm Jewish."

"No shit?" Max said in mock surprise.

"Always with the jokes," Moe said, picking up the menu. "Are we gonna eat, or what?"

———

After lunch, as they were crossing Fifth Avenue, Max said to Eddie, "This place'll be a holy mess after the parade."

"What do you care? You'll be in Miami."

Each year for the past five years, Max headed for Miami in time to miss St. Patrick's Day. He wanted to avoid the inevitable debacle of running into someone like Colin Feeney, a rotund second cousin who'd once tracked him down at Pecky's and insisted on raising a few pints with his famous cousin and crooning "How Are Things in Glocca Morra"—until he threw up on Max's shoes.

That was a first, Max had complained to Eddie, though it wasn't uncommon for some drunken adolescent to vomit in his general vicinity on St. Paddy's Day, and he'd had enough. So instead of sticking around the city, he started making a pilgrimage each year to Hialeah Park, which in his words was "the most beautiful thoroughbred racetrack God has ever smiled upon."

Max had written eloquently of his broken heart when Hialeah was shut down in 2001. It was only fitting, he reasoned, that he should honor the racetrack with a column rather than celebrate the feast day of a saint who wasn't even Irish.

"Got any idea what you'll write about?" Eddie asked.

"I'm going to observe the flamingos as they prance in the pink around the infield lake. Not many people are aware they're still there."

Eddie laughed. "Shit, Max. Last year you communed with the ghost of Seabiscuit. That was weird enough. But this?"

"Yes, this," Max said testily. "I want to write about them before the bastards tear down the grandstand, drain the lake, and put up another fucking condo complex."

"When're you leaving?" Eddie said.

"Tomorrow night. I'm on the ten o'clock out of LaGuardia. You know where to find me before then."

Back at the paper, Eddie listened to his voice mail and retrieved a phone number from a guy in the MTA's publicity department. His name was Martin Gaines, and he said he was told by his boss to tip Eddie off about an incident that pertained to eating on the subway.

"We got a caller who swears he saw a rat with a slice of pizza in its mouth running along the tracks," Gaines told Eddie.

"Oh, man, this is too good to be true," Eddie said. "What subway stop?"

"He was at 103rd and Lex, waiting for the number 6, going downtown."

"He sound legit or off his meds?"

"Legit, for sure," Gaines said. "He said he's a nurse at Mount Sinai, works the late shift, and I believed him. His name is Gordon Sinclair. I told him you might call."

Eddie interviewed Sinclair over the phone and got a few more details. He said he saw the rat a little after midnight, and so did several other people on the platform. "I have only one correction I'd like to make," Sinclair said politely. "The rat wasn't running. He was sort of dragging the pizza in his mouth. That slice was twice his size, and he was having a tough time of it."

"Did you see what happened to the rat? Where it went?"

"I don't know. The train came, and we got on." Sinclair chuckled. "I'll tell you what, though—nothing was gonna stop that little guy from enjoying his slice."

"Check out my column on Wednesday, Gordon. You'll have a starring role."

Eddie planned to make another call to the MTA for an update before lunch the next day and cleared the afternoon to write in his office. He bought himself a roast chicken for dinner and ate it on the coffee table in his living room while watching CNN. When he was done, he flipped through the magazines he'd stacked on the round mahogany end table next to his couch, and then started reading *The Stranger*.

Within half an hour, he was sound asleep.

CHAPTER 8

BASIC WALKED INTO EDDIE'S OFFICE, his right thumb raised in the air. "Phoebe liked the column even more than I did," he said.

"Love that Phoebe," Eddie said with a wide grin.

"I never imagined that you could write about linguini and clams and a pizza-eating rat in the same column and it'd make sense."

"That's why you ought to pay me the big bucks."

"Speaking of big bucks," Basic said, "accounting's on my ass about your expense account. Or rather, the lack of it. You haven't filed a single one all year. Don't you want your money back?"

"It's such a pain in the ass. I'd almost rather go broke."

On his way out to meet Max at Pecky's before his flight to Miami, Eddie handed in his expense account for January and promised Basic he'd do February by the end of the week.

Max had a mojito waiting for Eddie when he arrived. "Here's to a free Havana," Max said as he clinked glasses with Eddie. "And here's to Hemingway, who fueled up on this delectable libation as he was writing the hell out of *The Old Man and the Sea*."

"I'll drink to that," Eddie said.

"Look what I found today while I was browsing at the Strand," Max said, holding up a creased and moldy copy of *Everyday Drinking* by the British author Kingsley Amis. "It's a collection of his newspaper columns on the art and principles of consuming adult beverages. I've heard it's required reading for literate imbibers such as ourselves."

"Just what we need—an intellectual approach to drinking. Come to think of it, I hate this sweet shit." Eddie placed his mojito on the bar and gently pushed it toward Max. "You drink it."

"Gladly," Max said, then shouted, "Pecky, the usual for my friend."

Pecky delivered a Dewar's on the rocks with a splash of soda, and Eddie happily consumed one more before it was time for Max to catch his plane.

"How long will you be gone?"

"Through the weekend," Max said. "You be a good boy. Don't think I haven't noticed you stealing glances at that filly over there. Can't blame you, though. Take care."

The subject of Eddie's attention was wearing a blue blazer over a white blouse.

She had red hair that fell around her shoulders, and the top two buttons of her blouse were unbuttoned, revealing a hint of a lacy black bra. She was eating a hamburger and drinking a beer while flipping through the pages of a magazine.

Eddie wondered why someone who looked like her was eating alone at close to nine o'clock in a joint like Pecky's. He had no intention of asking her—until she closed the magazine and flashed him a smile. It wasn't exactly an invitation to join her, but it was enough for Eddie to take a deep breath and approach her table.

"Excuse me," Eddie said, "but I just have to tell you—you're the loveliest woman who's walked into this place in a very long time."

She looked at him for several seconds, her wide-set green eyes demanding his attention, and then she said, "Sit down."

"Thank you," Eddie said, sitting opposite her and introducing himself.

"Liz Coyne," she said, smiling and shaking Eddie's hand. "I'm a reader of your paper."

"Good to know. We need all the readers we can get."

"I read all the papers. Have to. I'm in public relations. And trust me when I say you deserve a better picture to go with your column."

"I think this could be the start of a beautiful friendship," he said.

Liz ordered another beer and Eddie another Scotch. They spoke until they finished their drinks, and without a lull in the conversation. She told Eddie she had randomly walked into Pecky's after escorting a client to the opening of his ex-wife's ethnic-fashion boutique. They talked about their jobs and their bosses, recent movies they'd seen, and how they were both hooked on *The Sopranos*. She was rooting for UCLA, her alma mater, to win the college basketball championships, while he'd picked Duke to go all the way, even though Max frequently warned him to avoid betting on teams whose players actually attended classes and took courses like medieval literature and organic chemistry.

After exchanging business cards and promising to stay in touch, Eddie helped Liz slip into her coat and hailed her a cab. As he walked to his apartment, a song came to him from out of nowhere, and he found himself singing under his breath about her lovely smile and how it was all right with him.

When Eddie got home, he played "It's All Right with Me," one of the tracks on *Sinatra Sings Cole Porter*, thinking of Liz Coyne again and singing out loud as the song was winding down, singing about the tempting lips that weren't the lips of the one he adored—but, hey, if some night she were free…

CHAPTER 9

TOWELING HIS FACE after a late-morning shave, Eddie stared at himself in the mirror and remembered what his new best friend had said about his picture in the paper. He never gave it much thought. After all, his picture was the size of a postage stamp. Then again, it was taken almost four years ago, and though his hair was still dark and thick and his jawline still taut, he believed his face had more character than the picture revealed. Or could it be he was simply looking older?

He stepped back to get a better look at his arms and chest, took a slight breath to suck in his stomach, and felt confident that if he lost a couple of pounds, he could still run the same course up in Van Cortland Park that he'd conquered as a cross-country runner in high school.

As he pulled a pressed shirt from his bedroom closet, the BlackBerry on his night table started ringing. It was Phoebe.

"I was just thinking of you," he said.

"My heart just skipped a beat," she said in a wise-ass voice.

"I have that effect on women. Listen, do you think I need a new picture for my column?"

"Maybe we'll take an online poll of our readers," she said, teasing him.

"Very funny."

"Changing the subject, handsome, we got a call on the desk from Father Keller over at St. Joe's. He left his number, said it's important he talk to you."

Eddie called Father Keller. "Some sonuvabitch stole the statue."

"What?"

"You heard me. When our handyman opened the church early this morning, he noticed the statue of St. Joseph was gone. I called the police…"

"Have they responded yet?"

"Two cops came by, and then a detective by the name of O'Grady— Dan O'Grady."

"What precinct?"

"The 19th."

"You tell Arena yet?"

"Of course," the priest said. "He stayed calm, but he's not happy about it. He wants the statue back for the Mass to celebrate St. Joseph's Day. It's on Sunday, and that's only four days away."

"Have you talked to any other reporters about this?"

"Nope, I'm handing you an exclusive on a silver plate. You owe me a damn fine cigar, and maybe even a drink."

Eddie called Detective O'Grady, who said he had almost nothing to go on. "All I got is that the statue was taken overnight. The handyman insisted he locked everything up, but the door to the sacristy was unlocked. The door opens into the school's playground. That's gotta be how they came in, because there's no signs of forced entry anywhere."

"Strange, huh? Stealing a statue that can't be worth much, except for its sentimental value."

"That's the thing," O'Grady said. "I read your column about the statue and the restaurant owner…"

"Nick Arena."

"Yeah. The only thing that makes any sense is that since the statue means a lot to him, maybe somebody figures he'll pay up big to get it back. You know, a ransom. We talked, me and Arena, and so far, not a peep from anybody."

Eddie's next call was to Arena. He left messages at both Nonna's and Filomena's, then hustled to the paper. He conferred with Basic and Phoebe, and it was decided that Eddie should write a quick, just-the-facts-ma'am story for the website. He could insert updates as he got them.

As Eddie was banging out the story, Arena called. "I guess you have heard from Father Keller. He said he would tell you about the statue."

"I'm writing a story now for our website, and I'd like a reaction from you about the theft."

"It is quite distressing, as I am sure you understand. I am hoping the police can recover the statue in time for the Mass on Sunday."

"And suppose they can't? What will you do then?"

"What can I do?" Arena said evenly. "Life goes on."

"Detective O'Grady told me that nobody has called demanding money. That still true?"

"Yes."

"Will you pay to get it back?"

"I have not made up my mind."

"You're considering it, then?"

Arena paused for a moment. "We are serving lunch now at Nonna's, and I am very busy. May we continue this conversation tonight? It would be my pleasure if you joined me for dinner at Filomena's. Eight o'clock?"

"I'm there," Eddie said, throwing one more question at Arena. "If someone does call you about money for the statue, please let me know right away, okay?"

"*Va bene.*"

Eddie sent the story to Basic when he was done. Basic gave it a quick read and had it posted online. He told Eddie that unless someone called Arena demanding payment before the final deadline later that night, or unless the statue was found and returned, the story would run as is on page four or five in tomorrow's paper.

With a few hours to kill before dinner with Arena, Eddie started to tackle February's expense account. He'd barely finished tabulating the month's first week when he had a reporter's itch he couldn't scratch until he made a phone call. He contacted a reliable source at the FBI's New York office and asked him what the bureau had on Nick Arena, if anything. He said he'd call Eddie back.

Twenty minutes or so later, the source kept his promise. Most of the information he had on Arena was gleaned from an internal FBI report completed in 1970. Arena was one of some 1,100 mafiosi and their associates listed in the document, and his brief entry contained the date and place of his birth, his parents' names, the date he arrived in America, his address at the time, and his criminal associates.

"It says here Arena has no criminal record," he noted, "and I checked: he's still clean, not even a parking ticket. It also says, and I quote, 'He bought Nonna's restaurant, in Manhattan, NYC, on May 17, 1968. He was the manager of one and possibly two bakeries owned by Giovanni "Long John" Vitale, who allegedly backed Arena in this restaurant venture.' You know who Vitale was, right?"

"I know he was called Long John because he wore an eye patch."

"Yeah, anyway, the report goes on to say, 'Arena himself is not known to have engaged in any illegal activities, but his close relationship with Vitale suggests he is more involved in mafia rackets than is currently known. It is likely that his restaurant is one source of income for Vitale.' And that's pretty much it."

"I was told he was never a made guy in the Vitale family."

"If he was a wise guy once upon a time, he was a ghost in the mafia machine. And since Vitale died almost twenty-five years ago, he's not getting anything out of Arena's place now, if he ever was. That's all there is on Arena."

"Those bakeries were a front for Vitale's numbers operation, am I right?"

"Vitale ran numbers out of bars, pizza parlors, candy stores, social clubs down in Little Italy—you name it. In addition to his bakeries."

"I was also told, and I quote, 'They baked more than bread in those bakeries.' That mean anything to you?"

A short burst of laughter skipped though the phone line. "Funny you should ask. I was just thinking of a story that made the rounds around here. It was about a guy who managed one of Vitale's warehouses in Brooklyn, where he stashed the goods that fell off the back of a truck. Know what I'm saying? Well, this guy skims some new blenders for a big party he's throwing, and they use the blenders to make peach daiquiris. So they baked the poor dumbass to show what happens if you steal from the *capo*."

"Peach daiquiris, you sure?" Eddie asked half jokingly.

"Could've been piña coladas, but there's no doubt about the moral of the story."

"You think it happened in one of the bakeries Arena managed?"

"I have no idea. But I know a guy I can reach out to."

When he'd finished talking with his source, Eddie tapped into Filomena's website, figuring he'd check out the menu, and found out that Arena had opened the restaurant three years ago, earning raves for his culinary homage to Tuscany. He also found what was likely the most recent photo of Arena. Trim and elegantly dressed, he was front and center among the restaurant's staff. According to the caption, his daughter, Filomena, was clutching her father's right arm and kissing him on the cheek. Eddie's eyes lingered over the languid slant of her body as she leaned into her father, and although her dark, shoulder-length hair swept across the right side of her face, he could see just enough of her chin, lips, and nose to wish he could see more of her.

CHAPTER 10

EDDIE GOT OUT OF THE CAB at Eighty-Second Street and Third Avenue, and walked west until he reached Filomena's blue-and-white-striped awning that extended from the front door to the curb. Entering the restaurant, he liked what he saw: a cozy bar with seats for only ten, and opposite it, four small, round tables lined up against the wall. The walls were sandy-brown, and on top of the bar, at the end nearest the entrance, sat a large, muted-green clay vase brimming with immense sunflowers.

After checking his coat, Eddie walked past the crowded bar, gave the maître d' his name and told him that Mr. Arena was expecting him. The maître d' led Eddie into an elegant, pale-yellow dining room with fresh flowers in smoky-gray porcelain vases that rested in recessed niches along the walls.

At the rear of the dining room sat Nick Arena, his back to the wall. He stood as the maître d' neared his table with Eddie in tow. "Eddie, welcome to Filomena's," Arena said, shaking Eddie's hand. "Sit down, please."

As the maître d' walked away, the two men settled into their seats, and Arena said, "I have taken the liberty of arranging our meal. I hope it will meet with your satisfaction."

"I'm sure it will."

With a nod of his head, Arena summoned a tuxedoed captain. "Please bring the wine now, Tomasso," he said.

Eddie was struck by Arena's imposing presence and the lyrical cadence of his accented speech, which seemed more pronounced in person. He wore a pinstriped, navy-blue suit—custom-made by Brioni, Eddie guessed, or some other high-end menswear fashion house—with a white shirt and a lilac silk tie. He had alert charcoal eyes behind black, horn-rimmed glasses, and the smooth olive skin of his face and the full head of silver-streaked dark hair gave him the appearance of a corporate lion out of Milan or Rome. He was sixty-nine years old, Eddie had read somewhere, and he'd aged gracefully, a man who doubtlessly appreciated the finer things in life.

The captain had set aside the two bottles of wine that Arena requested earlier for dinner and arrived back at the table within seconds. The red was a 2003 Brunello di Montalcino Altero Poggio Antico, and the white, a 1997 Robert Young Chardonnay.

The captain poured Arena a splash of the Brunello to taste, and he nodded approvingly. He had Eddie taste the chardonnay.

"Delicious," Eddie said.

Arena smiled and said, "Two wines. One Italian and one American. A truly magnificent combination."

A waiter delivered two plates of figs with paper-thin slices of prosciutto di Parma. "The figs are fresh," Arena said. "You know, Eddie, in ancient Rome, figs were considered a sacred delicacy and offered to the gods."

"Which wine should I drink with this?" Eddie asked.

"With good wine, I do not stand on formality. Which wine with which food does not concern me, and it should not concern you."

"Suits me just fine." Eddie chose the Brunello to drink with his figs and prosciutto. "I haven't tasted figs this fresh since I don't know when."

As both were finishing their first course, Eddie said, "I assume you haven't heard anything new about the statue."

"Not a thing," Arena said, sighing sadly. "Tell me, Eddie. What manner of man steals a statue from a church, the house of God?"

Before Eddie could respond, a busboy came around to clear the empty plates, and the waiter replaced them with two plates of linguini heaped with tiny Manila clams and bathed in olive oil, garlic, and parsley.

Eddie breathed deeply, his face inches from his plate. "The aroma is enough to bring me close to heaven."

The men ate their linguini and clams without saying much, and as soon as their empty plates were whisked away, the next course was served: osso bucco alla Milanese. Taking his first bite and savoring the meat's tenderness, Eddie shook his head, letting loose a low chuckle.

"I hope it is my food that makes you so happy."

"Yes, it is, Nick, because I'm reminded of something my father used to say at the dinner table. He'd be devouring my mother's rigatoni or her eggplant parmigiana, and he'd pause and he'd say to us, me and my brother and sister, 'Don't you feel sorry for people who aren't Italian?'"

Nick laughed along with Eddie. "Was your father born in this country?"

"Yes, but my grandparents were born in Trapani."

"Ah, Sicilian, like me. Trapani is only fifty kilometers or so to the west of Alcamo, where I was born."

Eddie took another bite of osso bucco and another sip of the Brunello. "About the statue, Nick. I know you want it back for the Mass on Sunday. But suppose nobody calls with a ransom demand, or the cops can't recover it in time? Still not sure about a reward?"

"Who can say what a little more time will bring?"

The conversation waned as the two men continued eating, and then Eddie said, "You know, Nick, I couldn't find out much about you between the time you came to America and when you opened Nonna's."

"There is not much to tell."

"You're being too modest. You worked in a bakery, didn't you?"

"It was a wonderful learning experience," Nick said in a cool voice.

"Look, Nick, I'm just curious. I'm not working here. In fact, whatever is said here tonight is between you and me."

Nick sipped his wine, his eyes fastened on Eddie's. Eddie felt an urge to fill the silence between them. "Did you know Giovanni Vitale?"

"Yes, I did," Nick responded without hesitation.

"He owned the bakery where you worked, right?"

"To be precise, I eventually managed two of his bakeries. If I can recall, I think he owned four in all. The finest in Brooklyn."

"I heard they were a front for his numbers operation."

Nick poured the remainder of the Brunello into Eddie's glass. "It was common knowledge. Even the bakeries I managed provided that service to our customers."

"I also heard the ovens were used to make an example of people who crossed Vitale. Any truth to that?"

"I used to hear those rumors as well," Nick said with a pinched smile.

"Just rumors?"

Nick nodded slowly, and Eddie followed up: "Did Vitale finance Nonna's?"

"I paid him back a lot more than he put up. It was the price of doing business with him. But I have no regrets. Who else would have bankrolled me? And when he died, Nonna's was mine. No other partners. That was our arrangement, and that is all I intend to say about Giovanni Vitale and Nicolo Arena. *Va bene?*"

"Okay, not tonight, anyway," Eddie said, swallowing his last bite of osso bucco as Nick looked on with an expression that was hard to read. "Do you eat like this every night?"

The question seemed to lighten Nick's mood. "Oh, no. I am much too vain about my weight."

"I know you have a daughter who works here…"

"Filomena. She is my manager."

"Your mother's name, you told me. Is your wife involved in your restaurants as well?"

"I do not have a wife," Nick said flatly.

"Oh, I'm sorry. I didn't—"

"There is nothing to be sorry about."

A bottle of Strega was placed on the table, along with espresso and biscotti. Nick filled two tiny glasses with the yellow liquid. "*Cent'anni,*" he said, raising his glass and wishing Eddie a life of one hundred years. Eddie repeated the toast, and then each took a sip of the bittersweet saffron liqueur.

"Do you speak Italian?"

"Wish I could," Eddie said, shaking his head. "But I'll tell you what I'd settle for. All night long I've been listening to you speak and wondering: Where the hell can I get an accent like that?"

Both men laughed, and as they did, a woman's voice came slicing through their laughter. "What's so funny, Papa?"

Nick glanced over Eddie's shoulder. "Filomena, what a nice surprise. I thought you would go home after the play."

Before Eddie could greet Nick's daughter, she had already bent at the waist to kiss her father on the forehead, and as she did, her dark hair cascaded down the side of her face, briefly concealing it.

Eddie didn't get a good look at her until she straightened up, and Nick said, "Eddie, this is my daughter, Filomena."

Filomena extended her hand. "Hello, Eddie," she said with an easy smile. "It's been a long time."

Eddie drew a sudden, sharp intake of breath, not quite a gasp but something close to it. He reached out and clasped her fingers as he tried to rise from his chair. His legs wobbled. He gave up and stayed in his seat, never taking his eyes off her.

"A very long time," he said.

"You haven't changed much at all."

"Neither have you, Phyl," he said, and there was a hush of wonder in his voice.

———

Phyllis Blake. That was her name when Eddie fell in love with her, and she was impossible to forget.

Phyllis Blake, who liked vodka gimlets, chocolate Labradors and yellow Mustang convertibles, and the autumn scent of fallen brown leaves. And Jane Austen and Glenda Jackson and Madonna and Nina Simone above all.

Phyllis Blake, who would slip her arm through his and bump against his hip when he walked her home; and who walked on the balls of her feet, like a ballet dancer, when she was naked; and who made him promise again and again that he would one day take her to Rome.

Phyllis Blake, who had black eyes shaped like almonds and hair, trimmed short and parted on the left side, that was blacker than her eyes.

Phyllis Blake, who loved him, and he loved back.

The last time Eddie saw Phyllis Blake, he was twenty-two years old. She was twenty-one. She had walked out of his life, and he never knew why, and as hard as he'd tried, he never could find her. He wondered if she had married and taken her husband's name. Maybe she had died overseas somewhere. He used his reportorial skills to rummage around courthouses and dig into city property records. Then, when the world went digital, he plugged into the Internet and its countless databases. He had even checked out her high school class's tenth-year reunion, pretending to cover it for his paper. But she never showed up, and no one there had a clue as to where she was or what had happened to her.

Eddie used to worry about his obsession with Phyllis. The memory of her had often scurried alongside his nights like a snapping dog, and he wondered at what point his obsession would turn to perversion. But he'd decided long ago he had it under control.

Sometimes months went by when he didn't think of her. Not many—just enough to get him right until another night came when, on his third or fourth Scotch, he would surrender to memory, giving up shards of his past with her to Max and Basic and Phoebe. Over time they came to know the name Phyllis Blake, and what she once meant to him.

And so there he was. After fifteen years without her—without even a glimpse of her, without hearing her utter even a single syllable—and when she walked into the room and stood before him with her eyes looking into his, she could still nail him to his chair.

CHAPTER 11

EDDIE HAD PRACTICALLY DRAGGED Phyllis to the bistro bar down the block from her restaurant.

"It's hard to know where to begin, Phyl..." Eddie paused at the mention of her name. "I don't even know what to call you. Phyllis? Filomena? What?"

"Only Nick calls me Filomena. To everybody else, I'm still Phyllis. It's simply an Americanized version of Filomena. No big mystery there."

"Oh, no? You don't think it's a mystery to me that your name is an Americanized version of Nick Arena's mother's name?" Eddie shook his head. "I feel like I've fallen down the rabbit hole."

After his initial shock at seeing Phyllis, Eddie had asked Nick if he knew all along that he and Phyllis were once in love. Yes, Nick admitted, she had told him many years ago. Eddie was furious with Nick for keeping Phyllis's identity from him, but he checked himself and said nothing. Instead, he simply thanked Nick for a splendid dinner, saying he hoped Nick wouldn't mind if he and Phyllis left to have a drink somewhere.

Nick did not mind at all, but Phyllis did. She wanted to go home, said they could have dinner in a couple of days and catch up.

Catch up? *Catch up!* His head was buzzing. You "catch up" with a friend you haven't seen in a few months, not the guy whose heart you etherized when you walked out of the picture half a lifetime ago and the picture faded to black. How could she be so cool, so aloof? Even if she knew he was having dinner with Nick when she walked in on them, what were the fucking odds that fate would throw them together the way it did?

She could've shown *some* excitement when she saw him, a crazy sparkling joy in her eyes or a breathless hiccup in her voice. Shit, she didn't even bother to fake it.

Anyway, he'd spent too many years wondering what the hell had happened to her, and he'd be damned if he wasn't going to get at least a few answers before he'd let her slip away into the night.

"I guess what I need to know first is, where have you been for the past fifteen—" Eddie interrupted himself again. "And how the hell is Nick Arena your father?"

"It's complicated."

"I'll bet it is. And what about that vanishing act you pulled on me?"

Phyllis hesitated, then: "I figured if you'd wanted to find me, you eventually would have."

"Not to be too dramatic or too clichéd, but I searched high and low for you. It drove me nuts. Were you living in Europe? California? I called Stanford, and they told me you didn't return for your senior year. Did you marry and have kids and wind up in another state?" Eddie sighed sadly. "After a while, I became less and less obsessed with finding you and moved on."

"I never doubted you would," she said, avoiding his eyes.

"Oh, no, wait," Eddie said, his back stiffening. "Please don't tell me you've been living right under my nose, right here in the city."

Phyllis tilted her head and smiled. "I've only been back in New York a little more than a year."

Eddie paused, and then, with a might-as-well-come-clean shrug of his shoulders, he said, "Every now and then I'd google you, just out of curiosity. You never popped up, and now I know why. I was always looking for Phyllis Blake, but you'd changed your name."

"A long time ago, yes."

The waiter arrived at the table with Eddie's Scotch and poured Phyllis a glass of Pellegrino. Eddie nodded at the green bottle of mineral water. "You used to drink vodka gimlets, straight-up."

"Not anymore, only drink wine now. I see you still drink Scotch."

"I tried switching to wine a few times, but it always made me feel like I was a couple of drinks behind the rest of the world."

"I know what you mean," Phyllis said, her dark eyes gleaming as she threw back her head and laughed an earthy laugh that conjured up the smoky saloons and the noisy sex of those years when they were young.

God, how was it possible? Even now, she seemed beyond beautiful—she *radiated* beauty. He was willing to concede that the city abounded with men who might find other women more alluring, more bewitching. But they'd be wrong. That plush mouth and those killer cheekbones. A short, straight nose he would describe as refined rather than ordinary, and her almond-shaped, tar-black eyes were like twin magnets that pulled you in and held your gaze. She wore her black hair a lot longer than she had when they were young, and it was now threaded with a few silvery-gray strands that seemed to sparkle like slivers of glass.

Her body was fuller, rounder here and there than the last time he saw her. He liked it. She still had a body that could rattle his senses, but he couldn't allow it, not yet, not before she'd filled in the years he'd endured without her.

"On the walk over here," Eddie said, "I remembered my mother always said that someday we'd meet when I least expected it, and I'd get the answers to a lot of the questions that—"

"How is your mom, Eddie?"

"She died three years ago. Cancer. But my father's going strong, still practicing law. What about your parents?"

"Both fine. Living in Florida now, in Naples. I see them whenever I can."

"They wouldn't tell me where you'd gone, said you needed time to find yourself. Something like that. And then they moved not long after you left, and I lost touch. So tell me—exactly who *are* the Blakes?"

"David Blake is my mother's brother. He and Molly adopted me when she died. I was only a few weeks old."

"How'd she die?"

"A cerebral aneurysm."

"So your real mother, your biological mother, was Nick's wife?"

"No, they never married."

"But Nick gave you up to the Blakes when she died?"

Eddie waited several seconds for Phyllis to respond, and when she didn't, he said, "Did you grow up knowing that you were adopted and that Nick was your real father? Was that something you kept from me?"

Phyllis took a deep breath. "June 14, 1991. It was a Sunday. I left P.J. Clarke's around six…"

"That was the last time I saw you."

"I caught the six-twenty to Douglaston. When I got home, my parents introduced me to their dinner guest, a middle-aged man I'd never met before. He was well-dressed and handsome, and he spoke with an Italian accent."

"Nick Arena," Eddie said. "That's when you found out? That night?"

Phyllis nodded. "A few days later, Nick and I left for Italy, and we spent the summer together, traveling and getting to know each other. He showed me the square in his hometown where American soldiers had gathered after liberating Sicily from the Nazis. He ran up to an officer and saluted him, and a wounded Sicilian partisan—he had a bloody bandage on his eye—he picked Nick up and kissed him on the forehead. He was only six, but at that moment, he made up his mind to come to America."

"Well, good for Nick," Eddie said, without bothering to hide the sarcasm in his voice. "But what I'd really like to know is why in hell you took off with Nick like that. Without even telling me. And what about the fifteen years after that summer? What happened to you?"

"Like I said, it's complicated."

"I'm a smart guy, try me," Eddie said, irritated. "You came by the restaurant tonight because you knew I was having dinner with Nick, and you wanted to see me. You had to know I'd want to find out where you'd been all these years."

"You're right, Eddie. I went to the restaurant because I knew you'd be there. I hadn't seen you in so long, and I was curious. I'd been reading your column…"

The sentence died and seemed to float away somewhere, and then Eddie said, "When I got the column, one of the first things I thought was that maybe you'd read it, and you'd be so impressed you'd call me or show up at the paper, and tell me how much you missed me. Something like that."

"Always the romantic, huh, Eddie?"

"Hopelessly so," Eddie said, lightly touching her left hand. "I don't see a ring."

"I don't see one on your hand, either."

"I'm not married."

"Neither am I. Ever been?"

"No. You?"

"Yes," Phyllis said.

"That's not the answer I was hoping for, but I knew in my bones that some guy wouldn't let you get away for too long. How did *he* lose you?"

"It was wrong from the start. Lasted less than three years."

"Who was he? Tell me about him."

Phyllis's lips barely parted to speak when Eddie said, "No, don't. I'm not sure I want to know." Eddie paused, then: "Children?"

"No."

"Any regrets about that?"

"I still have a little time left," she said. "And besides, I now have the hips for them. Or haven't you noticed?"

"Your hips look damn good to me, lady."

Smiling ruefully, she said, "If I'd walked in here fifty pounds heavier and missing a few teeth, you'd still think I looked good, wouldn't you, Eddie?" Then, without waiting for an answer: "Please, I really should go."

"There's still so much you haven't told me," Eddie said.

"You know where I am now," she said. "What chance do I have against the best columnist in the city?"

"None."

"I truly believe you are, Eddie. The best. You're a terrific writer. And I've been so happy for you, actually realizing your dream."

"Thank you, Phyl," he said, wanting desperately to wrap her in his arms. He settled for a quick, glancing kiss on her cheek instead.

CHAPTER 12

STROLLING DOWN SECOND AVENUE, his overcoat buttoned against the windy morning air, all Eddie could think about was Phyllis. He smiled, picking up the pace. She had appeared to him out of nowhere, like a vision, and he liked what he saw as much as he ever had.

At the paper, Eddie checked his voice mail. Assorted crackpots and jokesters reported seeing the statue in various neighborhoods around the city—on Queens Boulevard directing traffic or in downtown Manhattan buying a round of beers in McSorley's. Then he hit a message that made his heart pump a little faster. It was from Phyllis. She'd called earlier that morning, said it was wonderful seeing him and looked forward to having dinner with him sooner rather than later. She left her cell phone number and her private number at Filomena's.

He replayed the message just to hear her voice again, then hung up the phone and leaned back in his chair. His elation was fleeting. What the hell was he doing? Out of thin air, she'd turned up in his life, and he was rolling over like a puppy. If he let himself fall for her as he once did, she could just as easily hurt him again. She'd had practice.

"Thinking great thoughts, or..."

Eddie bolted upright in his chair. "Hey, Basic, what's up?"

"Got nothing better to do at the moment, so I thought I'd bother you. Any ideas for Sunday's column?"

"Thinking about the statue. Also thinking about a backup, in case it doesn't pan out."

"Cops any closer to finding it?"

"Not that I'm aware of."

"If you dig up anything about the statue today, or if they find the thing, I'll get you space for a column. If not, you go again on Sunday."

"You got it. Thanks, Basic."

When Basic left, Eddie's mood took another quick turn. He called Phyllis at Filomena's. She had barely said hello when Eddie cut in: "I'd love to have dinner with you tonight. Tomorrow night too, if you'd like."

"I'm working tonight," she said, a note of disappointment in her voice. "Maybe we can have a late drink, but don't hold me to it."

"I won't."

"Promise?"

"Hand to God," he said, reflexively raising his right hand.

"Now, I've got to get ready for the lunch crowd, Eddie. Call me later, okay?"

"Count on it."

Eddie stopped by Basic's desk on his way out, telling him he'd decided to make a pit stop at the police station rather than calling for an update.

"If the statue turns up, don't forget to call for a photographer," Basic said.

When Eddie arrived at the 19th Precinct, he was directed to Detective O'Grady's desk. O'Grady was brown-bagging it, egg salad on whole wheat. The sleeves of his blue shirt were rolled up to his elbows, and he'd tucked a paper napkin under his chin. He shook Eddie's hand, then offered him a can of Diet Coke from the six-pack on his desk.

Eddie popped the top and said, "Got anything on the statue?"

"Not a thing," O'Grady said. "We questioned everyone at the church with a set of keys and everyone with access to a set of keys. Nothing. Nada. And it doesn't look like anyone stole any keys either. All sets were accounted for, none missing."

Eddie spent another fifteen minutes with O'Grady, quizzing him to get more specifics, like a list of all the people he'd interviewed and the questions he'd asked them. He thanked O'Grady, asked him to keep him on top of things, and hoped the detective wouldn't mind if he talked to the people on the list himself.

"Knock yourself out," O'Grady said.

By the time Eddie stepped outside the precinct, the wind had died down. The sun felt warmer than it should have in the middle of March, and the sky was an elegant blue, dappled with a few drifting clouds. He carried his overcoat on his arm and loosened his tie, and hadn't walked two blocks before the sun and the sky seemed to conspire to turn him into a gobsmacked teenager again. Within another block, he decided he wouldn't take the chance that Phyllis might be too busy to have a drink with him tonight. He'd show up at her restaurant and order something to eat for lunch, and hope she wouldn't think he was crowding her. She could totally ignore him, act like he wasn't even there. He wouldn't hold it against her. He'd be perfectly content just to catch a glimpse of her face when she happened to come into view.

Eddie walked the fourteen blocks or so uptown to Filomena's. The lunch crowd had thinned, and no sooner had he sat at the bar than the maître d' was at his side.

"Good afternoon, Mr. Sabella. Are you here to see Mr. Arena?"

"Yes," Eddie said, and then quickly turned his awkward little lie into a half-truth. "And Phyllis too. I just want to say hello."

The maître d' smiled slyly. "Very well," he said, and pivoted toward the dining room.

Eddie ordered a bottle of Pellegrino, and before the bartender could bring it, he spotted Phyllis heading his way, dressed in an orange blouse, black leather skirt, and a beige jacket with large gold buttons that hugged her like a glove. He couldn't name the designer of the jacket, but it smacked of money. It also smacked of sex.

"I wasn't expecting you until maybe tonight," Phyllis said, kissing his cheek.

"I was hungry, and this place was like a magnet. Great food, gorgeous manager."

"Flattery will get you the best table in the house," she said, accepting the compliment with a smile.

"Can I just eat at the bar?"

"Of course."

"I was thinking of something light, maybe a caprese salad."

"Good choice," Phyllis said. "We get the *mozzarella di bufala* fresh every morning, and our olive oil is imported from a farm outside of Pienza, in Tuscany. You can't get any better in the city."

"Running a restaurant seems to suit you better than...uh, what did you study at Stanford?"

"Clinical psychology, and isn't that just like you to remember what cocktail I liked, but not my major."

Phyllis threw him another smile before turning to walk away, then stopped after a few steps. "Oh, I almost forgot. You wouldn't believe who ate here the other night—Ginny Paley. Remember her?"

"Yeah, cute little blonde, from your high school."

"Cute little slut," Phyllis said, and then, batting her eyelashes and quoting the blonde in an exaggerated, girlish voice: "'You look just like Al Pacino, Eddie. Really you do.'"

Eddie laughed. "You did that very well."

"Ugh, she made my skin crawl," Phyllis said, faking a shudder, and went to get Eddie his lunch.

A few minutes later, Eddie's caprese salad arrived in the hands of Nick Arena. "I'm honored—the boss himself," Eddie said as Nick served him a dish of creamy mozzarella and sliced tomatoes, drizzled with olive oil and sprinkled with fresh basil.

Nick and the bartender then spoke to each other in Italian, and the bartender poured Eddie a glass of wine. "Try this one," Nick said. "Please."

Eddie sipped the garnet-red wine and sighed, closing his eyes in a dramatic gesture that he knew would please Nick.

"At its core, you can taste the hints of ripe blackberry and raspberry, no?" Nick said, his face aglow.

"Yes, and at its core, it also tastes expensive. I must insist on paying for this."

"This one small glass of wine is on the house, and that is all. I will not object if you pay for everything else." Then, with a quick laugh: "After all, Eddie, I have to earn a living."

"How can I refuse?" Eddie said, raising his glass to Nick and taking another sip.

After Eddie had eaten a bite, Nick said, "I have been thinking about our conversation last night, and I have decided to offer a reward for the return of the statue."

"How much you thinking?" Eddie said, holding a forkful of tomato and mozzarella in midair.

"Twenty-five thousand dollars."

Eddie whistled softly. "I know what it means to you, but that's an awful lot of money for an old wooden statue."

"I will pay even more if I have to, but let us keep that to ourselves. *Va bene?*"

"Okay."

"And I do not intend to press charges. Perhaps that will make my offer more attractive."

"That's your call. It's your money."

Arena poured himself a glass of wine and clinked glasses with Eddie, who said, "I intend to write about this when I get back to the paper. When the story goes up online, you might have a lot of press calling and coming here to the restaurant. Local TV too. Could be a real pain in the ass."

"I have friends in the police department. They will send me someone to keep the press outside. I do not intend to talk to anyone but you."

"Thanks, Nick."

Eddie swallowed his last morsel of lunch, then pulled out his notepad. "Where do you want the scumbag to contact you?"

"Here at Filomena's."

"Get ready for the shit to hit the fan."

CHAPTER 13

EDDIE CONFERRED WITH Basic and Pheobe as soon as he returned to the paper. "Any chance of getting the front page?" he wanted to know.

"You're a greedy bastard," Basic said with a slight smile. "You've got five hundred words. Get it up online, pronto."

Moments later, Eddie was on the phone with O'Grady, informing him about the reward. "One more thing—Arena doesn't want to press charges. He just wants the statue back."

"What about the priest? Technically, it's the church's statue, no?"

"You got me," Eddie said. "I'll call Father Keller when I hang up with you, and I'll let you know what he says."

"If the priest says he won't press charges either, don't bother. It's out of my hands. They gotta deal with the DA's office."

After talking with Father Keller—who was mildly surprised by the amount of the reward and said he would stand by Arena and refuse to press charges as well—Eddie called a college buddy at the DA's office. Jimmy Wisnewsky was a respected assistant DA in the trial division. He and Eddie were roommates in their freshman year at NYU, and through the years had kept up a solid friendship.

Eddie laid out the latest wrinkle in the stolen-statue story, and Wisnewsky said, "We'd probably decline to prosecute if we're not going to get any cooperation from either Arena or the priest. The statue can't be worth much in real dollars, so why would we waste our time, other than the fact we took an oath to lock up the bad guys. Which means you can't quote me."

"Okay, I won't, but what the hell? I'll just flat-out say it's unlikely the DA's office would prosecute a case like this."

"That'll do it."

It took Eddie a little less than half an hour to tap out the five hundred words Basic had asked for. Meanwhile, Phoebe assigned a photographer to take exterior shots of Filomena's to supplement the photos of the statue already on file. She also wanted Arena to pose for a photo. When Eddie passed along Phoebe's request, Nick politely declined, forcing her to use a grab shot from the restaurant's website.

A few hours later, Eddie was working on February's expense account when Basic stepped into his office and said, "You've got the front page."

"Wise decision," Eddie said with a smile from here to there.

"Last Sunday's column was a big hit with our readers, so we thought we'd go to the well again. We're gonna bill it as an exclusive."

Later that evening Basic and Phoebe met Eddie at Pecky's, each carrying a couple of copies of the paper. "Hot off the presses," Basic said to Pecky, holding up the front page of the paper. The headline blared:

EXCLUSIVE: $25K REWARD FOR RETURN OF STATUE

Beneath it, in smaller type, a two-line subhead read: *Restaurant Owner Says He Won't File Charges Against Thief if St. Joseph Is Returned Unharmed!*

The first twenty-five words of Eddie's column, along with his thumbnail-sized photo, ran on the front page, then jumped inside to page three, laid out with pictures of the statue, Nick Arena with his staff, and the façade of St. Joseph's Church.

"That's hot shit, my friend," Pecky said, pouring Eddie another Scotch. "On me, and here's hoping you keep those exclusives coming."

"From your lips to God's ears," Eddie said.

Nodding at Eddie's copy of the paper, Phoebe said, "So, is it up to your high standards?"

Eddie scanned the front page and complimented his editors on the layout inside. "Somehow, some way, this story is gonna get bigger. I can feel it in my gut."

Basic bought his pals another round, then went home before they could talk him out of it. When Phoebe made a move to leave a little while later, Eddie asked her to stay. He needed to talk to *someone* about Phyllis.

"I ran into Phyllis Blake last night," he told Phoebe. "Or I guess I should say she ran into me."

"The one and only Phyllis Blake?"

Eddie nodded, and Phoebe said, "Oh, this has got to be good."

"You're not gonna believe how good. Turns out, she's Nick Arena's daughter."

A wide-eyed Phoebe said, "Tell Mama all about it, please."

Between sips of his drink, Eddie recounted Phyllis's out-of-the-blue appearance at his dinner with Nick and their conversations over drinks afterward and at lunch today.

"Do we have a problem here?" Phoebe said. "You've been carrying one heavy torch for this gal for years and years. Now she's back, un-attached. She wants to see you for dinner, and seems to be interested in getting something going again. Yet...you don't seem terribly happy about all this."

"Should I be?"

"Hey, you're the one who couldn't keep away, couldn't resist slink-ing over to Filomena's for lunch, just to glance at that glorious face. And that's a direct quote. What am I missing here?"

"I don't know, Pheebs. When I first laid eyes on her, she completely undid me, and all these years later, she's done it again, and I can't fig-ure out why she's the one—the one with such a hold on me."

"Some mysteries can't be solved, and maybe they're not meant to be. But if you want to talk about it, I can play Oprah as well as any-one."

Eddie drained the last of his Scotch. "Let's get another drink," he said, motioning to Pecky with his empty glass. When Phoebe decided to switch from white wine to a vodka and soda, he said, "You're really enjoying this, aren't you?"

Phoebe smiled. "You don't see me running home to watch CNN, do you?"

Eddie knew Phoebe would listen. She always had. And she was good at it—it was one reason why she was once the paper's best city-side reporter, a pint-sized dynamo who went drink-for-drink with the boys at night and then whipped their asses on a story the next day.

After two childless marriages and two divorces, she figured it was time to slow down, and when Basic asked her to be his deputy some six years ago, she readily accepted. On the far side of fifty now, she still had the kind of taut body that could make a bishop's heart knock against his rib cage. She had faultless, caramel-brown skin—a blessing bestowed by the union of her African American father and French-American mother—and she wore her short, dark hair in a jagged cut that made her look like she'd just tumbled out of bed. A friend of Eddie's once admiringly described her hairstyle in a single word: *wicked*.

Phoebe had a string of men within easy reach—more than a few younger than she, a lot younger—who escorted her to the latest trendy restaurants and hit plays. Some got close to her, but she never believed the third time could be the charm and remained single.

"Before we get deep into it," Phoebe said, hopping off her barstool, her pocketbook in hand, "a girl's gotta do what a girl's gotta do."

"Give me the cigarettes," Eddie said.

Phoebe clutched the pocketbook to her chest, joking, "You will have to pry it from my cold, dead hands."

"C'mon, Phoebe. I know you're going to the ladies room to sneak a cigarette."

"No, I'm not."

Eddie's expression plainly noted he didn't believe her.

"I'm going to sneak a cigarette in the kitchen."

"I wish you wouldn't," he said as Phoebe sashayed toward the back of the joint.

CHAPTER 14

AFTER PHOEBE LEFT PECKY'S, Eddie settled the check, then realized he'd forgotten his BlackBerry on his desk. Back in his office, he checked his email. It was ten thirty. Phyllis would be closing the restaurant around eleven, and he'd have to call her before then to see if she wanted to meet him for a drink. She'd warned him that she might not be up for it, and he was in no mood to be turned down. Maybe he shouldn't even call her, put her on notice that this time around, he would be calling the play-by-play.

The newsroom was nearly empty and uncommonly quiet, and he knew that each minute he waited to decide whether to call her would seem like three. He knew, too, that she'd soon come stealing back into his head—and he'd wish he could feel exactly how he felt when he first caught sight of her.

———

She was dripping wet, walking along the pool deck in a blue one-piece swimsuit that clung to her in all the right places, revealing a body that was built for summer. Her smooth skin was buttered in a coppery tan and glistening with tiny bubbles of water streaming down her body, from her toned arms to her finely sculpted legs.

"Oh, sweet Jesus," Eddie said barely above a whisper, and hoped nobody had heard him.

He watched her grab a towel and run it through her short, dark hair, and as she did, she looked across the pool. He was sitting in his tall lifeguard chair, and she smiled at him just long enough for him to glimpse the large black eyes and full lips that accentuated the beauty of her face. His pulse quickened, his ears tingled. He was seventeen, and he'd never felt like this before.

That evening Eddie jogged the six blocks to his home. He burst into the kitchen and kissed his mother. "Mom," he announced, "I'm in love!"

"That's wonderful, dear," she said evenly. "What's her name?"

"I don't know."

"Don't you think you ought to find out?"

The next day Eddie found out her name was Phyllis Blake, and the following day he walked home with her and several friends after Sunday Mass. He learned she had very recently moved with her family to Douglaston, a town of tall trees and lush lawns, gracious homes, and waterfront vistas on the eastern edge of Queens. She was sixteen and had just completed her sophomore year at St. Mary's. She already knew he was going into his senior year at Holy Cross, where he was the editor of the school newspaper and ran track—and he was secretly thrilled that she'd obviously asked about him.

Within only a few days, he and Phyllis were inseparable for the rest of the summer, and for two years after that. The first time they slept together, he said, "You'll always be my girl, nobody else's. Deal?"

"Deal. I love you to pieces."

They began growing apart when Phyllis chose to attend Stanford over Columbia—which would have been only a subway ride away from Eddie at NYU—putting thousands of miles between them. Eddie had a nagging suspicion she was concealing an uncertain heart. He could always ask her, he supposed, but he was afraid she would give it to him straight and turn him inside out.

A little more than a year later, she came right out with it, gave him the old line about needing her space.

"You've been three thousand miles away—how much more space do you need?"

Over time, the answer became sadly clear. They had kept in touch, a phone call now and then, a drink or two during the holidays. A couple of months into his senior year at NYU and Phyllis's junior year at

Stanford, she called Eddie to tell him she was home for a few days and asked to meet him for a drink at the Regency Hotel on Park Avenue.

Eddie never saw it coming. She wanted him to know she was getting engaged, and once she said it, her sentences began picking up steam. He was a senior at Stanford, a computer science major, his name was Bill Paulson, he was meeting her parents tonight, she wanted them to remain friends…

"*Friends?*" Eddie said, a slick piece of anger working its way into his throat. "You couldn't tell me in a Dear John letter? What? You had to see the expression on my face as you stuck the knife in?"

"Eddie, you're being irrational, I just—"

He turned and started walking out before she could finish the sentence.

It took him several months, but Eddie finally called Phyllis to apologize. "I was such an asshole, Phyl. I've regretted what I said ever since."

"I didn't think I'd ever hear from you again," she said softly. "I hope you didn't beat yourself up too much. Bill and I had one of the shortest engagements on record. We split. He was a jerk."

"A jerk, huh? I was hoping you'd say you couldn't live without me."

"Oh, Eddie…"

He never forgot how each beat of the long silence that followed was like a jab to his chest.

Eddie was happily surprised when Phyllis reached out to him shortly after he landed a job on the city desk at the newspaper. She was home for the summer and wondered if he'd like to meet for a drink. He was nursing a Scotch when she arrived at P.J. Clarke's wearing a white linen dress with lilac polka dots that flattered her tanned arms and legs. He gave her a quick kiss, pulled up a stool, and ordered her a vodka gimlet, straight-up, not too sweet.

Eddie asked for another Scotch on the rocks with a splash of soda, and when they clinked glasses, Phyllis said, "I can't stay too long."

"I was hoping I could take you to dinner."

"My parents are having a guest for dinner, and they want me there. Another time."

"I'd like that, Phyl," he said. "Ever since you called…well, I've been thinking it'd be a crying shame if we didn't give ourselves another shot."

"And what happens when I go back to Stanford in September? Being apart hasn't worked out very well for us."

"As a great writer once put it, 'When two people love each other, they can sleep on the blade of a knife.'"

"Always the romantic, huh, Eddie?"

"Let's get a room, and I'll show you."

The brassy sound of Phyllis's laughter delighted him like it used to, and after Eddie had her laughing again and then again, he waved at the bartender for another round.

"I've got to go, Eddie, really."

"One more drink, please."

"You really don't give a damn about my liver, do you?" Phyllis said with a smile, sliding off the barstool.

"It's your heart I'm after."

"Try poetry."

"'How do I love thee? Let me count the ways. I love thee to the depth and—'"

Phyllis put a finger to Eddie's lips, kissed his cheek, and said goodbye.

"I'll call you soon, okay?"

"Okay, Eddie," she said with a generous smile that seemed like a gift.

When she walked out the door, he never imagined it would be another fifteen years before he'd see her again.

———

"Fifteen fucking years," Eddie said in a whisper, slowly shaking his head in disbelief and regret. He poured himself another drink and checked his watch. It was ticking toward eleven o'clock.

CHAPTER 15

PHYLLIS SAT AT THE BAR, sipping red wine as she studied the next day's reservations. It was ten thirty, and she found herself wondering if Eddie was coming. He hadn't called to see if she were free for a drink, as he'd said he would earlier in the day.

Phyllis chatted with the last customers to leave, an elegantly dressed couple who'd been regulars at Filomena's since the day it opened. After escorting them to the door, she checked her watch. Another fifteen minutes had passed, and still, no Eddie.

Well, what did she expect? He seemed eager enough to be with her that afternoon, but he'd probably come to his senses. It couldn't have been too hard to do. When they got together last night, they hadn't seen each other in years, and now twenty-four hours later…what? Did she really think he'd come bursting through the door, his heart on his sleeve?

After so many years apart, it was ridiculous to assume she knew him as well as she once had. Eddie didn't strike her now as the kind of guy who'd roll over just like that for another chance with her. Yeah, he got a little flirty, so what? That's what men did around her. Maybe he even wanted to sleep with her. But she had to get real here: what Eddie really wanted from her were a few answers. She had to accept it. Too many years had passed. He'd moved on.

Phyllis glanced at her watch again and then at the door. Where was he? She poured herself an inch more wine and pictured his face, stronger and handsomer with age. And those eyes, so dark and beguiling, set wide on either side of the slight bump on the bridge of his nose.

She had to laugh. Another late night, and there she was, drinking alone. Since leaving her life as a Blake behind, she'd glided from one man to another, like an exotic butterfly: falling in love with an Italian student in Florence, living with a restaurant critic in Santa Barbara, marrying a piano player in Reno. Jack the Piano Man, a nice guy who wanted to be a concert pianist, but ended up in Los Angeles scoring movies. Started playing around a lot, and not just on the piano. She filed for divorce when she realized she really didn't give a fuck what he was doing or with whom.

When she thought about Eddie, she'd tell herself that what she once had with him was no different from all her other failed romances, but she always suspected she was fooling herself. What she'd had with Eddie was different, because *Eddie* was different. A few of the others may have loved her, granted. But Eddie? He was mad for her—deeply, absolutely, illogically, with every molecule in his body.

"Powerful stuff," Phyllis thought out loud. That kind of madness, the kind that drilled into the marrow of your being, was perhaps the biggest reason why she had fallen for him. She couldn't resist it as a young woman, and she wasn't sure she could resist it now that she'd allowed herself to see him again. If Eddie walked through that door and showed even a touch of the crazy love he'd once had for her, she might let herself fall for him all over again. Truth be told, she was halfway there already.

Phyllis finished her wine and walked to the kitchen with her empty glass. She said good night to the clean-up crew and Tomasso, one of the captains who made a few extra bucks by hanging around and locking up the place. She considered calling Eddie at the newspaper, thinking maybe he was working on a story and couldn't get free. *Yeah, right*, she said to herself. Who was she kidding? Eddie didn't show up and didn't even call because he didn't want to.

Swathed in a belted, dusky-gray overcoat, Phyllis stepped out into the night, and her red beret almost flew off her head. She caught it before the wind could carry it away, and as she did, she spotted a man leaning against a car a few yards from the restaurant. He was wearing a dark overcoat, his hands shoved in its pockets, his hair blowing across his brow, and he was staring at her. The street was empty, except for him.

Phyllis took a quick step to her right, an instinctive first move to walk the other way or maybe back to the restaurant.

"Hey, Phyl, it's me," he half shouted, and she froze.

Finally, she said, "You didn't call. I didn't think you'd come."

"Neither did I."

Her voice cracked with emotion. "What now, Eddie?"

He walked toward her, his arms opened wide. "Come in from the cold."

She went to him, and he pulled her in. She tilted her head back and said, "Why didn't you call? Why didn't—"

Eddie kissed her, a deep, lingering kiss. A tear slipped down her face, glazing their lips. "If you only knew what I'm feeling right now," he said.

"I do," Phyllis said, circling her arms around his neck.

"You can't, trust me," Eddie said, smiling tenderly, "unless you can feel your blood cells colliding."

"The white ones or the red?"

"Good question. But I don't think it really matters."

"If you say so," she said, pressing her mouth to his and going limp as a willow.

CHAPTER 16

A T E I G H T T H I R T Y O N A C O L D St. Patrick's Day morning, Roger Bustamante walked east on Eighty-Ninth Street, bopping to the song shooting from his iPod earbuds directly into his brain, seemingly impervious to the wind that whipped his face and tossed his wispy black hair. Dressed in jeans, black high-top sneakers, and a pea-green army surplus jacket, he carried a dozen green carnations in a glass vase wrapped with a green grosgrain bow.

He liked people to call him Buster, a nickname he'd picked up in New York—not in Cebu City in the Philippines, where he grew up and learned to speak fluent English in high school. Buster was twenty-five and had been employed as a delivery boy at the Flower Shop Around the Corner on Eighty-Fifth Street and Lexington Avenue for four years, or some three years since his visa had expired. He shared a room with two other undocumented immigrants from Cebu City in the basement of a home in Woodside, Queens, that was owned by a distant cousin. Each young man paid Buster's cousin two hundred dollars a month in rent. In cash, of course.

He couldn't complain. He was as close to happy as a delivery boy could be, having saved enough money to bring his younger brother to New York one day soon.

At his destination, he climbed the stoop that led to the vestibule of the tenement building and searched the panel of names for the one on his delivery receipt. He pushed the little black button next to Cecilia Bello's name. Speaking into the intercom grille, Buster identified himself, and when she asked him to step outside onto the sidewalk so she could see him, he readily granted her request. Judging from her voice, he figured she was an old lady who just wanted to be extra careful.

Once outside, Buster scanned the third-floor windows, and when he spotted Cecilia Bello looking down at him, he held up the vase of carnations. He saw her wave, and then she buzzed him in.

————

Cecilia sat back down in her living room, waiting for the delivery boy to come up. She was drinking a cup of tea and watching a rerun of *Law & Order* on the Sony television that she'd once joked would outlive her. That was ten years ago, and it wasn't funny anymore. Thank God, though, she was having one of her good days. She hadn't had one of those in...oh, she couldn't remember when. At least a few weeks. Could it really be that the statue had something to do with it? Had to be, she thought. Her faith in St. Joseph was paying off, and she was going to take advantage of it, to keep praying as often and fervently as she could before she had to give the statue back.

She had cooked up a batch of scrambled eggs and bacon for Johnny before he went off to play basketball, even ate some herself. She showered and touched up her powdered face with a hint of red lipstick. She put on a white cable-knit sweater and green wool pants in honor of St. Patrick, and even thought about taking a walk around the block after *Law & Order.*

When she heard the expected knock, she went to the door, and the delivery boy said, "If you're Cecilia, ma'am, then this basket's for you."

"Oh, yes, green carnations," she said, taking the basket and placing it on a small round table next to the chair by the window. She didn't have to open the card. "That dear man never forgets. They certainly do brighten up the room, don't they?"

"Yes, ma'am. Can you please sign this for me?" the delivery boy said, handing her a pen with the delivery receipt.

"Of course," she said. She sat on the couch, signed the receipt on the coffee table, and handed it back along with the pen.

"Thank you, ma'am," he said.

"Now, wait just one second, young man, while I get you a tip,"

Cecilia said, getting up from the couch. When she did, she felt woozy and staggered a little.

"You okay, ma'am?" he said.

Rubbing her forehead, she said, "I'll be all right."

She walked to the hallway as if she were stepping on glass, then she stumbled near the entrance to her bedroom.

She was on one knee, trying to pick herself up off the floor, when the young man rushed to her. He gently helped her to her feet and half carried her into the bedroom.

"Is there anyone I can call?" he said as she laid herself down on the bed.

"No, that won't be necessary, really," she said. "But I'd be grateful if you could get me a glass of water from the kitchen."

"Sure thing," he said.

When he returned, he pointed toward the bureau at the foot of Cecilia's bed. "That's a fine statue. St. Joseph, isn't it?"

"Yes, it is," Cecilia said. "How do you know?"

"I'm Catholic too."

"God bless," she said. "If you bring me my pocketbook from the chair over there, I can give you your tip."

Cecilia gave him two dollars and thanked him for being so kind.

"My pleasure, ma'am. You take care of yourself."

Alone now, Cecilia was left to wonder if he had recognized the statue. He didn't act like he had—but how could he not? It was all over the newspapers and the local news on television. He seemed like a personable and well-mannered young man, the type who had an education, the type who would read a newspaper if only for the sports, and maybe the story of the reward for the stolen statue caught his attention on the morning's front page.

Oh, what a fool she'd been. She should have had Johnny put the statue in the closet before he left to play basketball. Then again, how was she supposed to know a nice young man would end up helping her into her bedroom?

"He knows, he knows," Cecilia said in a voice shaken by anxiety, and then she clasped a hand over her mouth and began to weep. As soon as Johnny got home, she vowed, she would make him return the statue to the church.

CHAPTER 17

FOR MUCH OF THE NIGHT, Eddie and Phyllis had tried to make up for lost time, both in and out of bed, and when Eddie awoke alone, he smelled coffee and called Phyllis's name.

She was gone.

He dragged himself into the bathroom and guzzled a glass of Alka-Seltzer to neutralize last night's booze. Smacking his lips, he looked at himself in the mirror and said out loud, "God, how I love the taste of Alka-Seltzer in the morning."

He splashed his face with cold water and brushed his teeth, then walked to the kitchen for a cup of the coffee that Phyllis had left for him. She'd also left him a message on a piece of notepad paper:

Dear Eddie, Thanks for listening. It's a long story and needs more time to tell it all. —Phyl xoxoxo

That was all she wrote, and Eddie was disappointed with the note's seeming lack of affection. Not even the slightest hint of the sex, which had been pretty terrific. And, my God, how he hated those cutesy *X*s and *O*s.

At least, Eddie thought, he'd gotten a few answers to questions that had eaten at him for fifteen years.

———

Nick and Phyllis's mother had met at a cooking school in Bologna, where they had a brief and passionate affair. Her name was Emma, a graduate of Vassar who dreamed of becoming a chef. Nick wanted her to return to America with him. He offered her a job at Nonna's, wrote her letters, called her, but she resisted. She never told Nick she was pregnant, never told him she'd had his baby. And if one day she intended to—as her sister, Molly, believed she did—she didn't get the chance. As she lay dying from a cerebral hemorrhage, she implored Molly and David to adopt Phyllis and raise her as their own until she was old enough to learn about Nick, probably never imagining they'd wait until Phyllis was twenty-one to tell her about her real father.

The Blakes, Phyllis explained, were unable to have children of their own, and they held on to her for as long as they could. They always knew where to find Nick, and when they finally told him about Phyllis, he broke down and cried, and then he lashed out in anger. But he came to appreciate how much the Blakes loved his daughter and how well they had raised her. She visited the Blakes each Christmas in Naples, Florida, where they'd settled after David retired, and she'd made a vow to bring flowers to her mother's grave in Boston at least once a year.

"Do you still grieve for her?" Eddie asked.

"Yes, but not simply because she was my mother. After all, I never knew her. I grieve for her because she was too young to die."

Eddie pressed her to explain how she could've left him hanging without even a phone call or a letter through all those years. She said, "I was so confused for an awfully long time. I didn't know who I was, who I should love and care for more—David or Nick? Molly or my real mother? So many questions. Suppose my mother had lived and married Nick and raised me? Would I have ever met you? Would I have gone to Stanford, or Vassar, like she did? Would I have worn my hair short, or long like her? And on and on…

"I felt I had to decide between being Phyllis Blake or Phyllis Arena. I chose to change my name, to bury Phyllis Blake and dig myself out as Phyllis Arena. You know—a fresh start, a clean slate. And to do that, I had to leave everything behind. It may not make much sense now, but back then, it seemed like the sanest thing in the world to me."

Eddie wasn't happy to hear that Phyllis had fallen in love in Florence, and that after Nick returned to New York, she'd stayed in Italy another year. When they were young, Phyllis made Eddie promise he'd one day take her to Rome, and he was pleased when she crossed her heart and told him she had never set foot in the city.

"How could I?" she said. "I was afraid it would have been too sad."

———

After showering and shaving, Eddie checked his BlackBerry for messages, and found one left by his FBI source. It read, "Sorry it took so long to get back to you about Arena and the bakeries. I got jammed up. Call me."

Eddie called his source, and they agreed to meet in fifteen minutes at a coffee shop across the street from the newspaper. On the subway ride downtown, he sat opposite a pretty young woman who'd dyed her hair green and was making out with a guy in a cheap, glittery-green top hat. When they got up to leave, the girl said to Eddie, "You Irish?"

"Afraid not."

"No problem," she said, kissing Eddie on the lips.

"Thank you," Eddie said, grinning as she and her top-hatted friend darted out of the subway car. It was much too early to start celebrating, and he hoped by the end of the night the two of them could still remember where they lived.

At the coffee shop, Eddie found Sebastian Harris in a booth. He was already eating a bagel with his coffee and reading Eddie's story about the reward for the statue. He was a twenty-five-year veteran of the FBI, a sturdy, drill-sergeant presence in a dark-gray suit, white shirt, and green-and-blue-striped tie. When he reached out to shake Eddie's hand, Harris said, "I don't have much time, but that shouldn't be a problem. I don't have much to tell."

"Then why am I buying you breakfast?" Eddie said, smiling sarcastically as he took off his overcoat.

"Don't be a cheap bastard. I could've hit you up for a fancy lunch."

"Lucky me," Eddie said. "Let's hear what you got."

"It's impossible to determine if Tieri or anybody else used any ovens in a bakery that Arena managed."

"Who's Tieri?"

"Oh, that would be Gaspar Tieri. Way back when—I'm talking

late sixties—the NYPD had flipped a guy who said he witnessed Tieri burn someone in one of Vitale's bakeries. But guess what? The witness disappeared before the trial, and nothing ever came of it. Tieri was a bad actor, the kind of dirtbag who always kept a shovel in the trunk of his car. Get my drift? He's still mobbed-up, but he's a lot older now and a lot more cunning. He operates a funeral home down on Sullivan Street. The Tieri & Sons Funeral Home."

"What's the bottom line here?"

"At the very least, it's hard to believe Arena didn't know Tieri and didn't know what was going on in some of those bakeries."

"I had dinner with Arena the other night, and he freely admitted running numbers out of his bakeries. I guess it's not surprising he denied that anybody was baked in one of his ovens."

"Where are you going with this, anyway?"

Eddie shrugged. "Probably nowhere. Until you called me for coffee, I'd almost forgotten about it."

CHAPTER 18

GUGLIELMO "WILLIE" STRACCI had the phone glued to his ear, taking the orders that poured in for shamrocks and green carnations and green roses and green every damn thing.

Willie operated four flower shops in Manhattan, all of them called The Flower Shop Around the Corner, all of them open seven days a week. A veteran of almost thirty years in the business, he once experimented with keeping his shops up and running around the clock. His pitch: "We're open all night—because you never know when you might fall in love!"

Within months, Willie realized that if a guy had fallen in love by two or three in the morning, chances were slim he'd be wandering the streets in search of a place to buy a dozen roses. He'd either be getting laid, or trying like hell to get laid. Willie's bid to create a new paradigm for his business was a bust. The money spent on electricity, wages, and other costs to keep the shops open all night exceeded the money earned on flowers by a wide margin.

Willie's favorite shop, and his smallest, was located on Eighty-Fifth Street and Lexington Avenue. It was a short walk from the brownstone where he rented the bottom floor, and it served as the base of his operation. Several years ago, he'd forbidden certain large pots of flowers and plants—the ones that concealed packets of heroin and cocaine—from being delivered to that shop. The other three shops picked up the slack and assumed the distribution that the Eighty-Fifth Street shop normally would have handled.

Willie was sixty-seven years old and feeling it, and was seriously thinking about retiring to Florida, maybe Boca Raton or Vero Beach, somewhere near the ocean. His cyclopean body had lost a slab of muscle here and there, his broad shoulders sagged a little now, and his stomach strained against the buttons of his shirts. But he still had the hard face and large, meaty hands of a man who could tear you apart in no time at all if he were so inclined.

Even at his age, everything about Willie screamed *badass*. Except for one thing: his toupee. His boyhood friend Gaspar Tieri had recently recoiled in something very much like horror when he saw Willie's newest hairpiece.

"The fuck, Willie! It looks like a rug."

"That's what it is, Gaspar," Willie said with a puzzled expression.

"I mean, it's like a real rug, a shag. And that fucking color!"

"What?" Willie said, lifting his eyes toward his brow. "It's brown."

"It's shit-brown, to tell you the truth," Gaspar said, scrunching his nose like he was actually smelling shit. "My God, Willie. This is like—what?—the seventh or eighth toup you bought since I've known you, and they never look right. You should've got the plugs years ago when I advised you to."

But Gaspar knew perfectly well that Willie would never go for transplants, because of the needles. When Willie was seventeen, he'd dropped out of high school and spent most days lifting weights and turning his six-foot-four, 250-pound body into a triumph of chiseled muscle. So impressive was Willie's ripped transformation that word had reached Gaspar Tieri, the coolest guy in their Brooklyn neighborhood.

Gaspar was a couple of years older than Willie, and Willie admired him from afar: he had the coolest hair, wore the coolest clothes, and drove the coolest car—a powder-blue Buick Roadmaster convertible. He was on his way to becoming a made man in the Vitale crime family, and acted the part with brio.

It was Gaspar who suggested that Willie enter the annual Mr. Coney Island contest on the Fourth of July. Gaspar was willing to bet a boatload on Willie, but he insisted that Willie first had to make a few visits to a certain neighborhood doctor for shots of a special medicine that was like vitamin B. He told Willie the shots would help with the definition of his muscles. Willie resisted, said he'd rather stick his head in a pot of boiling olive oil than go anywhere near a doctor with a needle.

Willie never did enter the Mr. Coney Island competition. Like Gaspar gave a shit, because he came to realize that Willie's muscles had endowed him with other talents—talents Willie himself wasn't yet aware he possessed. Talents that the Vitale crime family could maximize to their fullest potential.

So one day Gaspar introduced Willie to the underboss of his crew. Willie was soon on track to becoming something of a legend in the Vitale crime family, thanks to his implacable willingness to maim and kill and the creativity with which he carried out his assignments, and he was eventually rewarded with an executive position in four flower shops.

When Willie was first installed in the floral trade, Gaspar was doubtful he could succeed. "You got a big public-relations problem, Willie. You look like a guy who doesn't know fuck-all about flowers."

Turned out, Gaspar was only half right. Willie may have had the cold sunken eyes and the clotted brow of someone whose ancestors nailed Christ to the cross, but he also had the verdant heart of a greenhouse guru.

Willie himself had sent Buster out with the first orders on St. Paddy's Day morning, as the retired fireman he employed to manage the shop, Joe Regan, had called in sick. Willie didn't believe him, but he figured if the guy wanted to celebrate his heritage by drinking and puking his day away, what the fuck. And anyway, no biggie. Willie enjoyed working out front. He couldn't explain why, but he was good at it.

"I swear to God, I don't know where I inherited it from," he'd tell anyone who marveled at his knack for picking the precise plant or floral arrangement that was sure to please any customer seeking his counsel.

Willie was almost done taking his umpteenth order of the morning when Buster burst into the shop, a rolled-up newspaper in his hands. "Mr. Stracci! Mr. Stracci!" he said breathlessly. "You gotta see this! Hurry up! Please!"

Holding the phone with one hand, Willie used the other to grab
Buster by his jacket collar, and threw him a look that sent a clear and
simple warning: shut the fuck up or else.

Buster shut the fuck up. Willie completed the order, and when he
hung up, Buster said, "Mr. Stracci, I saw the statue! Saw it myself. It's
the one! The old lady over on Eighty-Ninth, it was in her bedroom! I
swear!"

"Calm down, Buster, you're gonna pop a blood vessel."

"She has the statue!" Buster said, laying out the paper on the counter and pointing to the photo of the statue that accompanied Eddie's
story about the reward. "That's the statue of St. Joseph I saw in her
bedroom when she fainted..."

Gazing at the photo, Willie said, "What the hell was it doing in
her bedroom?"

"I don't know, Mr. Stracci. I only know there's a big reward.
Twenty-five thousand dollars. See? It says so in the newspaper. You
have to get it for me."

"The fuck you talking about?"

"If I tell them where the statue is and pick up the reward myself, I'll
have the papers and the TV cameras all over me, and they'll find out
I don't have my green card. I don't want to be deported. You get the
reward for me, I'll give you five thousand dollars."

"Very fucking generous of you, Buster, but I don't need the publicity
either—hear what I'm saying? And anyways, when they ask me how I
knew where the statue was, what the hell am I supposed to tell them?"

"We gotta think of something, Mr. Stracci," Buster said, despera-
tion in his voice.

"I can't think of anything until I read the fucking story."

As Buster paced in a tight circle, Willie started reading the paper.
Within a few seconds, a widening smile animated his face, lingering
there until he finished the story.

"You stay here and handle the phone," Willie told Buster. "I'll fill
the orders when I get back."

Willie grabbed his coat and headed for the door. He took Buster's
newspaper with him.

CHAPTER 19

WHEN HE ARRIVED AT THE NEWSPAPER after talking to his FBI source, Eddie promptly tapped into the voice mail on his office phone. He quickly ran through another collection of cranks and nutjobs until he landed on a voice that was high and thin and exceedingly polite. Within seconds, he was positive it belonged to an elderly lady:

"Hello, Mr. Sabella, this is...oh, excuse me. My grandson brings me the paper first thing every morning, and I always read your column. You are a fine writer. I am calling to assure you that the statue was not taken by anyone who means it harm. Nor was it taken by anyone who is looking for a reward. No crime was committed, not really, not in a strict legal sense, I don't think. The statue is...well, Mr. Sabella, it was borrowed. It is safe and being well taken care of and will be returned to the church very shortly. And we won't ask for a single cent. You needn't worry, and neither should Father Keller. He is a fine, God-fearing man, isn't he? I am very happy you wrote so nicely about him. Uh, that is all, I guess. Thank you very much for listening. Goodbye."

Eddie immediately transferred the message to his digital recorder and transcribed it on a file in his computer. He then called Basic.

"What's up?" Basic said, standing in Eddie's doorway.

Eddie waved him in. "Listen to this," he said, and replayed the message.

When it was done, Basic pounded Eddie's desk with his fist. "Yes! I love it. Is this a great country or what?"

"Hold on, Basic. I don't want to bring you down, but how can we be sure it's not a crank call?"

"Aw, shit, Eddie, she's a little old lady. Can't you tell? And little old ladies don't make crank phone calls."

"Says who?"

"Says the city editor who's gonna run that message on the front page. You just got yourself a column for tomorrow's paper."

"You're the boss, but we have to assume she's not the one who snuck into the church, grabbed a ladder, climbed it, and carried off the statue. If she's legit, then she knows who's got the statue."

"I'll buy that."

Eddie picked up his phone.

"Who you calling?"

"If you listen carefully to the message, sounds like she knows Father Keller," Eddie said. "I'll play it for him, maybe he'll get a hit off the voice."

Eddie called the rectory and was told that Father Keller had attended a St. Patrick's Day communion breakfast and wouldn't return for at least another hour. "Does he have a cell phone? No? That's what I figured. If he happens to call in, please tell him I'm looking for him. If not, I'll see him at the rectory when he gets back. Thanks."

When Eddie hung up, Basic said, "By the way, what about the cops in all this?"

"I won't call O'Grady until I get to Father Keller. If he knows who the old lady is, I want to make sure I get to her first."

"Seems only fair," Basic said, smiling impishly.

CHAPTER 20

GASPAR TIERI DRANK HIS COFFEE, smoked his cigarettes, and read the newspaper. He always enjoyed mornings here at his funeral home, so quiet and peaceful before the crowds of mourners arrived after lunch. He had bought the establishment on Sullivan Street in Little Italy from Alberto Basirico in 1975, thanks to a loan from Don Giovanni Vitale. It wasn't Gaspar's idea of a business he could wholeheartedly embrace, but Vitale was keen on diversifying his portfolio of legitimate investments, and he handpicked Gaspar to front the funeral home because, he said, his loyal soldier was blessed with a serious nature. Back then, it was called the Basirico & Sons Funeral Home, and after Gaspar purchased it with Vitale's money, he renamed it.

The Tieri & Sons Funeral Home also served as Gaspar's headquarters, where he conducted other, more profitable businesses for the Vitale crime family. Gaspar was one of the family's toughest and longest-serving members, but an unfortunate incident many years ago had weighed on his ascension through the ranks. It wasn't until he started collecting social security that he was elevated to acting underboss, a temporary replacement for Frank "Blue Boy" Azzurro, who was on the mend from open-heart surgery.

When he got the news of his promotion, he told his old friend Willie Stracci, "Just my luck the fucker will recover with all his facilities, but at least I'll have my day in the sun."

Gaspar had a sharp nose and chin, and a full head of steel-gray hair, neatly slicked back with the same Wildroot Hair Cream he used as a kid. Back then, everybody called him "Ducks," a reference to the greasy ducktail haircut he was constantly combing. But then, one day Vitale told him to lose the nickname; it showed disrespect toward Anthony Corallo, who was gaining prominence as Tony Ducks because of his knack for ducking prosecution.

When Vitale gave him the order, Gaspar was visibly upset. "Wipe that look off your face!" Vitale screamed at him. "It's only a bird, for fuck's sake. It's not like I'm asking you to lose your baptized name. We're talking about a fucking bird here!"

Thus, Gaspar became the only wise guy in the long history of the mafia whom anyone could ever recall losing a nickname.

Decades later, the memory of that slap at his manhood still made Gaspar's small, scornful eyes blink rapidly behind his wire-rimmed aviator glasses. But hell, he'd outlived Tony Ducks, and that gratified him. At sixty-nine, he was a wiry five-foot-eight. He thought of himself as a sharp dresser. He favored dark suits and black cap toe shoes, white shirts with starched collars and French cuffs, and powder-blue silk ties; he'd switch to black silk ties during business hours, out of respect for the dead and the grieving families that assembled in the four parlors of his funeral home.

Gaspar was working on his second cup of coffee and third Lucky Strike when Willie walked into his office and laid out Buster's newspaper on his friend's desk.

"See that?" Willie said, pointing to the picture of the missing statue. "I know where it is."

"How the fuck do you know?" Gaspar said in a rush of words that sounded like his larynx was paved in wet pebbles.

Willie told him about Buster and the fallout from the delivery of a vase of green carnations to a Cecilia Bello at 372 East 89th Street.

"Buster's hoping I got a way to secure him the reward so nobody knows it's him and he don't get deported," Willie said.

"What's it mean to my life if he gets deported?" Gaspar said.

"Nothing, but I had to keep him quiet before he did something stupid."

"What're you thinking?"

"Maybe you could give him a few thousand for the information."

"He'll be happy with that?"

"I'll explain it to him."

"Let's hear."

Willie shrugged. "I'll tell him it's how it's gonna be. Take the money, and don't make waves."

Gaspar paused, lighting another cigarette. "I'm getting a hard-on right now for that statue," he said, grabbing his crotch. "Now that you tell me where it is, I want it real bad, Willie."

"I figured."

"Get rid of him," Gaspar said.

"What?" Willie said, his head jerking back a little.

"You heard me. Get rid of your boy."

"The fuck, Gaspar. He's a good kid, hard-working."

Gaspar drilled Willie with his beady eyes. "What must be done, must be done, my friend. I gotta have that statue."

"But he don't know about you, about our connection. I didn't say shit I was coming over here with the information."

"Listen to me, Willie. Use your fucking brain. The kid delivers flowers to this old lady, and not too long later, the statue goes missing from her apartment. The cops ain't that stupid. You gotta assume they trace the kid to your shop. The kid's connected to you, and you're connected to me. Even if you give me a hundred to one the kid plays dumb, like he don't know nothing about any statue, I don't like the odds. He's dead, he don't talk. Even better, he's dead and they don't find the body, they can't prove a fucking thing. Now, those odds, I like. Can't beat 'em. You hear me?"

"Yeah, yeah. It's just that I'm feeling bad about that poor fucking kid. I didn't mean for this to happen to him when I come in here."

"Do me a favor, and stop with the sympathy shit," Gaspar said, suddenly launching into a coughing jag that made Willie squirm in his chair.

When Gaspar's hacking cough finally subsided, Willie asked, "Who you gonna use to get the statue?"

"Outsourcing it, someone from outside I like. I don't wanna involve anyone in my crew in this type of personal situation."

Willie's face curled up like a fist. "Hold on, Gaspar. You're involving me, wanting me to get rid of Buster."

"That's different."

"How's that different?"

"It just is. Take my word for it."

Gasper rose from his chair, gently grabbed one of Willie's ham-hock biceps, and steered him to the entrance of the funeral home. He spoke in a whispery voice: "Look, Willie, I know this'll be hard on your emotions. But if I know human beings, the kid's not gonna settle for two or three thousand. He'll end up being a big fucking problem, trust me. You gotta nail the loose lips before they can sink the ships."

Back at his desk, Gaspar unlocked the bottom right-hand drawer and pulled out one of the half-dozen prepaid cell phones he stored there. He called Arnold "Kat" Katcavage, a freelancer he often hired when he had business of a personal nature that needed attending to. He was reliable and resourceful and a clean deal, not a single arrest on record. Which put him at the top of the list when Gaspar needed to outsource a job.

After discussing the assignment with Kat and settling on a price, Gaspar said, "You know the drill. You never mention my name, and you ditch your people before you pull in here. I don't want to see anyone in that fucking car but you."

"I know, I know…"

"And when you get the statue, take the FDR Drive on your way down here. All those goddamn drunks that are in for that parade can fuck up a wet dream."

"When you want it?"

"Like that, I want it," Gaspar said, snapping his fingers. "I can't take a chance the cops get to the old lady first, or she calls the priest and confesses her sin for stealing it. Like I said, looks like she lives alone. Piece of cake. And leave her alone. Understand? Not even a scratch. I don't need this to turn into a big fucking headache."

A smile slowly spread across Gaspar's face when Kat promised him he'd have the statue after lunch.

One of the many virtues Gaspar admired about Kat was the respect he showed for another man's privacy. He never asked why. Like now— if he read the papers, maybe he thought Gaspar was after the reward, but he really couldn't give two shits why Gaspar wanted the statue. He just got the job done. He was the real deal.

The call ended, and Gaspar wandered into the parlor where a cousin of his—a trombone player who had died suddenly of a heart attack—was laid out in a top-shelf, black, walnut-and-steel casket. He knelt before the corpse and offered a quick Hail Mary for the repose of his cousin's soul. He then tucked the cell phone he'd used to call Kat in the pocket of the dead man's snazzy plaid jacket. Gaspar had once lent him a couple hundred bucks to get his trombone out of hock, and now it was his cousin's turn to return the favor and take the cell phone—along with any trace of his conversations with Kat—with him to his grave.

"Thanks, Cousin Jimmy," Gaspar murmured, patting the corpse's shoulder. "I really appreciate this."

CHAPTER 21

EDDIE WAS WAITING for Father Keller in the visitor's room off the foyer when the priest returned to the rectory.

"Finally," Eddie said. "Must've been a helluva communion breakfast, huh? It's almost time for lunch."

"Nice seeing you too," Father Keller said. "To what do I owe the honor of your esteemed presence?"

"Can we go to your office?"

Eddie followed Father Keller down the hall. "Tell me, what's so important?" the priest asked as he sat behind his desk.

Eddie played the message on his digital recorder. The priest listened intently, and when it was over, Eddie asked, "Recognize the voice?"

"Am I supposed to?"

"Well, it sounds like she knows you. I'm betting she's one of your parishioners."

Father Keeler sighed, rubbing a hand over his gray-haired head. "And one of the kindest and most faithful, at that."

Eddie tried to contain his excitement. "Who is she?"

"Looking for another front-page story, are you?"

"Guilty."

Father Keller rose from his desk and said, "Let's go."

Eddie and the priest walked side by side toward Eighty-Ninth Street. "Her name is Cecilia Bello. You interviewed her grandson, Johnny Bello, a few days ago."

"The altar boy, right?"

Father Keller nodded. "A very sad story. She's been Johnny's sole guardian ever since his parents died in a car accident three or four years ago, and now she's got some sort of blood cancer. When she goes, I don't know what'll happen to the kid."

"Tough break," Eddie said. "I'm thinking maybe the kid took the statue."

"I assume so. He's been questioning me an awful lot about what happened the other day. He's convinced the statue actually cried, that he witnessed a miracle. And he was really upset that his grandmother was too weak to come to the church and pray to the statue."

"So he brought the statue home to her. And if she prayed to the statue..."

"He probably thought she'd be cured of the cancer," Father Keller said. "Breaks my heart. Johnny's a solid kid. He's just desperate, and so is his grandmother—she doesn't want to leave him alone in the world. Is that a crime? Do you have to splash their story all over the paper?"

"Father, you know better than to ask me to bury a story."

"We can just take the statue back to the church and say that some anonymous soul left it outside the sacristy door. The police will buy it, I'm sure. What's the harm in that? Nobody gets hurt. You'd still have the story before anybody else."

"You're asking me to lie, Father. A big lie, a lie that'll deceive an awful lot of people who read the paper."

"Come to confession," Father Keller said with an elusive smile, "and I'll absolve you of your sin."

"I'll need that in writing," Eddie said with an elusive smile of his own.

The priest and the columnist turned west on Eighty-Ninth Street. A few paces later, and they were climbing the stairs to the building's lobby. Father Keller rang Mrs. Bello's bell three times before she got on the intercom and, recognizing the priest's voice, buzzed him and Eddie in. The door to her walk-up apartment was ajar, and when they stepped inside the living room, they found Mrs. Bello sitting on the couch, her arms wrapped around herself, sobbing.

"Now, now, Mrs. Bello, what's wrong?" Father Keller said, sitting next to her and patting her on the shoulder.

As Father Keller tried to console Mrs. Bello, Eddie's eyes darted around the room in search of the statue. He spotted a couple of green carnation petals that had fallen on the carpet from a bouquet on a small table near the window. He picked them up and absentmindedly put the petals in his coat pocket.

"They took the statue, Father," Mrs. Bello said through her tears. "I'm sorry, I'm so sorry."

"Who took the statue?" Eddie said.

Mrs. Bello turned to Father Keller. "Is he a friend of yours?"

"Yes, that's Eddie Sabella. I think you know who he is."

"Oh," she said, looking at Eddie. "Did you get my message? I left it early this morning."

"I did. Father Keller recognized your voice. That's how we knew to come here."

"You said the statue was safe with you," Father Keller said. "What happened?"

"Two men barged in here and took the statue. They never even buzzed."

"How long ago?" Eddie said.

"Twenty minutes, maybe half an hour," she said, kneading her hands. Then, to the priest: "I was going to call you, but I've been in such a state."

Taking notes, Eddie said, "What did they look like?"

"I don't know. They were wearing those wool masks that cover your head and your face."

"Ski masks," Eddie said.

Mrs. Bello turned to the priest. "Oh, Father, what will we do?"

Before the priest could answer, Johnny entered the apartment, a basketball under his arm. "Johnny!" she cried.

Johnny hustled to his grandmother's side, knelt before her, and held her hand. "What's going on, Grandma? You okay?"

"Oh, Johnny, the statue's gone. Two men came in here and stole it. It's gone."

Father Keller got up from the couch, went to Eddie, and said in a low voice, "This puts a different slant on things, doesn't it?"

"We gotta call O'Grady."

CHAPTER 22

WHEN THE WHITE HONDA ACCORD pulled into the Tieri &
Sons Funeral Home parking lot, Gaspar was waiting. Kat had called
ahead, and Gaspar told him to park the car alongside the double doors
in back, where the bodies were delivered. Kat, he knew, had dropped
off his associate at La Mela's on Mulberry Street and planned to join
him when his business with Gaspar was done.

Kat slid out of the car, cradled the black garbage bag in his arms,
and followed Gaspar through the brightly lit, white-tiled embalming room. As they walked past the four empty mortuary tables, Kat
rubbed his nose. "What's that smell?"

Gaspar pointed to a large, shiny metal tank in the far corner.
"Comes from the embalming fluid in there. It's got formaldehyde and
methanol and some other shit mixed in. I keep everything clean as a
whistle, but after you use that stuff a few years, you can't get rid of
the smell."

"Gives me the creeps, this place," Kat said. "You ever watch them
making up the bodies when they're here?"

Gaspar shrugged. "I've seen a lot worse, believe me." He led Kat
into his office and locked the door. "Let me see it," he said.

Kat placed the black garbage bag on the desk and lifted it off the
statue, like he was unveiling a painting or a priceless vase. "That's one
good-looking statue," he said.

Gaspar ran a gentle hand over St. Joseph's head, and his eyes delighted in the craftsmanship and subtle coloring. "You're telling me?

It was made in the old country, that's why. They're real artists over there."

"Listen, Gaspar, I gotta bounce, okay?"

Gaspar unlocked the top drawer of his desk and handed Kat an envelope. Kat shoved it in his back pocket without counting the $1,500 he was owed. That was another aspect of their business relationship Gaspar appreciated: trust.

"You enjoy the statue, Gaspar, and I wish you the best of luck with it."

"Thank you, Kat."

Gaspar pulled the black garbage bag over St. Joseph's head and body, and Kat helped him place the wrapped statue on its side behind the couch to the right of his desk. Then, locking his office door behind him, he led Kat out the same way they'd come in.

As he watched Kat drive away, Gaspar allowed himself a satisfied smile. He had managed to deprive Nick Arena of something that was of great value to him. If he had known about the statue and how much it meant to Arena before reading the story in that morning's paper, he would've snatched it from the church himself years ago.

Then again, maybe not.

Gaspar realized destiny had kissed him on the cheek, giving him the opportunity to snatch the statue from an old lady in her home. He hadn't had to take it from God's own house and risk bringing down a terrible curse on his head.

All in all, everything had worked out just fine. It was never too late to even an old score.

CHAPTER 23

"I don't know how they got in, Detective," Mrs. Bello said, sitting on her couch between Johnny and Father Keller. "Like I told Father Keller, they never buzzed me from downstairs, and they didn't knock or ring the bell on my door. The first time I saw them was when they came into my bedroom. I was lying down, resting."

"You said they had ski masks on," O'Grady said. "Can you tell me anything else about their appearances? What they were wearing, things like that?"

"One was wearing a leather coat, brown leather. The other one...he was taller and skinnier...he was wearing a heavy black jacket."

Eddie stood near the window, taking notes, letting O'Grady ask the questions without any interruption from him.

"Did they say anything?"

"Only the taller man. He handed a big black trash bag to the other man, the one in the leather coat, and said, 'Open it.' And while he held it, the taller man put the statue in. I must say, he handled the statue very gently."

"Did they say anything else?" Father Keller said.

"No, nothing. I said, 'Please don't take it. It's not mine. It belongs to the church.' But they just went about their business, as if they didn't hear a word I said. And then they were gone."

"You got any questions, Eddie?" O'Grady said.

Eddie held out the palm of his hand to Mrs. Bello, showing her the green carnation petals he had kept in his pocket. "I found them on the floor when I came in. They came from that arrangement over there. Was it delivered this morning?"

Mrs. Bello's right hand fluttered against her chest. "Oh dear." She shifted her eyes to O'Grady. "I would have remembered eventually, but in all the excitement, I forgot to mention it sooner."

"Mention what, Mrs. Bello?" O'Grady said.

"Well, when I was watching *Law & Order* this morning, a young man delivered those carnations, and when I went to get him a tip, I fainted. The next thing I knew, he was helping me onto my bed."

"Did he see the statue?" Eddie said.

Mrs. Bello nodded. "He admired the statue, and he knew it was St. Joseph. He told me he was a Catholic."

"But did he know it was the same statue from our church?" Father Keller said.

"I can't say for certain, but I think he did."

After Mrs. Bello provided a description of the delivery boy, Eddie said to O'Grady, "You think he tipped off those two jabonies?"

"Very possible," O'Grady said, and then, turning back to Mrs. Bello: "Who sent you the flowers?"

With the help of her grandson, Mrs. Bello got up from the couch. "I never opened the card, but I know who sent them," she said, walking toward the carnations.

She opened the card and read it aloud: "'Happy St. Patrick's Day, and may you have the luck of the Irish. Oliver.'"

"He sends them every year," she said. "He's my doctor. Oliver Taylor. I'm a McGrath from Far Rockaway, you see. Bello's my married name."

"There's no indication of the flower shop on the card," O'Grady said. "Did you sign something, get a receipt?"

"Oh dear, he never gave me one."

O'Grady was plainly disappointed. Then, looking at Johnny, he said, "Now it's your turn, young man. Did you tell anyone that you had taken the statue and brought it here?"

"No, sir, nobody."

"How'd you get the statue out of the church?"

Johnny said, "I hid on the floor under one of the pews and waited for Mr. Walker to lock up and leave. Then I took the ladder out of his closet in the back. That's what I used to climb up and get the statue. It wasn't heavy. I could carry it easy."

O'Grady said, "The sacristy door was unlocked when I checked it. That how you left?"

"Yeah, I walked out into the school yard. It was late, and it was dark, and nobody saw me. I wrapped it in my coat to make sure."

"One more question, for the record," O'Grady said. "Why'd you take the statue?"

"He did it for me," Mrs. Bello said in a sorrowful voice, pulling her grandson close to her. "He was hoping for a miracle. Don't blame him. He's only a child, a frightened child. Blame me. I should have known better. It was my responsibility to return the statue, and I didn't. It's my sin, not his."

"Johnny, the statue never cried, did it?" Father Keller said.

"No," Johnny said, bowing his head. "Not that we saw."

"One more thing," O'Grady said to Mrs. Bello. "I'll need to reach your doctor. I'm sure he can tell us where he ordered the flowers from."

Mrs. Bello gave O'Grady her doctor's phone numbers. "That's it for me," O'Grady said, and then, turning to Johnny: "And you'll be hearing from me, young man."

On the street, Eddie said, "It's gotta be about the money, right? I doubt those two thugs took the statue for prayer meetings."

"They probably figure," O'Grady said, "if Arena's willing to pay as much as twenty-five grand for the statue, they could squeeze him for more."

Father Keller joined Eddie and O'Grady, and said to the detective, "They're scared as hell up there. I hope you can cut them a break."

"I presume you're not going to press charges against the boy," O'Grady said.

"For what—believing in miracles?"

"You'd make a helluva defense attorney, Father," O'Grady said, breaking into a smile for the first time since arriving on the scene. "Shouldn't be a problem."

"When you get ahold of the doctor, let me know pronto, okay?" Eddie said to O'Grady.

"I know you're gonna try to get to him first, so don't forget to share," O'Grady said. Then he turned to the priest and shook his hand. "I hope to have something for you soon, Father."

As O'Grady walked away, Father Keller looked hard at Eddie. "You're really going to write a column about all this, aren't you?"

"We've already had this argument, Father. It's my job."

"In my opinion, only a cold-hearted bastard would expose that sweet old lady and her grandson to public ridicule. And I don't think you're that kind of guy."

"Thanks, Father, good to know," Eddie said. "Look, the best I can do is maybe not use their names or their address. I can't promise anything until I talk to my editors."

"Whatever you can do for them, I'll take it."

"By the way, Father, why did you ask the kid if he saw the statue cry?"

"I hoped he'd realized once and for all that the statue hadn't cried, and that he didn't witness a miracle."

"A few minutes ago, you implied there was nothing wrong with believing in miracles, didn't you?"

Father Keller gave Eddie a look that revealed nothing and finally said, "This is off the record, Eddie. I had Floyd—you know him, my handyman—check that stain above the statue where I thought the leak had come from. It was bone-dry."

"When did he check it?"

"Right after I got down from the ladder and started walking over to the rectory with you."

"What're you trying to tell me?"

Father Keller shrugged. "Take it for what it's worth."

"What does that mean? Are you starting to believe it cried?"

"No, never heard of a St. Joseph statue crying. The Blessed Mother, yes, but not St. Joseph."

"Well, that settles it, then," Eddie said in a sarcastic tone.

CHAPTER 24

THE SECOND EDDIE WALKED into the newsroom, coffee and sandwich in hand, he conferred with Basic and Phoebe, filling them in on the morning's events.

"But here's the thing," Eddie said. "On the way over here, it started to dawn on me that we've got a problem."

"Tell me about it," Basic said knowingly. "Soon as we put up anything online, we'll alert every newspaper in town, not to mention the local TV assholes. They'll be buzzing around the old lady and the priest and the cops for any scrap of information they can get."

Phoebe weighed in. "They'll do anything to advance the ball. Suppose they get wind of the delivery-boy angle? It'll be a mad scramble, and somebody else could get to the bottom of the whole thing before we do."

"I was thinking about writing a story without using the Bellos' names or where they lived. But how do I get away without mentioning O'Grady and Father Keller?"

"Look, we still have about seven hours until deadline," Basic said. "Maybe something will break with the doctor, and we can have the whole story wrapped up in a beautiful exclusive package."

"What if nothing breaks?" Eddie said.

"Nobody knows anything but our small circle," Phoebe said. "Get to Keller and O'Grady and Arena and whoever else and tell them to keep quiet. Think they'll do that for you?"

"Yeah, I do," Eddie said. "But aren't we forgetting something?

Like the anonymous message I got this morning—we now know it's Cecilia Bello."

"I haven't forgotten," Basic said. "We can't run it, not yet. It's one thing to hold a story because it needs more reporting. But we know who sent you that message, and if we print it, we can't pretend we don't. You start working the phones, maybe something will shake loose."

First, Eddie called Dr. Oliver Taylor at his office and was told he'd be in surgery all day and maybe into the night at Memorial Sloan Kettering. He left his cell phone number with the doctor's service. He then called O'Grady, who'd also left a message for Dr. Taylor. He also phoned Father Keller, who said he wouldn't tell a soul about anything to do with the statue.

"I spoke to Nick," the priest added. "He's very upset. You should call him, though I'm certain he won't be blabbing about what's transpired."

When Eddie got Nick on the phone, he said, "Some of your customers may ask you about the statue. Please tell them nothing's changed, and the reward is still in effect."

"Detective O'Grady told me the thieves may contact me and ask for more money. He said I should tell them I will think about it and to call back in a few hours. Then he wants me to call him. We will see."

As he was finishing his coffee and sandwich, Eddie got a call from Sebastian Harris, his FBI source. "Got another piece of information for you, and this one might get me that fancy lunch. There was bad blood between Tieri and Arena. My guy didn't have any specifics, except to say it was a very long time ago when they were both young men on the make."

"'On the make'? You're not saying Arena was mobbed-up, are you?"

"No, no, just that their paths crossed. And I guess they didn't care much for each other. You like?"

"Let's see where it gets me."

Eddie thanked Harris, and no sooner had he hung up the phone than he called the Tieri & Sons Funeral Home. A sandpapery male voice answered.

"This is the Tieri & Sons Funeral Home, and we are here to help you in your time of grief."

Eddie's gut told him the man he wanted had just answered the phone. "Mr. Tieri?"

"Yes, speaking."

"I'm impressed, getting the owner himself without even asking."

"My assistant's on the other line. What can I do for you?"

"I'm Eddie Sabella. I write a column for—"

"I know your name, I can read," Tieri said brusquely.

Eddie figured Tieri wasn't the sort of subject you could soften up with a few softball questions. He decided on the spot to see if he could catch him off guard by asking out of the blue: "Do you know Nick Arena?"

"Personally?" Tieri asked.

"Yes, personally."

"What's it to you?" Tieri said, a nasty hook in his voice.

"I don't know if you've been reading my stories the last few days, but Nick Arena's the owner of the statue that was stolen from St. Joseph's..."

"No shit, I must've missed that story," Tieri said in a stunned tone genuine enough to impress a theater critic.

"So, Gaspar, you have—"

"Ay, what happened to 'Mr. Tieri'?"

"Okay, then...*Mister* Tieri," Eddie said, exaggerating his pronunciation.

"That's more like it," Tieri said, suddenly launching into a coughing jag that made Eddie wince.

"Hey, you okay?"

"Like you give a shit," Tieri finally responded. "This phone call is fucking *finito*."

"You never answered my question about Nick Arena," Eddie said quickly. "I hear there was bad blood between the two of you."

"You should ask him."

"I will, and then I'll let you know what he tells me."

"I'll be waiting on fucking pins and needles," Tieri said, and hung up.

So much for that, Eddie thought. Going into the interview, he hadn't known what to expect from Tieri, and coming out of it, he'd learned nothing new—except that he was done trying to find out anything sinister about Arena and the bakeries. Neither his FBI source nor the streetwise bookmaker Moe Vogel could link Arena to any crimes, and Tieri didn't seem to give a shit about Arena, their past history, or the stolen statue.

CHAPTER 25

BEFORE LEAVING THE PAPER, Eddie discussed a game plan with Basic and Phoebe then called O'Grady, who still hadn't heard from Dr. Taylor.

When he got home, Eddie completed a two-mile run in his condo's gym, showered, then dressed in a white shirt, blue blazer, and gray gabardine pants. He'd been too absorbed in his reporting to give Phyllis much thought, but in the fast-fading light, she invaded his senses as he looked for a cab. He figured he'd grab a bite and a few drinks at Pecky's with Basic and Phoebe, and then he'd head to Filomena's around ten o'clock, when the dinner crowd had thinned and Phyllis wouldn't be too busy.

A cab pulled up, and out stepped a stylishly dressed blonde, followed by an older man. He was wearing a gray overcoat with a black velvet collar and had a black patch over his left eye. "It's all yours," he said to Eddie.

"Thanks," Eddie said. Sliding into the cab, he gave the driver the address for Filomena's—not Pecky's, as he'd intended only seconds earlier.

Eddie called ahead to Filomena's to warn Nick he was coming armed with a couple of questions, and when he arrived, Nick was waiting at the bar to greet him. They shook hands, and Nick said, "What will you have, Eddie?"

"Dewar's, rocks, splash of soda," Eddie said to the bartender as he took off his overcoat and laid it on the high-backed stool next to him. "Thanks for seeing me."

"You amaze me, Eddie. Always working, always questioning, always prowling for a story."

"Let's just say I'm a curious guy, and sometimes I get an itch I have to scratch. For example, I was planning to have drinks and dinner with some friends of mine. But then this guy gets out of a cab—a distinguished-looking guy, and he's wearing a patch over his eye. So I get into the cab, and I forget about meeting my pals, because I need to talk to you. You following me, Nick?"

"Yes."

"Anyway, the guy with the patch made me remember a story Phyl told me about her trip to your hometown in Sicily…"

"That was a long time ago."

"She said you vividly recalled the day American soldiers liberated Alcamo from the Fascists. You were six years old, and you saluted some officers in the town square, and a young man with a bandage over his eye picked you up and kissed you on the forehead."

"It is true, yes. But what is the point, Eddie?"

"I am willing to bet you knew Giovanni Vitale a lot better than you let on the other night."

Nick's smile faded as he pinned Eddie with a steady gaze and drummed the bar with the fingers of his right hand. "It is an interesting story, and sometimes it is hard for me to believe that I actually lived it."

"I'd like to hear it."

Nick shrugged, his expression indicating that he'd think about it.

"Does Phyllis know about the connection between you and Vitale, about how far back it went?"

"Of course."

"Funny, she forgot to mention it."

"I am sure she told you as much as she thought was prudent without violating my trust and my privacy."

Nick eased himself off the barstool. "Wait here," he said, and then walked to the back of the restaurant.

Moments later, Eddie watched Phyllis blow across the dining room like a soft sea breeze, cool and fragrant. As she moved toward him, he heard in his head the half-remembered lyrics of a song—*I'd be the shadow of your dog / If it would keep me by your side.*

Phyllis kissed Eddie on the cheek. "No phone call, no flowers," she said, and then she whispered in Eddie's ear, "Screw 'em and forget 'em, huh?"

She smiled as she cocked her head at Eddie, but he thought he'd detected a chilly edge in her voice, as if she were only half teasing him.

"You know that's not true, Phyl," he said, reaching for her hand.

"My father told me he's taking you out for a drink, somewhere you two can talk and won't be bothered. What's going on? Any news about the statue?"

"I'm sure Nick told you what happened this morning."

"You can't imagine how much that statue means to him, Eddie. He won't show how depressed he truly is about it. I hope you can lift his spirits."

"I'll try, Phyl. And what about you? When will you be through here?"

Phyllis's voice was gentle as she said, "Can we skip tonight, Eddie?"

Eddie worked his mouth into a frown that seemed to fall somewhere between bewilderment and disappointment.

"It's just that...well, I need some time to think," she said.

"Think about what?"

"I feel like we're moving too fast."

"For you, maybe. Not me," Eddie said.

"Eddie..."

"I won't forget to send flowers in the morning, I promise. I'll fill this whole damn place with flowers."

Phyllis barely smiled. "It's not that, Eddie. Last night was crazy. It wasn't like me. I was so...I just don't fall into bed with a man after a night or two."

"What the hell are you talking about?"

"Please, Eddie, not so loud."

Eddie lowered his voice, even as his mood darkened. "I'm the man who's loved you since he was a kid. I'm the man who kept on loving you after you crapped out on him. I'm not just any man, and it pisses me off you'd say something like that."

Phyllis's eyes darted nervously toward the end of the bar and the dining room. "I almost forgot about that temper of yours," she said, heading for the door. "Come on."

Eddie followed her onto the sidewalk.

"You want me to say I'm sorry?" she said, wrapping her arms around herself as the wind kicked up the chill. "Okay, I'm sorry, Eddie. Yes, I crapped out on you, like you said. But I won't keep apologizing to you for the rest of my life."

Eddie took off his sports jacket and threw it around her shoulders. "I don't want your apologies. I want *you*, and I want you now—and if I can't have you now, I'm not taking any chances. I'll flush you out of my system for good, I swear I will."

"Oh no, you won't," Phyllis said, her eyes blazing with anger now. "Flush me out, and where does that leave you? Think about it, Eddie."

He turned to walk away, and she grabbed his arm. "Don't be such a jerk and just listen to me! I'm sorry for what I did, Eddie, but let's be honest here. As long as you could convince yourself that you were still in love with me, you didn't have to make a commitment to another woman. No responsibilities, no complications. You were safe."

"*Safe*? Well, Dr. Phyl, I guess you've got it all neatly figured out. All these years, it wasn't about loving you, it was about fearing commitment." Eddie slapped his forehead in a mock gesture of sudden enlightenment. "Shit. If I had only known, I could be a happy, well-adjusted father of two right now."

"Go ahead, be sarcastic all you want."

"You really think I was safe?" Eddie said. "I lived in the shadow of your absence for a helluva long time, Phyl, and it wasn't a safe place. It was hell."

"Please, Eddie," she said, her voice faltering. She reached out to touch him, but he waved her off and walked back into the restaurant.

CHAPTER 26

"We should eat something," Nick said to Eddie.

They were sitting alone in a small room off the main dining area at Amelia's restaurant, named after its colorful proprietor, Amelia Kramer.

Shortly after Nonna's opened in 1968, a few friends had taken Amelia to the new restaurant, and when she was done with her meal, she complimented Nick profusely and invited him to dine at her place on the Upper East Side.

Since then, Nick and Amelia had frequented each other's restaurants, and through all those years, they greeted each other in almost precisely the same manner. With a grand flourish, Nick would say, *"Che bella, signora!"* And as he hugged her ample body and kissed her on both cheeks, she'd say, "You're such a handsome devil," and surreptitiously pinch his ass.

And so, whenever Nick needed privacy over drinks or during a meal, he knew he could count on Amelia to provide it for him in an alcove near the kitchen, a gesture he especially appreciated on a night like this one, when half the city, it seemed, was drinking to St. Patrick.

As the wine arrived, Nick set a few ground rules. "I have a very good memory, Eddie, and I will tell you about my relationship with Giovanni Vitale and more. But it is between you and me, all of it. *Va bene?*"

"Okay, but if anything you tell me appears in someone else's story about the recovery of the statue…well, you'll be hearing from me."

"You are confident about its return?"

"One way or another. Either you'll end up paying the reward, or O'Grady will catch the pricks who stole it before they can collect." Eddie smiled broadly. "With my help, of course."

Nick smiled back and then summoned the waiter. He ordered for both of them—fried calamari to start, then veal chops and broccoli rabe sautéed in olive oil and garlic. Before he left to place the order, the waiter refilled their glasses with the 2001 Gagliardo Barolo Cannubi that Amelia had sent to the table.

"Splendid, no?" Nick said, raising his glass toward Eddie and taking a sip.

"Did you always want to own a restaurant? I mean, was that your dream when you came here?"

Nick shook his head. "My dream was to come to America and find out. You must remember, I was only nineteen when I arrived here. The date will always be etched in my heart and my mind—September 22, 1958."

"What else do you remember about that day?"

"When I landed at the airport—it was called Idlewild International Airport back then, not JFK."

"Yes, I know."

Nick slightly bowed his head and, with a glancing smile, said, "But what you do not know is that when I got into the taxi, Elvis Presley was singing a song called 'Hard Headed Woman' on the radio."

After another sip of wine, Nick continued to reminisce, and the story he told over dinner was even more captivating than Eddie had anticipated, beginning with the first time he met Don Vitale.

It was July 24, 1943, Nick remembered, and American troops from the 504th Parachute Infantry Regiment entered Alcamo without opposition and freed the town from the Fascists. Not a single person was harmed, not a single home or church damaged.

Hundreds of Alcamese, the Arena family among them, gathered in the Piazza Ciullo to cheer the soldiers. On the steps of the church of Sant'Olivia, little Nicolo spotted two American officers talking with a young man who had an old hunting rifle slung across his shoulder and a bloody bandage over his left eye. He was shorter than the officers, and thin and coarse as twine. And although he wore a dirty white shirt and frayed gray pants, the Americans treated him with respect.

"I was only six years old. I was so excited, I broke free from my father, who was holding my hand, and I ran through the crowd. When I reached the soldiers, I stood very straight, like a soldier, and saluted the American officers." Nick snapped off a crisp salute for a smiling Eddie. "And then the officer saluted me. The Sicilian with the bandage on his eye laughed out loud, picked me up, and kissed me on the forehead. He shouted, *'Fantastico!'* and pinched me on the cheek. That young man was Giovanni Vitale."

According to Nick, a few months later, Giovanni Vitale settled in Brooklyn, thanks to the intercession of the U.S. Army. It was their way of rewarding him for his bravery; he'd lost his left eye in a fierce gun battle against the Fascists that was pivotal in the army's victory in Sicily.

When he came to America years later, Nick got a job as a presser in a dress factory that was owned by Vitale, who had become a rising power in the New York mafia. One day Nick's boss told him that the owner of the dress factory, Don Giovanni Vitale, wanted to see him at the San Cologero Social Club on Roebling Street in Brooklyn. Vitale was feared for his brutal leadership and admired for the Byzantine complexity of his mind, as well as for the dazzling success of both his legitimate and illegitimate investment portfolio.

"You see, Don Vitale was from Alcamo like me, and he had heard I was a hard worker. He personally took special care of the Alcamese in America. He offered me a job in one of his bakeries. A very good job that paid good money. I accepted, of course, and then I asked him if he remembered a little boy he had raised in his arms on that glorious day in Alcamo. You should have seen the expression on his face when I told him it was me. *Marron!*"

Nick went on about his years in the bakery business, how he'd secured a loan from Vitale to open Nonna's, and then opened Filomena's. "And now, here I am, a proud and prosperous American citizen who loves this country beyond measure. I owe Don Vitale a lot, don't you see?"

"From what I recall, Vitale died in '83. Right?"

"Yes, that is correct."

"You were lucky he kept his word, and you got to keep Nonna's when he died."

"Giovanni Vitale always kept his word," Nick said, and Eddie sensed that Nick was mildly offended that he'd presumed otherwise.

"You sound like you regarded him as an honorable man."

"It is almost impossible for someone of your generation to fathom such a thing. I am neither proud of my association with the man, nor am I ashamed of it. I have known men like Don Vitale all my life, and I understand them. Men who come from nothing, men who fear they will be nothing all their lives. Once they have power and money, they will hold on to it with everything that is in them.

"Judge me if you will, Eddie, but I thank God to this day that Don Vitale financed my restaurant. Who else would have? It was the way of the world for many immigrants like me."

"And if Nonna's had failed? Do you think he would've asked you to join the family?"

"I had no intention of failing."

"That's not an answer, but I suspect you've convinced yourself of that."

"I had not come to America to live half my life in the light and the other half in shadow. If I had ambitions to be a gangster, I would have stayed in Sicily, where the mafia thrives on the greed and brutality of men who were born poor and dumb and hopeless. I did not want to become what I detested."

Finished with their meal, Nick and Eddie were drinking small snifters of anisette with their espresso when Nick leaned forward on his elbows, his hands laced just beneath his chin. There was a moist gleam in his dark eyes that Eddie hadn't seen before. "May I ask you a very personal question?"

Eddie nodded, and Nick asked, "Do you love my daughter?"

Eddie paused, his sad, distant smile in tune with his response. "I have loved her since the first time I saw her. I was seventeen then. I am thirty-seven now."

Nick was about to say something when Eddie cut in. "The more pertinent question is: Does she love me?"

Nick smiled confidently. "This afternoon my daughter asked me why I seemed to like you so much. After all, we have just met. I said, 'Oh, he is a fine fellow, but I like him mostly because you love him.'"

"And what did she say to that?"

"She asked me how I could be so sure, and I told her that a father knows these things. That is why I invited you to dinner the other night. I had to meet the man I know my daughter has loved for much of her life."

"I wish I could be as certain as you are."

Nick let a few seconds go by. "One night, before Filomena found her own apartment, she was listening to one of her records in my library. When I walked in, she quickly wiped away some tears and turned the record off. I asked her what was wrong, and I remember she said it was sometimes difficult getting past the second song. It reminded her of someone she used to know." He raised an eyebrow at Eddie. "Perhaps you know the record? Nina Simone was the singer..."

"*At the Village Gate*, probably. It was her favorite album when we were kids. She was just being nostalgic, Nick, that's all."

"More than that, Eddie. She told me about her relationship with you. She spoke with such affection for you that when she suddenly showed up at our dinner, I knew. She had to see you. I knew right then that you were the someone she used to know."

Nick reached across the table and patted Eddie's forearm. "I cannot say why she is hiding her heart, why she will not surrender to you—"

"Whoa, Nick. You're getting a little operatic here."

"Ah, Eddie, love *is* operatic, is it not? Take my advice—to win her, you must not waver."

Eddie poured a splash of anisette from his snifter into his espresso and said, "My turn to get personal. Phyllis's mother—were you in love with her?"

"Yes, I loved her once, but our affair was very brief. I know Filomena told you about us, how I wanted Emma to come to Brooklyn with me, but she would not." Nick shrugged. "She never told me she was pregnant and had my baby. I will never know why. And there is another thing I will never know—why she named our child Phyllis. A customer once told me that Phyllis is the American version of Filomena, my mother's name. Did she think that one day we would be together, the three of us, a family?

"Filomena prefers to believe I never married because I could not find a woman I loved as much as her mother. Truthfully, Eddie, I never married because I was too ambitious and too selfish to share my life with another person. And then Filomena came into my life, and… well, I am truly blessed."

Both men drained what was left of their drinks, and Nick poured them a little more. He loosened his tie and unbuttoned his shirt, revealing a scar, a faint pink zipper about two inches long, running from below his left earlobe down the side of his neck.

"That scar on your neck…how'd you get it?" Eddie said casually.

Nick touched the scar. "It happened a very long time ago—an accident in the kitchen. Now, we must finish our anisette. It is late, and I am not as young as you."

After a brief argument over the check, Eddie was forced to let Nick pay when the waiter refused to accept his credit card. "You want me to lose my job?" the waiter said to Eddie. "Amelia said Nick's the big shot here, not you, even though you got a column."

On the way out, Nick kissed Amelia, and Eddie shook her hand. "You should come here more often," she said to Nick, and then to Eddie: "You too."

"Not unless you let me pick up the check the next time I'm with Nick."

"Don't be such a wise guy, you," Amelia said, and as Eddie turned to leave, she pinched his ass.

CHAPTER 27

IT WAS A FEW MINUTES before eleven when Eddie walked into his apartment, and it was a few minutes after that when his phone rang. Max was on the line.

"What're you doing home so soon?"

"Some business to attend to. How'd you like my column from Hialeah?"

"I didn't know flamingoes could talk."

"It's called poetic license, dipshit," Max said. "I need to see you."

"Everything okay?"

"No complaints, but it's kinda important we have a drink."

"Where are you? Pecky's?"

"You hear any assholes singing and vomiting in the background? I'm at the Colonial on Fifty-Seventh. Figured I wouldn't find any Irish wannabes at a French-Vietnamese joint, and I was right."

Eddie found Max sitting alone at the mahogany bar on the second-floor lounge, sipping a tall, orange-colored drink he supposed was a screwdriver. Soft music was playing in the background, and Eddie counted maybe a dozen people drinking at small tables around the room.

Eddie ordered his usual. Max asked for another screwdriver, and said, "You look beat to shit."

"She's back," Eddie said, dipping a finger in his drink and swirling the ice around.

"Who's back?"

"Phyllis Blake."

"The big one who got away?"

"The same. Except now she goes by her real name—Phyllis Arena."

"Her real name? You mean her married name?"

"No, she's not married."

Max raised his glass to his lips but barely sipped a taste before saying, "Wait a minute. Don't tell me she's related to Nick Arena?"

"His daughter."

"Christ," Max said, then downed half his screwdriver. "I always figured she was married with four kids and living somewhere in New Hampshire, or Colorado, or one of those fucking nowhere states. How the hell did you find her?"

"It was the other way around," Eddie said, and proceeded to tell Max how Phyllis had walked into his life again. How it seemed likely that she'd fuck him over like she did fifteen years ago, only this time, the pain would be even more exquisite because she'd be living and working only a few blocks away from him at Filomena's, and he'd constantly have to fight the temptation to beg her for mercy and plead for a few crumbs of her affection.

"Shit, Eddie, it must be exhausting being you."

"Any advice?"

"Look on the bright side. If you had married her way back when, you'd probably be divorced by now, paying half your salary in alimony and feeling shitty because your bratty kids don't want to spend any time with you."

"Seriously, Max."

"What the hell do I know? I'm a two-time loser. Three, if you count Mia, who I should've married."

"I liked Mia," Eddie said, placing his elbows on the bar and holding his face in his hands.

Max patted Eddie on the shoulder. "Enough about you, my friend," he said, taking a deep breath, and then: "I'm going to ESPN."

Eddie's face went blank. "You're leaving the paper?"

Max nodded. "In another couple of weeks. They call it a 'multiplatform' deal. What horseshit. What it really means is they want me to work my ass off—a column in the magazine and a blog on the web site and regular appearances on various shows. Radio too. You name it. But they're willing to pay me close to three times what I make at the paper. Good deal, huh?"

"*Great* deal, Max! Take the money and run," Eddie said in a persuasive voice. "Every fucking day, readers are moving to the Internet. That's where they're getting their news, and their sports, and their entertainment, and the advertisers are following them. Talk to Basic. He'll tell you. Everybody's under tremendous pressure to cut costs, and there's rumors of another round of layoffs and buyouts."

"Fuck, Eddie, you're making it sound like the paper is going to fold any day now."

"Circulation's down, and it keeps going down. It's 2006. Who knows what the newspaper business will look like in 2016 or 2020? But I bet it won't be pretty."

"I need another drink," Max said, signaling the bartender. "You're making me feel like a rat deserting the ship."

"I'm sorry, Max. I don't mean to, honestly. I'm happy for you."

"Thanks, Eddie."

"ESPN is lucky to have you."

"God love 'em. I never thought I could make the big bucks being on television, but ESPN doesn't give a shit if you're old and fat."

"Old, fat, *and* bald, actually."

"Almost bald, to be accurate," Max said.

Eddie grinned nostalgically. "You know what Breslin told me back when I was starting out? He said, 'Reporting for a newspaper is the greatest life in the world. Anybody who doesn't go into it is a sucker.'"

"And he was right, Eddie. In spite of how it's going now, we did the right thing."

"Max," Eddie said, staring at his friend for several beats before raising his glass and clearing a knot of melancholy in his throat. "I'm going to miss you."

Max raised his glass too. "To us, Eddie, a couple of ink-stained wretches and proud of it, no matter where we may end up."

"I'll drink to that."

CHAPTER 28

WILLIE SCREAMED SO LOUD in his sleep that he woke up his wife, Janice, who dug an elbow into his side to shut him up. He opened his eyes and shot straight up, choking on his own breath.

"The fuck, Willie?" Janice grumbled. "You forget to take the Zantac?"

"I took it, like always." Willie spat out the words in a rapid-fire burst and then made a sucking sound as he gasped for air.

"You having a nightmare?"

"Nah," Willie lied between gasps, shaking his head.

"Then the Zantac didn't work. Take a couple more," she said, turning on her stomach and burying her head in a pillow.

Willie got up, grabbed his black silk bathrobe off the foot of the bed, and shambled into the kitchen. He poured himself a glass of cold water from the refrigerator and cursed himself for sticking with a job that triggered such horrible dreams.

Willie had killed a lot of men in his time, using an abundant variety of weapons, methods, and locations. In addition to shooting his victims with firearms of all types, he'd stabbed them with knives and ice picks, hacked them with machetes, decapitated them with axes, and disemboweled them with an assortment of surgical instruments. He'd bludgeoned them with baseball bats. He'd hung them with rope, strangled them with piano wire, and smothered them with pillows. He'd thrown them off rooftops and out of windows. He'd drowned them in toilet bowls, bathtubs, and drums of oil. He'd baked them in ovens, poisoned them with strychnine, and once even arranged for a fifteen-foot-long, 350-pound reticulated python to squeeze the life out of a postal worker who'd accidentally run over Gaspar's pet cat with his truck.

That was some kill—legendary among men who appreciated such things. Gaspar had loved that cat, a green-eyed little blimp that had lived longer than any of the other cats he'd owned since he was a kid. When one cat died, he immediately bought another, and he named them all Skoonj, a tribute to his boyhood idol, Carl Furillo, the right fielder of the Brooklyn Dodgers during their glory days in the fifties. Furillo got tagged with the nickname Skoonj—short for *scungili*, snail in Italian—because he was so slow on the bases and in the outfield. If the nickname was good enough for Furillo, Gaspar often explained, it was good enough for a fucking cat.

Gaspar was heartbroken when his long-lived Skoonj got run over by the UPS driver, and in his grief, he lashed out. "I want the life squeezed out of that fucking murderer," he told Willie through his tears.

That was where the python came in.

It belonged to a Thai importer of exotic animals who operated on the margins of the law. Willie contacted him through one of the Vitale family's soldiers, who had used the importer to obtain a month-old Burmese python as a birthday present for his twelve-year-old son. "He's your guy," the wise guy said. "You can't look him up in the Yellow Pages, on account of all the weird shit he does with the animals."

The Thai went by the name of Mhu, and after learning of Willie's special mission, he invited him to his warehouse in Patterson, New Jersey. Willie arrived with the UPS driver bound and gagged in the trunk of his car, and two of Mhu's fellow Thais checked him out at the door. Mhu himself was short and fat and dark, and was missing three fingers on his right hand. When he caught Willie staring at the hand, he smiled a creepy smile and said, "This can be a dangerous business."

Mhu had erected a sturdy cage in the warehouse, as big as a jail cell. Coiled in a corner was the Burmese python, its black-and-brown-patterned body as thick as a telephone pole. When the UPS driver saw it, he went bug-eyed and fainted. Mhu ordered his men to bind the UPS driver's feet and put him in the cage. Then, turning to Willie, he held out his hand, the one with all five fingers. Willie opened the briefcase he was carrying and gave Mhu $10,000 in cash for services about to be rendered.

Once they had locked the driver in the cage, Mhu's men started sprinkling some sort of grain on the floor outside the bars. "What's that?" Willie said.

"Chicken feed," Mu said.

"What for?"

"The chickens."

There were four of them, and they strutted around the outside of the cage, happily pecking at the feast. Their scent aroused the Burmese python, and it slowly uncoiled and slithered toward the body of the UPS driver. "You see," Mhu explained, "the python is now in a feeding frenzy. He smells the chickens, and since it has very poor eyesight, it will mistake the young man for his prey. Watch."

As if sensing the terrible fate that awaited him, the UPS driver came to and desperately tried to squirm away. But the python caught up to him, slowly wrapped its fifteen feet of muscle around its prey's torso, and opened its mouth so wide, it managed to clamp the UPS driver's head, from ear to ear, between its teeth.

"What the fuck?" Willie yelled at Mhu. "It's eating him!"

"Please, don't fret," Mhu said.

"I paid for it to squeeze the life out of him, not to eat him!" Willie said, drawing his gun. "You stop it, or I will!"

"Put the gun away," Mhu said calmly. "It is acting on instinct, grasping its prey so he cannot run away. It will be over very soon. Please, watch."

The python continued to wrap itself around the UPS driver, now almost completely immobilized, blood dripping down his neck from the puncture wounds on either side of his head.

"You see," Mhu said to Willie, "the python is contracting its muscles, which will constrict the young man's ability to breathe, and he will suffocate."

Mhu looked at his watch. A little more than a minute later, he said to Willie, "You see, as you wished, the young man has had the life squeezed out of him."

"Will the snake eat him now?" Willie asked in awe.

"Oh, no," Mhu said. "It will soon realize that its victim is much too large for it to ingest. But I have other animals that would have no such problem. May I keep the body?"

Willie slept like a baby that night, as he did most nights back then. But then came the millennium, and there was no escaping the nightmares. He thought that maybe he was entering a new phase of his life, that maybe he really did have a conscience and it was finally kicking in. Due to his advancing age, he'd been assigned only six kills since 9/11, and yet each time he'd wake up in a cold sweat because his bloodied and mutilated victims had invaded his dreams. Sometimes the nightmares would linger for several nights in a row, scaring the hell out of him.

And now this: he'd shot Buster with a handgun just once behind the left ear, and the delivery boy had died on his feet, dropped to the floor quicker than a knocked-out boxer. Buster never saw it coming; he didn't suffer. So what if Willie had liked the kid? He reasoned that if a merciful kill like Buster's was going to drill him with another fucking nightmare, then he had to seriously consider packing it all in and moving to Florida, like Janice had been nagging him to do.

CHAPTER 29

BETWEEN WRESTLING WITH a throbbing hangover and recalling pieces of his conversation with Nick about Phyllis, Eddie decided it was useless to lie in bed any longer. He swallowed two aspirin with a cold glass of Alka-Seltzer, made himself a pot of coffee, and showered. After splashing his face to wash away the last flecks of shaving cream, he examined himself in the mirror with a hard stare, trying to figure out why he'd gotten so angry with Phyllis. What did she say that was so awful, so offensive? Why did he let his temper get away from him?

Eddie splashed his face again. How did he end up like this? And then he thought, shit, she was wrong about him. He hadn't carried the torch for her as a wedge against making a commitment to another woman. He wasn't so different from a lot of other guys. You could fall in love ten, twenty times, but you'd never recapture the sheer lunacy of the first time, never reach the same demented heights of ecstasy or depths of despair. Maybe he was just trapped in his adolescent emotions, when nothing else had mattered to him more than Phyllis, when he was on top of the world because the girl he loved had loved him back.

God, he hoped not.

Ain't first love a bitch?

Eddie was almost done reading the paper when his cell phone rang. It was O'Grady, who'd finally gotten a call from Dr. Taylor last night and learned where he'd ordered the flowers for Mrs. Bello.

"I told him I'd call you in the morning with the information. Meet you at the flower shop…Eighty-Fifth and Lexington…ten o'clock."

Eddie beat O'Grady to the flower shop, but not by much. He spotted the detective walking up Lexington and waited for him. Inside, they introduced themselves to the man behind the counter. He said his name was Joe Regan, and identified himself as the shop's executive assistant. After the detective described the delivery boy, he said, "Sounds to me like it's Buster."

"Buster who?" O'Grady said.

"Bustamante. Buster Bustamante. He do something wrong?"

O'Grady ignored Regan's question. "Can you check yesterday's receipts, see if you had a delivery for Cecilia Bello at 372 East Eighty-Ninth Street?"

Regan quickly found the receipt. "Here it is. Yep, it was Buster who made the delivery."

"I'd like to talk to him," O'Grady said.

"He hasn't come in yet. He's already late, and I can't get him on his cell phone."

"You know where he lives?" O'Grady said.

"Somewhere in Queens."

O'Grady raised an eyebrow. "Can you be more specific?"

"Sorry, Detective, but I really don't know. You gonna tell me if he's in trouble?"

"No."

Eddie said, "You must have his social security number or his payroll and tax records—*something* that lists his address. Can you check your books?"

Regan hesitated, shifting his weight from one foot to the other and brushing a hand through his fading red hair. His blue eyes turned grim as they nervously darted from Eddie to O'Grady.

"Give me a break, okay, Detective? Any questions about the books, you should talk to the boss."

"He's paid off the books, right?" Eddie said and, without waiting for an answer, turned to O'Grady. "Buster is an illegal, count on it."

"Like I say, you should talk to Willie. He was taking orders yesterday because I had a wedding to go to."

"Who's Willie?" O'Grady said.

"Willie Stracci. He's the boss."

"And where is Willie?"

"Don't know, Detective. He called me before I came in, said he had to run some errands for the wife and should be here around eleven."

"He have a cell phone?" Eddie asked.

"Yeah, sure."

O'Grady laid his opened notebook on the counter, tapped the blank page with his finger, and said to Regan, "Write down the number."

"I don't have it."

"You gotta be kidding," O'Grady said. "How the hell do you run a business nowadays without your boss's cell phone number?"

"No, no, it's not like that. If he's not coming in, he calls and gives me a number where I can reach him."

"So whenever he gives you a cell phone number," Eddie said to Regan, "it's always different, right?"

"That's what I said, yeah. And since he'll be here around eleven, he didn't give me the new one."

"Thank you for making it perfectly clear," Eddie said in a lightly mocking tone. He handed Regan his card. "If you hear from your boss before he comes in…"

"You tell him I want to talk to him," O'Grady said, giving Regan his own card and shooting Eddie a smirking, sideways glance. "And he should call me first. Same goes for Buster."

Looking at Eddie's card, Regan said, "Hey, you doing a story about Buster being an illegal?"

"We don't give a shit if he's illegal," O'Grady said. "I just want to talk to him, and to his boss, and I don't have all day."

"You said he was running some errands for his wife," Eddie said. "Maybe she knows where he is. What's his home phone number?"

"It's unlisted. He don't give it out."

"You gotta be fucking with me," O'Grady said. "You really don't know it?"

"Honest."

"I've had enough of this shit," O'Grady said in an exasperated voce. "Does he live anywhere near here?"

"Yeah, a few blocks," Regan said warily.

"Give me the address," O'Grady said sternly.

"Over on 175 East Eighty-Second, between Lex and Third. He lives on the bottom floor of a brownstone there. You didn't get it from me, okay, Detective?"

CHAPTER 30

BEFORE DROPPING IN at the Tieri & Sons Funeral Home, Willie stopped for espresso and biscotti. He wore a new camel-hair overcoat over his best black sharkskin suit, a white shirt, and a hand-embroidered Countess Mara pink-and-blue paisley tie that he bought in the late eighties. Even back then, the tie set him back $250, and he wore it only when he wanted to make an impression.

Back on the street, he reached into his pocket for a mint and started the five-block walk to Gaspar's. He had made up his mind. He'd reached the end of the line. At his age, when he took into account the life he'd led, he was lucky he wasn't dead or rotting away in a federal prison.

Willie hastily crossed himself, then kissed the tips of his thumb and index fingers, thanking God. The nightmare he'd had about Buster was a sign. It convinced him to take advantage of his luck and give up the business that was coming very close to driving him *pazzo*. Look at fucking Gaspar. He'd ordered him to kill a harmless little Filipino. For what? A fucking statue? At least in the old days, it was kill or be killed. If it wasn't that, it was usually about something that had a real, professional purpose behind it.

Nothing but nothing was making much sense to him anymore. The only thing that did make any sense was getting his and Janice's asses down to Florida as soon as possible. And he told Gaspar just that.

"You know what Boca Raton means in English?" Gaspar said, sitting behind his desk and leaning across it toward Willie.

"No."

"Mouth of the Rat."

"What?"

"Boca Raton is a Spanish name. It means 'Mouth of the Rat' in English."

"How do you know that?"

"I just do, that's all," Gaspar said sharply.

"I believe you." Willie's tone had an edge of its own, implying that Gaspar should lighten up.

"Why the fuck you want to live in a place called Mouth of the Rat?"

"It's good as any place down there, and Janice can be near her sister. You remember her—Pauline."

"Who could forget?" Gaspar said with a lewd grin. "Nice rack."

"No more," Willie said, frowning. "It's a shame."

"Getting old's a bitch."

"No, it's not, Gaspar. That's the thing. I got to be sixty-seven, and I'm recognizing I could be seventy-seven or maybe eighty-seven if I retire and get out of this life."

"Willie, Willie," Gaspar said, shaking his head. "I don't have to tell you, Willie. There's no U-turns in our life."

"Yeah, but you and me, Gaspar, we go back to when we was teenagers, and there's nothing we won't do for each other."

Gaspar smiled appreciatively. "You always had my back, Willie. Who was ever gonna fuck with you?"

The sound of Gaspar's laughter gurgling in his throat sometimes ignited a spark of fear somewhere in the recesses of Willie's belly, even when they were kids. This wasn't one of those times, though. At that moment Willie realized just how fed up he was being at Gaspar's mercy, being in his debt and in his shadow, being his second banana when he could crush him like a bug if he wanted to.

Some fucking friendship.

"See, that's what I'm talking about, Gaspar. We go back so far, I was hoping you'd represent my case with the bosses. I been loyal a long time, and you and me both know that there's loyal guys out there who been allowed to make a U-turn."

"Very, very few. But tell me why, Willie. Why now?"

"I'll tell you why, Gaspar. Strip away everything, and all this life ever give me was *agita*."

"You got the flower shops."

"Fuck the flower shops. They're not mine."

"The family's paid you pretty good to run them. It's not attractive to be so ungrateful about money like that."

"Money, fuck the money. The *agita* is killing me. Sometimes it gets so bad, I can feel it blowing out my ears, my nose, my asshole. And it ain't the food. Janice only cooks with the best ingredients. It's the tension, the pressure. And nights like last night, not even Zantac'll fix it."

Gaspar slowly nodded, giving Willie an understanding smile. "You got a knack for getting down to the nub of things, Willie. You always did. So I'll do the same. One more job, and I'll see you get to make your U-turn."

"Look, Gaspar, I didn't tell you everything about why I want to quit and such. You see, I had a terrible nightmare last night about Buster, and I—"

"Who?"

"Christ's sake, Gaspar, the kid who worked for me, who saw the statue and I had to make go away because of you."

"What're you getting so upset about? So I forgot his name, so fucking what? It's not like he was some acquaintance of mine. Get to the point."

"Like I said, I had a nightmare last night about Buster, and it's not the first time this happened. The last three or four kills—every time I got a nightmare. Scares the shit out of me. I'm afraid if I do anybody else, they'll come to me in a nightmare too. It's like God finally cursed me for the things I done. And if I'm cursed, Gaspar, I'm really fucked."

"Look, if it was up to me, I'd personally buy you the plane tickets and throw in a bathing suit. But this new job is coming down from the top. Very soon. I'll let you know."

"I'm feeling terrible about this, Gaspar."

"Willie, Willie, *marone*, you talk about *agita*, and I'm the one starting to feel it right here," Gaspar said, lightly pounding his chest with a fist. "I'm through debating this issue with you like this. Don't make me fucking beg."

What bullshit, Willie thought. He couldn't recall a single instance when Gaspar had begged for anything. Beg? He'd have been happy with a *Please, Willie* every once in a while. But what were his options here? Gaspar had him by the balls. All the years they ran together didn't mean a goddamn thing to him. If he flat-out refused to do the job, he believed deep down that Gaspar would fuck him up with the bosses, see to it that he never got permission to make his U-turn into the sun. And if he left without their blessing, they'd hunt him down for sure. Better to risk suffering more nightmares than to die like a dog on a beach in Boca.

"Okay, Gaspar," Willie said in a soft voice, his shoulders sagging. "I will wait to hear from you."

"That's my old pally!" Gaspar said, springing from his chair and extending his hand to Willie. "Like I always said, you're the best that ever was. A real artist, and that's no bullshit."

Willie got up and shook Gaspar's hand. He turned to leave, and as he walked a few paces toward the door, he heard Gaspar jump-start one of his bone-rattling coughs. Willie kept walking without looking back.

CHAPTER 31

JANICE STRACCI ANSWERED the door in blue cashmere pants and a white angora sweater that fell several inches below her waist.

"Mrs. Stracci?" O'Grady said.

"The one and only," she answered pleasantly. "And you?"

"I'm Detective Dan O'Grady."

"Oh really?" she said unpleasantly, placing a hand on her ample hip. "What's this about?"

Eddie could tell she'd had her blue eyes done and God knew what else. It was good work, though, and he made her to be in her late fifties. He had a harder time giving a name to the color of her hair; it was somewhere between red and orange. Maybe that was what they used to call flame-haired in Hollywood.

"I just want to have a word with him," O'Grady said.

"He's at work, at the flower shop on Eighty-Fifth."

"We just came from there, and we were informed that he was out running errands," O'Grady said.

"Could be. He left before I got up."

"So you haven't any idea at all where he might be now?" O'Grady said.

"I don't keep him on a leash."

"Do you have a cell phone number where we might reach him?" O'Grady said.

"He's got a lot of them. I can't keep track."

O'Grady glanced at Eddie with a sardonic smile, then said, "Why am I not surprised?"

She shrugged one shoulder and, with a puckered curve of her lips and a roll of her eyes, indicated she didn't give a shit what O'Grady thought.

"Maybe you'd know—"

"Who're you?" she said, cutting Eddie off.

Eddie identified himself, and she said, "How do you like that? I been reading your stories in the paper. Anybody ever tell you you're better-looking in person?"

"That's nice of you, Mrs. Stracci."

"Don't mention it. And you can call me Janice."

"Okay, Janice. Tell me—has Willie been reading my stories too?"

"As a general rule, Willie don't read the papers."

O'Grady said, "Can you tell me what you know about a young man named Buster Bustamante? Anything at all."

"I don't know any Buster whatever."

"He works for your husband," Eddie said. "He's the delivery boy."

"Willie never brings his work home with him," she said, sounding annoyed, as if she were airing a chronic complaint. "There's not a single fresh flower in the whole damn house. You don't believe me, you can see for yourself."

Janice stepped to the side of the open door with an inviting gesture. O'Grady declined, and instead gave her his card. "He can call me any time."

"Yeah, sure. Like he got nothing better to do."

Eddie and O'Grady hadn't walked some fifteen yards up the block when they heard Janice call after them. She was now standing in front of the brownstone.

O'Grady turned and said, "Yes, ma'am?"

"I got a question I forgot to ask Eddie about the statue."

"She's all yours," O'Grady said to Eddie. "I've got to check in at the precinct."

Eddie walked back to Janice, who said, "I know the priest thinks it was a leak, but do you think it's possible the statue really cried? I was talking about this with Willie last night."

"Anything's possible, I guess. What do you think?"

"Willie thinks it's possible, but I don't. I used to believe in things like that, but no more. Not since my sister-in-law Gerri got cancer of her ovaries and went to Lourdes for the cure. She died three months later. I never seen Willie so sad. She was the baby of the family."

"That's tough, losing a sister like that."

"But thank God, he's got three others still alive. He loves those girls. Has lunch with them when he can, has them to the house for dinner a lot. Good girls."

"Could Willie be having lunch with one of his sisters today?"

"He could be anywhere—visiting one of his other shops, having coffee with an old friend. That's what I'd bet. Don't ask me where, 'cause I don't know, but he has coffee with old friends more than with me."

"Old friends, huh?"

"Yeah, from when he was a kid in Brooklyn. Those guys—Lilo and Benny and Gaspar—they stayed real close."

"Oh, is that Gaspar Tieri, the guy who owns the funeral home?" Eddie said, affecting a casual tone.

Janice blinked, and Eddie noticed something flicker in her eyes. "What's with all the questions?"

Before Eddie had a chance to respond, Janice said, "Nice to make your acquaintance," and hurried through her front door.

———

Willie called Janice when he got in the cab. "Listen carefully, Jan, and do what I tell you. Start packing enough clothes for you and me. We're gonna drive down to Florida when I get home, so hurry up."

"What's going on, Willie? This have anything to do with that detective and newspaper writer that was just here?"

"A cop was there? What did he want?"

"I don't know, but he asked about a guy who works for you named Buster."

"Shit."

"Willie, you're making me very nervous."

"Don't worry about a thing, Jan. I'm gonna get a massage and a steam, maybe have lunch on the West Side with Lilo. When I get home, I wanna see everything packed. We're gonna drive down. I'll see you later."

"Willie, wait. If I don't have to worry about anything, how come you want to go to Florida all of a sudden?"

"I'm gonna buy us a house in Boca, and I was thinking we could stay down there forever. Just like you want."

"Did you tell Gaspar?"

"Fuck Gasper. Fuck them all. Trust me, life's too short. I got to thinking about Gerri—"

"Funny thing, me likewise."

"Yeah, anyway, what am I waiting for? Until I get cancer like her, or my heart explodes? You do what I say, Janice. Start packing, and let me worry about everything else."

CHAPTER 32

EDDIE HAD PHONED AHEAD to the paper and assigned a crack intern to search Google and LexisNexis for Guglielmo "Willie" Stracci's police record. The research was waiting for him on his desk.

Willie was a reputed member of the Vitale crime family, with a criminal record dating back to 1957, about the time he dropped out of high school. A series of petty crimes, including street fighting and selling stolen property, twice landed him for brief periods in the county jail. Several of his arrests during that period were in the company of two other men, Gaspar Tieri and Lilo Abarno.

"Gaspar Tieri, wouldn't you know it," Eddie whispered to himself.

By his early twenties, Stracci had become a highly regarded Vitale family enforcer and labor goon. Considering Stracci's arrest record, it was damn near miraculous he'd served only one stretch in a federal prison: from 1986 to 1993 on a manslaughter conviction. Through the years, he'd amassed a diverse record of criminal activity: assault and battery, illegal possession of firearms, truck hijackings, extortion, gambling, conspiracy to commit sports bribery. He was also a suspect in three murders of "reputed members of rival criminal enterprises of the Vitale crime family."

Willie was also arrested twice on suspicion of laundering mob money through his flower shops, which were allegedly funded and controlled by the Vitale family. Nothing ever came of the charges, and while Willie was sometimes questioned in connection with various Vitale family rackets, he hadn't seen the inside of a jail cell of any kind in some ten years.

Eddie leaned back in his chair, laced his fingers behind his head, and shut his eyes in thought. He started connecting the dots. Many years ago, Arena worked in one of Vitale's legitimate business, and Eddie's FBI source had told him of "bad blood" between Arena and Tieri. Tieri and Stracci were made members of the Vitale crime family. It seemed odd to Eddie that both Tieri's and Stracci's names would come up in his reporting about a stolen statue owned by Arena.

Considering the fact that Buster Bustamante worked for Stracci and delivered the carnations to Mrs. Bello, Eddie was certain that somehow Stracci had to be involved in the stealing of the statue. Why? The $25,000? And what about Tieri? What was his role—if he indeed had one—in this escapade? He'd have to run their names by Nick and see where it took him.

Eddie called Filomena's to speak with Nick, but he was at his apartment. He asked the maître d' if he wouldn't mind reaching out to Nick and telling him that Eddie Sabella needed to see him. Within minutes, the maître d' phoned Eddie, who quickly grabbed his coat and his notepad.

"Where the hell are you going?" Basic barked as Eddie rushed past his desk. "And where's tomorrow's column?"

"Still got plenty of time. We'll talk when I get back."

CHAPTER 33

THE CAB DEPOSITED EDDIE near the corner of Eighty-First and Fifth Avenue. The doorman alerted Nick to Eddie's arrival. Nick greeted Eddie and hung his coat in the foyer closet.

"Will you join me in a little brandy?"

"Just a little," Eddie said, following Nick into his den, where the blend of antique and contemporary pieces suggested the work of an interior decorator to Eddie. The walls were painted in a quiet tone of yellow, two of them lined with built-in cherry-wood bookcases. Looking at the watercolor sketch that hung above the fireplace, Eddie didn't have to see the artist's signature to know it was Picasso. On either side of the square glass-and-iron coffee table—nearly completely covered with art and photography books—were a pair of large, distressed-leather armchairs, and next to each armchair was a round side table containing a Saladino lamp with three little shades.

Eddie walked past the ornately carved desk near the window and gazed down at the vast expanse of Central Park. "It must look spectacular when it's lit up at night," he said.

As he turned to take a snifter of brandy from Nick, his eye caught an eight-by-ten photograph of Phyllis, framed in sliver, on the desk. Smiling wistfully at someone off-camera, she was wearing a white peasant blouse, her dark eyes and thick black hair as lustrous as the purple bougainvillea that climbed the trellis behind her. Eddie felt his heart lurch as he lifted the snifter to his lips and took a sip.

"That picture was taken in Florence," Nick said, "the summer we traveled around much of Italy." He paused. "A crazy thing, Eddie. We never got to Rome. Roma! She always wanted to go somewhere else. Have you ever been to Rome, Eddie?"

"No, I haven't," he said, wondering if he should tell Nick about the promise he and Phyllis had made to each other.

"You must. It is the most magnificent—"

"Sorry to interrupt, Nick," he said, forgetting about Rome. "But we gotta talk."

"Certainly," Nick said. "Please, sit."

Nick sat in one of his large leather armchairs, and Eddie sat in the other opposite him.

"Back in the day, did you know Gaspar Tieri and Willie Stracci?"

Nick took a slow sip of his brandy. "Why do you ask?" he said in an even voice.

"That wasn't exactly the answer I was expecting," Eddie said with a forced smile.

Nick crossed his legs and looked at Eddie for a couple of beats. "Yes, I knew them. We barely spent any time together. As I am sure you know, they worked for Don Vitale in quite a different capacity than I did."

"I happened to come across their names in my reporting—"

Nick's doorbell rang. He got up and excused himself. When he returned, he held a package the doorman had delivered. It was the size of a shoe box and wrapped in brown paper.

Nick unwrapped the package as Eddie watched from his leather armchair. "It is very light," he said, lifting the top of the plain white box and finding a wad of folded tissue paper with Scotch tape around it.

Nick retrieved a pair of scissors from the desk drawer, carefully snipped the Scotch tape, and unfolded the tissue paper. It contained a small piece of wood, less than an inch in diameter, in the shape of a flower and painted a pale shade of white. Nick placed it in the palm of his hand, gently stroking it with an index finger, and murmured, "What can this be?"

"Let me see," Eddie said, getting up off the chair.

Nick extended his open palm to Eddie, who bent to see it up close and then turned his attention to the box. "You missed this," he said, handing Nick a small card that had been pressed flat against one side of the box.

Eddie could see the cords in Nick's neck plump and throb. He took the card from Nick. Printed by hand in blue ink, the writing on the card read: *THE DEFLOWERING OF YOUR STATUE BEGINS PIECE BY LITTLE PIECE.*

"Shit," Eddie said. "Looks to me like one of the white lilies on the branch St. Joseph is holding."

"Yes, I am sure of it," Nick said.

"Can you call your doorman for me?" Eddie said, and when Nick handed him the phone, he questioned the doorman about the package.

"He's no help," Eddie said, hanging up. "The package was delivered by a kid he figured was a teenager, and maybe Hispanic. He simply handed the doorman the package and ran out. We've got nothing."

"Not nothing, Eddie. We know now the statue was not stolen for the reward."

"Could be, or maybe they don't think that twenty-five thousand is enough. Maybe they'll contact you and demand more, and this is a warning: you'd better pay up, or else they'll destroy the statue."

"Yes, that is possible," Nick said, swigging his brandy and pouring himself another shot. "It is...well, I do not show my emotions very often, but...you know, Eddie, as much as the statue means to me, I did not imagine I would feel this terrible, this empty, if I did not get it back."

Nick's body seemed to sag, and he sat back down in his chair. "What do you suggest we do now?"

"I'll call O'Grady. He'll want to check the box and the wood for prints, though we might've screwed things up by handling them like we did."

After alerting O'Grady, Eddie called Basic and Phoebe, filled them in on the latest development, and asked Phoebe to send over a photographer. He told them he'd be back in the office within an hour to write his column.

Sitting down again in the leather chair opposite Nick, Eddie said, "Let's assume the statue wasn't stolen to collect a reward, like you suggested. Who'd want to hurt you like this?"

"I do not know. At this moment, I cannot think of anyone."

"Maybe it's someone from your past. Like Willie Stracci."

"I told you, we were not well-acquainted. Stracci was a big, dumb *animale* who killed people. Perhaps he still does. That is all I can tell you about him."

Eddie laid out the relationship between Stracci, Buster, and the stolen statue. "Can you think of any reason why he might want the statue—other than the reward? Anything personal?"

"None," Nick said. "I am certain of this."

"What about Gaspar Tieri? Tell me about him."

Nick's eyes jumped like a flame off a match, and his jaw tightened. "Gaspar Tieri was always a cruel, treacherous man," Nick said, his face contorting like he'd just swallowed something bitter. "He had a taste for inflicting pain. He needed to hurt people like you and I need to breathe."

Eddie sat up a little straighter in his chair. "That bad, huh?"

"Knowing that piece of shit for even five minutes was to despise the ground he walked on."

The moment had come for Eddie to hit Nick with the question he'd been waiting to ask: "I have a source who told me there was bad blood between you two. True?"

"You have a good source," Nick said, without saying anything else.

A few beats later, Eddie said, "That's it? I'd like to hear more than that."

"Bad blood, as you put it...yes, many years ago. I have not even seen that pig since Vitale's funeral."

"In 1983. Right?"

Nick nodded. "Why are you so curious about Gaspar Tieri?"

"If we go on the theory that someone stole the statue to hurt you, someone from your past...anyway, tell me more."

Nick hesitated, and then: "It is an ugly story. It must be off the record. Otherwise, I will not speak of it."

"You're holding all the cards, Nick."

Nick cupped his snifter and gently swirled the brandy, staring at the whirlpool of golden-brown liquid. "What happened between Gaspar and me involved something I am ashamed of to this day."

Setting down his glass, Nick loosened his tie and unbuttoned the color of his white shirt, revealing the scar that ran down the left side of his neck. "Last night you asked me about this," he said, tapping the scar with two fingers. "It was Gaspar Tieri—he gave it to me."

Nick told of a night when Vitale treated a number of his young associates to a dinner in a brownstone on the Upper East Side. "Don Vitale asked me to come with him, and I knew it would be unwise to refuse him. Where we ate…they called it a club, but it was actually a whorehouse. There were women everywhere, some naked, some not.

"After dinner, Don Vitale went home, and he said I should stay. I stayed."

Nick shrugged regretfully. "We went to a large room with an enormous chandelier where a bar was set up. Gaspar was there. I remember Gaspar had a whore on each arm, and he ordered some crazy rum drink the bartender did not know how to make. So the son of a bitch pulls out his gun and holds it to the bartender's head. He threatens to shoot him if he does not drink the whole bottle of rum without stopping to breathe."

"What was the reaction of the other people in the room?"

"The animals—they thought it was some kind of joke. Even the whores laughed and cheered the bartender as he started to drink from the bottle. The poor bastard, he was shaking like a scared rabbit."

Nick picked up his glass and sipped his brandy, swallowing uneasily. "To make a longer story short…"

"No, don't. I have the time."

"But I do not have the stomach for it. The memory still sickens me. Please, allow me to finish."

Eddie nodded once, slowly, and Nick continued, his lips twisting in disgust as he spoke. "The bartender drank maybe half the bottle, and then he vomited. Gaspar grabbed him by his shirt and pistol-whipped him. Nobody said a word or tried to stop him. Including me, Eddie. It was a miracle he did not kill the man.

"A few nights later, Gaspar and I happened to run into each other at a joint on Mulberry Street. I was feeling very guilty for not helping that bartender, and I got into an argument with Gaspar. I called him a coward for the beating he gave that man, and he lost his temper. He smashed a glass against my neck. We fought, and I left him broken on the floor. There is nothing more to the story."

"So you and Tieri get into a fight. He breaks a glass against your neck, and you whip his ass. That's as far as it goes between you two?"

"Gaspar was deeply embarrassed when I hurt him, and word got back to Vitale that maybe Gaspar was not so tough after all. It hurt his reputation in the family."

"Yeah, but we're talking—what? Forty years ago?"

"Maybe a few years less," Nick said, breaking into a smile. "Have you never heard about Sicilian Alzheimer's? You forget everything *except* the grudge."

"Yes, I've heard the joke."

"It is funny, Eddie, because it has the ring of truth. And still, people underestimate the grip that a desire for revenge can have on a man. Understand this, Eddie: after so many years, he might not even know he is in its grip. Sometimes it is like a parasite in the pit of your stomach that suddenly comes alive again and eats at your insides."

"What makes it come alive again?"

"An opportunity to strike. Gaspar reads about the statue in the paper, and what it means to me, and his desire for revenge is aroused. It can drive a man *pazzo.*"

"But why wait all these years to get his revenge? Why didn't he just wait for the right moment and then kill you?"

"Gaspar is not a stupid man. I was making Don Vitale a lot of money in his bakeries and with the numbers, and Gaspar was not foolish enough to risk the Don's wrath by fucking around with my ability to keep earning."

Eddie shook his head, trying to grasp the logic behind Nick's various theories. "But Vitale died in '83, and Tieri still waited more than twenty years to exact his revenge? I've heard it said over and over that revenge is a dish best served cold, but this one's frozen in time. And if Tieri still wants revenge so badly, help me understand why he doesn't just shoot you, rather than go to all the trouble of stealing a statue?"

"Sicilians understand that sometimes it is more effective to keep your savage impulses in check when settling old scores. Revenge is not always achieved with piles of corpses and rivers of blood."

"Now that you've put it that way…do you think Tieri's got that kind of diabolical mind? That he would think of sending you pieces of your statue rather than simply killing you or paying someone to?"

Nick allowed himself a short laugh. "He is not so clever."

"Then you don't believe Tieri had anything to do with stealing the statue?"

Nick polished off his brandy. "I think it is unlikely."

"Very?"

"Highly."

"I was beginning to think you really did suspect Tieri."

"I never really—"

Nick was interrupted by the sound of two short rings from the phone on the desk. He lifted himself from the chair to answer the call from the lobby. "Send him up," he said.

It was the photographer from Eddie's newspaper, a lanky young Korean-American named Albert. He wore low-rise jeans, a gray pin-striped vest over a white shirt, and rings on several fingers.

Eddie and Albert quickly eased into a smooth working relationship. Albert followed Eddie's lead and got all the shots he might need for the story—the box, the note, the lily chip—except the one he wanted most: Nick reading the note, standing at the window of his den with Central Park in the background.

Nick had refused to pose, once, twice, three times, until Eddie stepped in and called off Albert, saying, "It's kind of an artsy-fartsy bullshit shot anyway."

"I don't agree," Albert said amicably. "But you're the reason I might get the front page, so you da man."

When Detective O'Grady arrived, Albert snapped off a few shots of him walking through the door.

"Did you tell him about Stracci?" O'Grady asked Eddie, who summed up his earlier conversation with Nick.

The detective then put on a pair of latex gloves and picked up the box with the chip in it, saying, "No way we'd get a print off this chip. Maybe off the box or the note, but I'd wager whoever has the statue, whoever wrote this note, wouldn't be careless enough to leave his prints."

"If it is at all possible, Detective, may I keep the flower from the statue?" Nick said. "It is so small, and like you say, it won't be of any use to you. I would hate to have the police misplace it."

O'Grady thought about it for a brief few seconds, then held out the box for Nick to take the chip. "Why not? But you safeguard it. I may need it back. It's one-in-a-thousand, but you never know."

Eddie and O'Grady left the apartment together. In the elevator, O'Grady said, "This the weirdest case I've caught in a long time. I can't make up my mind whether it's just silly or really perverted."

"It's turning into a helluva story, that's all I know."

Since O'Grady never specifically asked about Gaspar Tieri—he hadn't yet linked Stracci to Gaspar—neither Nick nor Eddie mentioned his name. Each had his own reason. It wasn't in Nick's nature, being Sicilian in his core, to volunteer information. Meanwhile, Eddie's competitive instincts persuaded him to keep Gaspar's name to himself for now, as he couldn't ignore the hunch that was still stirring in his gut.

It wouldn't be the last time he'd sidestep the cops to lock up another exclusive for himself.

CHAPTER 34

EDDIE WAS DEEP INTO his exclusive front-page story about Willie Stracci, Buster Bustamante, and the package containing the lily chip and the note when Father Keller returned his call.

"Holy Mary, Mother of God," the priest said. "Some sonuvabitch intends to take the statue apart piece by piece?"

"That's what the note says."

"What the hell is wrong with people today? Too many deviants and assholes in this world. And you can quote me word for word on that. I don't give a damn."

"Guess you won't have the statue back for tomorrow's Mass."

"It's a prohibitive long shot, certainly. I'll replace the old statue with a white limestone statue of St. Joe that's here in the rectory. What a damn shame."

Eddie also warned Father Keller that he couldn't write the column without including Mrs. Bello and Johnny Bello, but he didn't use their names or their specific address—they were referred to as the elderly lady and the grandson. The priest thanked him and said he hoped to see Eddie at Mass in the morning.

The first thing Basic said to Eddie when he got back to the office was, "How fast can you get me that column?"

"Like I'm double-parked outside," Eddie said.

Less than forty minutes later, Eddie sent the column to Basic. Gaspar Tieri's name didn't make the cut. While he'd still lay odds on Gaspar's involvement in the theft of the statue, he had no proof. He'd likely have to wait until Stracci or Buster surfaced and were questioned by O'Grady. Until then, he was keeping Gaspar in the crosshairs.

Eddie called Moe Vogel. "I need to talk to you about a guy named Gaspar Tieri. I'm betting you know him."

"Yeah, off and on for years," Moe said. "He's one mean, ruthless piece of business."

"I've heard."

"Whatever you heard, multiply it by ten. His mantra was, 'You wound me, I don't stop bleeding until I make you bleed.' And he always kept his word. Why're you asking about him?"

"His relationship to Nick Arena."

"Hard to talk now. I'm at the Rangers game tonight. Want to join me?"

"Hockey? I'd rather eat my spleen."

"Ha! Good one," Moe said. "I gotta remember that line. After the game, then, the bar in that hotel across the street from the Garden."

Striding out of the newsroom, Eddie bumped into Max at the elevator bank. He was wearing a tweed sports jacket over a beige polyester shirt adorned with jockeys atop racehorses.

"Love the shirt," Eddie said, only slightly concealing the smirk in his voice.

"It's what they call vintage, my ignorant friend. I bought it at the '78 Belmont to celebrate Affirmed's Triple Crown."

"Special occasion?"

"Nothing to write home about. Hey, listen, I'm having drinks tomorrow night with some ESPN execs. Should be free by eight thirty. Let's do dinner, grab a steak at Pecky's. Sound good?"

"I'm there."

Out on the street in the waning light, Eddie was headed for Grand Central to grab a subway uptown when his cell phone rang. He answered it as soon as he saw his father's number on the display screen.

"Hey, Pop, how's it going?"

"Fine, I'm fine. Just called to tell you how much I'm enjoying your latest string of columns."

"Thanks, Pop. Sorry I haven't called lately. It's been kinda hectic."

"I can imagine."

"You won't believe who I was with the other night."

"Who?"

"Phyllis Blake."

"My God, where's she been all these years?"

"It's a long story, Pop, a very long story."

"You know, Eddie, your mother always had a feeling you two would get together again. You think that's in the cards?"

"Who can say?"

"Well, if that's what you want, your mother would be so happy for you. Me too."

"I know, Pop," Eddie said softly.

As he entered Grand Central Station, he said goodbye to his father, promising to have dinner with him soon. When he hung up, he felt a flare of sadness in his throat. He didn't see or talk to his father often enough, and he knew his mother would be disappointed in him.

Rather than rushing home to kill time in an empty apartment, Eddie decided to grab a drink at Michael Jordan's oval bar overlooking the cavernous sweep of Grand Central. His mind soon wandered back to his conversation with Nick. He pulled his notepad from his overcoat pocket and reviewed his notes. Since Nick had spoken off the record, Eddie had kept his pen and notebook out of sight. But in the cab back to his office, he'd dashed off some notes from memory, notes he would never turn into a story unless Nick gave him permission—or dropped dead. They were scribbled in a kind of shorthand that Eddie often used: *revenge, people underestimate, grip, parasite, comes alive...*

Eddie paid for his half-finished drink, and a few moments after hailing a cab on Lexington Avenue, he heard himself telling the driver, "Take me to the Tieri & Sons Funeral Home, downtown, on Sullivan Street."

What was Nick up to? Eddie wondered. What was his angle? He had to be more suspicious of Tieri than he let on. It was in his nature. Had he inadvertently tipped Eddie off with that quote about man's undying desire for revenge? Or had he thrown it into the conversation on purpose, to keep Eddie on the scent, just in case Tieri was indeed in possession of the statue?

Eddie also wondered what the hell he thought he'd find out by going face-to-face with Tieri. Would he even get the chance to ask a question or two before Tieri clammed up and told him to get the fuck out of his funeral home? Eddie shrugged off his doubts. This was what reporters did when they had time on their hands. They chased stories, sometimes like a dog chasing his own tail.

The cabbie, wearing a tattered old flat cap and barely able to see over the steering wheel, drove like he was guided by radar. As the cab rolled to a stop behind a hearse parked in front of the funeral home, Eddie said, "Geez, that was quick."

"Not my first time here," the cabbie said. "This place been around for years."

CHAPTER 35

EDDIE WALKED PAST clusters of mourners. Business was booming. Each of the four parlors was occupied, and judging from the crowds, each of the deceased had been the life of the party or had come from large, extended families—or both. The suffocating scent of flowers reminded Eddie of his mother's wake, which was the last time he'd stepped inside a funeral home. The sickly sweet smell seemed to settle in the pit of his stomach, and he swallowed hard to keep from gagging as he perused the directory letter board in the lobby. He then checked his watch.

It was just past seven o'clock. *Shit,* he thought, he'd probably acted too hastily. He should've called ahead to make sure Tieri...

"Excuse me, can I help you?"

Eddie turned around to face a woman dressed in a black skirt and a black long-sleeved blouse with tiny white polka dots. "I hope so," he said. "I'm looking for Mr. Gaspar Tieri."

"May I ask what this is in reference to?"

"It's a private matter. And your name is?"

"Margaret Mary Gaffney. I'm Mr. Tieri's executive assistant. And you are?"

"I'm an acquaintance of Mr. Tieri's."

"No, you're not. I recognize you from your picture. You're Eddie Sabella, and I very much doubt that you're an acquaintance of Mr. Tieri's."

Eddie lifted his hands shoulder-high, palms out, as if to say, *Don't shoot.*

Margaret Mary gave Eddie a beguiling half smile. A smile like that came naturally to her, Eddie guessed. She had blue eyes and a dusting of freckles across her nose and cheeks. Her thick strawberry-blonde hair was tied back with a small black bow in a half-hearted ponytail. He figured she was in her mid-forties, unmarried—she wore neither an engagement ring nor a wedding band—and that she carefully monitored her weight. Another eight or ten pounds would push her from full-figured to chubby, and she carried herself with too much aplomb to let that happen.

"He's down the end of that hall, the office on the left," she said, pointing.

"You think he'd mind an uninvited visitor?"

"Probably, but I won't stop you," she said, and as she turned to walk away, there was that smile again.

Eddie knocked on the door and heard Gaspar call out in the gravelly voice he recognized from their phone conversation: "Come in, it's open."

"Hello, Mr. Tieri," he said, stepping into a nicotine haze that enveloped the office. "I'm Eddie Sabella."

Gaspar's wire-rimmed aviator glasses were a little too large for his pale, creased faced. But it was his black eyes—dull and darting and small as a reptile's—that held Eddie's gaze as he reached Gaspar's desk and extended a hand across it.

"What do you want?" he said, ignoring Eddie's attempt to shake his hand.

Gaspar stubbed out his cigarette in a square ashtray already filled with butts smoked to such a nub that Eddie wondered how Gaspar hadn't scorched his lips. He was pretty sure that Gaspar was defying any one of the city's anti-smoking laws, but he doubted Gaspar gave a shit. Considering his criminal record, smoking where he shouldn't be had no chance of cracking Gaspar's personal top ten list of felonious activities.

"Mind if I sit down?"

"You planning to stay awhile?" Gaspar lit another cigarette and gestured indifferently toward one of the two chairs facing him on the other side of the desk.

Eddie sat down, and before he could utter a word, Gaspar said, "If you got more questions you want to ask me, I'm really not interested in hearing them."

"I did warn you that after talking to Nick Arena, I'd be back to tell you about it. So here I am."

"Oh, this oughta be good. What he tell you?"

"I'll get to that. First, let's talk about Willie Stracci. A friend of yours, right?"

"That's not a state secret," Gaspar said casually. "And besides, I got a lot of friends."

Gaspar barely completed the sentence when a loud, hacking cough erupted from somewhere deep inside his chest. It shook his body and brought tears to his eyes, lasting maybe seven or eight seconds, but seeming much longer. He inhaled a few short, trembling breaths to get straight, and took off his glasses, using the fingers of one hand to wipe his eyes dry, never letting go of his cigarette in the other hand.

"Let me ask you a question, Mr. Reporter. Did Arena tell you about the numbers run out of his bakeries?" he said, every few words punctuated by a wheeze.

"Actually, he did. He said it was a service they provided to their customers."

"I bet my balls he didn't talk about the ovens in his bakeries, did he?"

Eddie flinched at the mention of ovens, though only slightly and likely unnoticed by Gaspar. "What about the ovens?"

"There were rumors they burned guys in those ovens."

"I happen to know that you were arrested for burning a guy—"

"That was a long time ago, sonny boy," Gaspar said in an aggressive voice, "and they couldn't prove a thing."

"Maybe that's because the witness against you disappeared before the trial."

Gaspar's smile was wet and wide, like a dog's. "Like I said, it was just rumors, and it would be a good thing if we left it at that."

"I'm curious. Did the rumors include the two bakeries that Nick Arena managed? Did he have a role in any of it?"

"Role? Like what, an actor?" Gaspar said.

"You know what I mean."

"If they burned guys in one of Arena's bakeries, that means he was like an accomplice or an accessory, one of those two things. I'm pretty sure about that."

"Nick says nobody was ever burned in one of his bakeries."

"You believe him?"

"Tell me why I shouldn't."

Gaspar inhaled a long drag of his cigarette. Before he could clear his lungs of the smoke, he started coughing again, all the while glaring at Eddie, whose pitying expression pissed Gaspar off. "You think I'm a fucking moron, smoking like this, don't you?"

"No, sir, you're not a fucking moron." Eddie looked at his watch. "I've been talking to you for almost ten minutes now, and you haven't told me shit."

"You tried," Gaspar said with a smug smile. "Don't blame yourself. I'm no virgin at this."

Eddie paused, then angled to take the conversation in a different direction by poking the mobster's pride. "By the way, I also believed Nick when he told me he kicked your ass in a barroom fight when you were supposed to be the toughest guy on the block."

"Fuck you. I got in my shots."

"Like a sucker punch to the neck with a glass."

Gaspar narrowed his eyes and hit Eddie with a mean-street stare, but Eddie kept pressing him. "We could go off the record if you'd like. Were any of Nick Arena's bakeries used to burn Vitale's enemies?"

"Off the record, on the record—fuck the record," Gaspar said. "You print anything I say here, you're a dead man. You got that? Dead fucking meat."

Eddie started to smile one of those oh-you're-such-a-kidder kind of smiles, but thought better of it. If there was anything in Gaspar's expression that indicated he was joking or maybe exaggerating to make a point, Eddie didn't see it. Then he summoned some nerve and said, "What the fuck world you think we're living in, threatening a journalist like that?"

"That was no threat," Gaspar said, his small eyes meeting Eddie's squarely. "I will spit you out like a bad clam."

At that moment, Eddie realized he had just experienced a first on the job: a subject expressing a preference for ending Eddie's life rather than merely stating a wish to go off the record. Still, he felt strangely calm. Maybe it was because he'd never heard of a wise guy killing a reporter in New York over a story he had written. No, wise guys didn't kill reporters—cirrhosis and lung cancer did. Or at least they used to.

"Then answer me this," Eddie said. "Why the hell did you even bother taking the time to talk to me?"

"I try to be a cordial person," Gaspar said, lifting a hand and checking out his manicured fingernails, glazed with transparent polish.

"And that's the only reason?"

"I been reading your stories, and I can tell you like Arena. He's got you wrapped around his little finger. Well, Nick Arena ain't no angel. You hear me? Nick Arena is a phony, stuck-up sonuvabitch."

Eddie noticed that Gaspar bared his teeth whenever he mentioned Nick's name, spitting it out like an owl would spit out the bones of small rodents.

"Give me an example why you think he's no angel and a phony."

But Gaspar had nothing more to say. He got up and grabbed his overcoat off an old standing coat rack. He was five-foot-seven or so, thin and properly funereal in a dark suit, white shirt, and black tie.

"Do you have the statue?" Eddie asked out of nowhere, hoping to provoke some sort of involuntary reaction that would signal Gaspar's guilt.

Gaspar continued putting on his overcoat without even the slightest hint of surprise in his eyes. "No. You happy? You should've asked me that when you walked in here. Saved us both a lot of time."

Eddie wondered if the aging gangster was acting too cool, as if he'd been lying in wait for Eddie to ask that precise question all along.

Outside the funeral home, a man dressed in black, including a black chauffeur's cap, was waiting for Gaspar. He was the driver of the hearse parked in front, and he opened the door for his boss. "Ay, it's a free ride," a grinning Gaspar said to Eddie as he folded himself into the front seat.

Eddie watched the hearse pull away from the curb, and a few moments later had a decision to make: Where to eat dinner? Uptown at

Filomena's, or somewhere nearby? He hadn't seen or talked to Phyllis in more than twenty-four hours, and they didn't exactly part on an upbeat note. What's more, Filomena's would be jumping with customers on a Saturday night. She'd be too busy to pay him much attention, and he'd wind up sulking at the far end of the bar like a needy mess of a man. The way things were going, he could imagine capping the evening by upsetting her again and then hating himself for doing just that.

Max was right about being Eddie Sabella, he concluded. It *was* exhausting.

He went back inside the funeral home. He spotted Mary Margaret Gaffney smiling at him, and he walked toward her. She kept smiling at Eddie with every step he took in her direction.

"Something else I can help you with?" she said, looking up at Eddie.

"I haven't eaten a thing since breakfast, and I'm starved. Can you recommend a good place around here?"

"You look like a guy who'd go for Italian."

"Am I that obvious?"

"Don't worry, it suits you," she said with a wink. "Giordino's, right around the corner on Thompson. Very Italian and very good."

"Can I get in at this hour on a Saturday night?"

"I know the owner. You hustle over there while I make the call."

"That's awfully nice of you. Thanks so much."

Eddie shook Margaret Mary's hand, and before he could let go, she said, "I might join you in a little while for a drink, so please don't eat too fast."

"I'll savor every morsel," Eddie said, and they both laughed.

CHAPTER 36

AS EDDIE ENTERED GIORDINO'S, his phone rang. He turned and walked back outside to answer it.

"Change of plans, my friend," Moe Vogel said. "I forgot Connie made a date for a late dinner in Brooklyn with her cousin after the Rangers game. No can do drinks. Anything we can take care of over the phone?"

"I just talked with Tieri at his funeral home. I can't shake this feeling that maybe he had something to do with stealing Nick's statue."

"Why?"

Eddie told Moe about the lily chip, and that he and Nick had speculated that perhaps the taking of the statue was motivated by revenge rather than money. "And when I pressed Nick about Tieri, he admitted that back in the day he kicked the crap out of him in a bar, humiliating him in front of other wise guys who were there."

"Did Nick tell you anything else about that night?"

"Like what?"

"I heard Gaspar was with his girlfriend. She saw Nick beat him up. She was Puerto Rican, a living doll. Don't remember her name. Gaspar was wild for her, acted like a puppy dog when she was around. If she said, 'Jump,' he'd say, 'How high?' Treated her like a queen.

"Next thing everybody knows, Nick snakes her away from Gaspar. They had a good thing going for a time, and then he dumps her. Then one day she overdoses.

"She was only a kid, maybe something like nineteen, or twenty.

Like that. Was she a junkie to begin with—there were rumors about her—or did she become a junkie and overdose because Nick dumped her? That's the question."

"What do you think?"

Eddie could hear the shrug in Moe's voice. "Who can say? But the word on the street was that Gaspar blamed Nick. He believed Nick fucked her up, broke her heart when he left her, and that's when she overdosed. Gaspar never forgave him."

"In terms of the revenge angle, that makes a little more sense to me. Blaming Nick for killing the girl he loved is a lot worse than losing a fight to him. At least that's my take."

"It's even worse than that. Gaspar ended up marrying a nice Italian girl from the neighborhood. Loretta Esposito. His mother pushed him to marry her. She was happy that he married Loretta instead of a P.R. But they had a miserable marriage. I guess Loretta was a constant reminder of the girl he really loved…"

"And lost to Nick," Eddie said.

"I once asked Nick whether the girl was already a junkie when he started going out with her. He practically gnashed his teeth at me and said, 'What the fuck difference does it make? She's dead.' Pretty cold, huh? Kinda surprised me."

"You know Willie Stracci too?"

"Geez, another blast from my past. Scary dude. Our paths only crossed a few times, but I can tell you he had half Tieri's brains, but twice the muscle. Make that five times the muscle." Moe chuckled. "Make that five times the muscle of any man who walked the earth."

When Eddie walked back inside Giordino's and got a better look, he'd bet even money he'd like the food. It was one of those old-school, red-sauce joints with checkered tablecloths and a large painting of the Bay of Naples over the bar, which was three-deep with folks waiting for a table. But as soon as Eddie gave his name to the handsome, middle-aged maître d' standing guard near the entrance, he was led to a table a few yards from the bar.

Eddie was almost finished with his veal picatta and sautéed escarole when he saw Margaret Mary approaching his table, followed by the maître d', who was carrying a second chair.

"How'd you like your dinner?" Margaret Mary said as she was seated at Eddie's table.

"Excellent," Eddie said. "Want something to eat?"

"No, thanks, I'm good. But a rye and ginger would hit the spot."

Eddie ordered Margaret Mary her drink, then asked, "So, what's it like working for Gaspar Tieri?"

"He's a prick," she said. "Pardon my French."

"That's it?"

"Isn't that enough? If I didn't need the job to help support my mother, I'd be out of there in a New York minute."

Margaret Mary took a long sip of her drink as soon as it arrived. "He's got a real bad temper. Oh, he never hit me or anything, but I've seen him get physical with other people."

"Like who?"

"Well, the gentleman who delivers the embalming fluid, for one. It comes in these big bottles, and the other day he gives us eleven bottles instead of the dozen we ordered. Gaspar went ballistic. He does that. You never know what will make him explode. Anyway, he started kicking the guy in his shins, and then he picked up an ashtray, one of those heavy ones, and hit him on the head."

"Christ," Eddie said in a semi-startled voice. "Then what happened?"

"The poor guy was out cold for, like, a minute. I thought Gaspar had killed him. When he came to, he ran out of there quick as he could."

Margaret Mary took another long sip of her drink as she listened to Eddie's follow-up question. "Didn't the company the guy worked for do anything about it?"

"What're they gonna do?" she said. Then, in a hushed voice: "He's in the mafia. You know that, right?"

"Yes, I do."

"By the way, Eddie, don't say anything about us having drinks. Gaspar'd probably fire me if he found out I was talking to the media."

"You have my word. And as long as we're off the record, can you tell me where Gaspar lives—just in case I might need to contact him outside the funeral home?"

"You're really putting me on the spot here," she said, and took the last swallow of her drink. "Okay, Eddie, you're lucky I like you. He lives at 205 Third Avenue, which is between Eighteenth and Nineteenth. But you'll hardly ever reach him there at night. He's a widower, you know. He spends a lot of time after work at the Ooga Mooga Lounge, in the East Village."

"The Ooga Mooga Lounge—you're serious?"

"I kid you not," she said. "And remember, mum's the word."

CHAPTER 37

WHEN EDDIE ARRIVED at the Ooga Mooga Lounge, he spotted Gaspar sitting alone at the bar. There wasn't much of a crowd, and Eddie got the impression there rarely was. The place was a dump.

Eddie sat on a stool next to Gaspar and got a whiff of Old Spice cologne. "I figured you for classier joints."

When Gaspar turned to see Eddie, he hung his head. "Why the fuck can't you leave me alone? I'm starting to think you got a death wish."

"Actually, I just think you're an interesting guy with a lot to say about a lot of things."

"Like that fucking statue you asked me about?" Gaspar said with a weary smile. "Look, you should really use your common sense. If I wanted to steal that thing, I'd of done it years ago."

"I'm betting you didn't know it even existed years ago. And if you did, you didn't know how much it meant to Nick Arena until the other day, when you read my column about the reward."

"Says you."

Eddie checked his watch. "I think you should know that in another hour or so, my paper hits the street, and you can read about your pal Willie Stracci and how he may know something about the theft of the statue."

"You write it?"

"Yes."

"I hope you get a raise," Gaspar said, a sneer in his voice.

Gaspar motioned to the bartender, a young, buff Black man in a Hawaiian shirt festooned with hula dancers and palm trees, his head wrapped in a red-and-white-patterned bandana.

"I'll have one more, *paisano*," Gaspar said.

"You?" The bartender nodded at Eddie.

"Dewar's, rocks, splash of soda."

"Who the fuck drinks Scotch in a tiki bar?" Gaspar said to Eddie, and then, to the bartender: "Make him one of mine. On me."

"What is it?" Eddie asked the bartender, flicking a finger at Gaspar's green-glazed mug, forged in the shape of a squat, piano-toothed savage playing a ukulele.

"A Tieri Tonga," the bartender said.

"Named after me," Gaspar said, beaming. "I invented it a long time ago. Had to teach my *paisano* here how to make it when he came on board last year."

"Will it kill me?"

"Just paralyze you a little," Gaspar replied. He gestured at the bartender. "Tell him what's in it."

"Vodka, rum, Curacao, and pineapple juice. If I told you the proportions, then I'd have to kill you. Right, Mr. Tieri?"

"Or maybe *I'd* have to kill *you*," Gaspar said to the bartender with a smile so thin it was barely visible.

The bartender laughed joylessly, and Eddie could have sworn he detected a spark of fear in his eyes before he walked away to blend two fresh Tieri Tongas.

"So, now we talked about the statue, what else do you want outta me?" Gaspar said in a voice without its usual tough-guy edge.

"First, let me see if I like my Tieri Tonga, and maybe I'll think of something."

"Well, I'll tell you something—you're like an iguana in the desert who bites you on your pants leg, and you can't shake it off."

"I'm offended," Eddie said, pretending to be insulted. "You're comparing me to something that crawls out from under a rock?"

"If the shoe fits," Gaspar said, not unpleasantly.

Eddie had the impression that Gaspar was starting to enjoy their banter, or at the very least tolerate it. He wanted to ask Gaspar about the young woman who'd left him for Nick, but he figured he'd wait and keep the conversation going for a little while longer.

Soften him up, if that was possible.

Until then, Eddie didn't want to miss the opportunity to shoot the shit with Gaspar. He had come across his fair share of singular characters as a city-side reporter and columnist—Father Arthur Keller being the most recent—and Gaspar seemed like he could be one of the more indelible, one of those guys who'd dropped his moral compass down a sewer before he was old enough to drive. If he could get closer to Gaspar, get to know more about him, unearth the kind of personal details you couldn't find by googling his name...then one day, when the old gangster kicked, he'd have the goods to write the kind of profile you could take to the bank.

"What's it about this joint you like so much?"

"The potential. It's a shithole, I'm not fucking blind. Just look at it..."

Eddie followed Gaspar's gaze as he scanned the entire room, from the speckled gray-and-green linoleum floor and the frayed red vinyl-covered booths to the plastic tiki heads and rubber palm trees and cheap straw hula skirts that were nailed along the dull-blue walls. And above the bar, hanging from the ceiling, the ugliest design scheme ever devised for brightening up a room—a series of lights in the shape of spiky, pinkish orange puffer fish.

"In the back room over there," Gaspar said, pointing to his right, "there's two pinball machines, which is bad enough. But there's also a big poster of Neil Diamond on the wall. Now, don't get me wrong. I like 'Sweet Caroline' and 'Forever in Blue Jeans' as much as the next guy, but what the fuck does Neil Diamond have to do with a tiki bar? Nothing makes any sense in this place."

The bartender arrived with two Tieri Tongas, and when Eddie had taken his first sip, Gaspar said, "How you like it?"

"Smooth, and tasty," Eddie lied. "So, Mr. Tieri—"

"Gaspar. Call me Gaspar. That's my name too."

"So, Gaspar, if it's got such potential, what would you do with the place?"

Gaspar's face told of his delight as he launched into his vision for the joint. "First thing, change the fucking name. The Ooga Mooga

Lounge, what's that about? I'd call it something like Bali Hai, something romantic like that. Then I'd make it like the old Trader Vic's in the Plaza Hotel. You're probably too young to remember it. A real top-shelf joint, before that fucking Trump bought the hotel for his wife and the Nazi bitch shut it down."

"If you're talking about Ivana, she's Czech."

"Czech, Nazi, who gives a fuck? They all sound the same to me," Gaspar said, taking a sip of his drink through a plastic straw. "Anyways, like I said, I'd make this like Trader Vic's, with dark-wood walls and fountains and real tiki heads and palm trees and canvas sails and thatched roofs over everything. I'd put leis made of fresh flowers on the tables every night, and I'd have all the good tiki drinks: Zombies and Mai Tais and Planter's Punch and Suffering Bastards and—"

Gaspar erupted in another one of his death-rattle coughing fits, his body twitching in spasms. He reached into his jacket pocket for a stained white handkerchief and held it to his mouth as he coughed.

The stains were red.

A few seconds later, he took another, longer sip of his drink and said, "You know what else I'd do?"

"What?"

"I'd serve great Hawaiian and Polynesian food—big fucking pupu platters with spare ribs and fried shrimp and chicken teriyaki on a stick. And for the main course, I'd roast whole suckling pigs, and I'd have a lot of fish, like salmon and tuna and mahi mahi. That's good shit, mahi mahi, when it's prepared right. Very healthful."

What a weird and yet oddly enchanting ambition, Eddie thought. It always amazed him when he stumbled onto a terrific story by asking simple and obvious questions. Crack open the shell of a stone-cold thug like Gaspar, an ex-con wise guy with a homicidal heart, and you'd never know what you might find. He hoped his suspicions about Gaspar and the statue were spot-on, so he'd have a reason to write about him in the very near future rather than wait for him to die—though that didn't seem too far in the future either, if that blood-stained handkerchief were any indication.

"Where the hell did your passion for this Polynesian thing come from?"

Without hesitation, and in a voice filled with such warmth and longing that Eddie had to remind himself he was listening to a gangster with classic psychopathic tendencies, Gaspar recalled a night when he was twenty-one years old and on a date with his girlfriend. "She was a beauty, *marone a mi*," he said, shaking his right hand in the air for emphasis. "Puerto Rican, but she had class, and sweet as anyone you ever met."

Never expecting Gaspar to bring up his lost love, Eddie saw he had an opening and jumped in. "What was her name?"

"Marisol. I used to call her Mary."

Gaspar sucked on the straw in his drink and then: "I was a kid after big things, had some pair of balls. Somebody told Don Vitale I was a reliable worker, and he wanted to do something nice for me. He was like that, could be very personable when he wanted to. He treated me and Mary to a dinner at Trader Vic's. The food was fantastic, sort of like Chinese, but better. Know what I'm saying?"

"Sounds like I would've liked it."

"Yeah, defintely. And the drinks? Jesus Christ Almighty! Ever have a Scorpion? It's got gin and vodka in it, and different kinds of rums and juices. They served it in a big fucking bowl, and it came with two long straws so me and Mary can drink it at the same time. And get this: there was a white orchid floating in the bowl. No shit. And when we finished it, Mary picked the orchid out of the bowl, dried it off, and pinned it in her hair."

Gaspar heaved a sigh, and he looked away. Moments later, his eyes moist with sadness, he cleared his throat before continuing. "We got hooked on the place, and went there a few more times. You know, they had a big-ass canoe in the lobby that was from *Mutiny on the Bounty*, the one with Brando in it. What a fucking nutjob he was, huh? Anyways, Mary loved Brando, and she loved that boat."

"That's a sweet story, Gaspar, really," Eddie said, and he wasn't conning him, though he *was* angling for Gaspar to keep talking. "Must've hurt something awful when she died."

"Fucking awful," Gaspar said. The words were barely out of Gaspar's mouth when Eddie saw something menacing ripple across his face. "Ay, how'd you know she died?"

"Take it easy, Gaspar. It's just that you seemed so sad talking about her."

Gaspar pounced again. "Must be somebody from the old days. C'mon, who was it? Nick Arena, wasn't it? That fuck-face Arena, right?"

Eddie held up a hand. "Swear to God, it wasn't Nick."

"I think you're full of shit," Gaspar said. "And just when it seemed we had a nice conversation going here."

"I didn't mean to upset you, Gaspar," Eddie said, hoping to placate the aging gangster and get him talking again.

"Yeah, sure," Gaspar said, and suddenly hopped off his bar stool. "I'm gonna catch some fresh air."

Eddie watched him walk to the door and debated whether to join him or give him some time alone to cool off. Before he could make up his mind, Gaspar turned and, holding the door open, said, "You coming or what?"

Outside, Gaspar lit a Lucky Strike. "Listen to what I'm telling you. Like I said back in my funeral parlor, I don't want to see any of this in print. There would be repercussions, *capisce?*"

Eddie nodded. "You must've loved her very much."

"She died too young. And I ended up having a lousy marriage. Oh, I don't blame Loretta—that was my wife's name. It's just the way things worked out. You can't win 'em all, know what I'm saying?"

Gaspar was starting to look and sound like a guy who'd been lugging around a fifty-pound bag of shit for much of his life.

"At least you've got your sons," Eddie said in a sympathetic voice.

"What sons? I got two daughters."

"But the name says Tieri & Sons..."

"I know what it says, but I thought the Tieri and Daughters Funeral Home didn't have the right fucking ring to it. I mean, who in their right mind ever brings their daughters into the funeral parlor business?"

"Any grandchildren?"

"No. My older daughter died of leukemia. Only sixteen when she passed, the apple of my eye. Loved the hell out of that kid. The younger one, we don't talk no more. Always disrespectful, born rotten. Drugs. Tattoos. Pins in her tongue and eyebrows. God forgive me for saying it, but she was a slut. Married a Lebanese boy from Bay Ridge just to spite me, and they moved to San Diego. Good riddance."

"I'm sorry for your loss, and who knows? Maybe you'll get back with your other daughter."

"Not a fucking chance in hell," Gaspar said, flicking his cigarette into the street and heading back inside. "What an asshole. I didn't wear my coat."

As the two men sat down at the bar again, Eddie decided against asking Gaspar about Nick and Marisol until he could sense the conversation winding down. Bringing it up would surely throw Gaspar into a rage of epic proportions, and Eddie wanted to keep him talking. "Why didn't you ever buy your own tiki joint instead of getting into the funeral business?"

"I had no choice," Gaspar said. "I asked Don Vitale to back me in a place, but he said a funeral home had more security than a restaurant, because people are always gonna die."

"Hard to argue with that logic."

"Bullshit. People are always gonna eat too. My wife called me a cliché. It's French, you know. Anyways, I asked what the hell she meant, and she said it meant I'd be just another mobbed-up wop running a funeral home. That hurt."

Gaspar finished the last few ounces of his drink and then signaled the bartender for another. "Fucking Vitale," he said, snorting his disgust. "He made me pay him through the fucking nose for that funeral home. I kicked back thousands every month until he died. And after all was said and done, he backed Nick Arena in the restaurant he wanted—but not me in the restaurant *I* wanted, even after all the loyalty I showed him."

"Maybe Vitale backed Nick because he had experience in the food business—you know, running the bakeries—and you didn't?"

"And what kind of fucking experience did I have in the funeral parlor business before he gave me a funeral parlor to run?" Gaspar said, slinging the words out of his mouth. "Ask me, experience wasn't the thing. Vitale fucked me and rewarded Arena for a whole different reason."

Eddie puckered his mouth around the straw in his Tieri Tonga for a quick taste and waited in silence for Gaspar to continue. After a long pause, as each man seemed to be ignoring the other and instead reading the labels on the bottles stacked in rows on the other side of the bar, Eddie finally said, half jokingly, "Time's up. Have you decided to tell me, or not? What was the reason?"

Gaspar pulled the straw from his drink and took a slow sip, his eyes peering above the top of his mug at Eddie. "Maybe you haven't noticed it, but I'm not the most likeable guy in the world. Arena is smooth, I'll give him that, and Vitale took a shine to him, treated him like a son. And Arena came from the same hometown in the old country. How the hell could I beat that?"

Gaspar raised his glass halfway to his mouth and held it there. A moment later, he turned to Eddie and said, "Ever see *The Godfather?*"

Gasper immediately answered his own question in a voice dripping with bitterness. "Sure you have, everyone has. Anyways, I think it was the second one, where Michael says, 'You should keep your friends close, but keep your enemies closer.' What bullshit! Who you really gotta be careful of is your friends, the ones you trust the most. They're the ones that'll betray you when you ain't expecting it. Guys like Vitale, their motto should be, 'Screw your friends first, they're the easiest.'"

Gaspar gulped the last of his drink. "Anyway, I made a decent living with the funeral home. Trouble was, Loretta and me got too comfortable, and every time I brought up the idea of opening my own tiki joint, she shot me down. No use bitching. I thank God I lived to be my age. A lot of guys I came up with didn't make it this far."

As Gaspar got up off his stool and put on his overcoat, Eddie said, "Why'd you tell me all this, Gaspar?" He tilted his head and knitted his eyebrows, his face a question mark. "Guys like you—"

"How old are you?"

"I'm thirty-seven."

"You print anything I told you, you're not gonna see thirty-eight. I can make that guarantee, know what I'm saying?"

At that, Gaspar laughed, and his laughter came in sandpapery staccato bursts that were hard to distinguish from the sound of his coughing. "And I'll be honest with you," he said. "It felt good to get some things off my chest. I don't talk to a lot of people no more."

Eddie followed Gaspar out the door. "Now don't get pissed, Gaspar, but I've got one more question."

Gaspar looked at Eddie. "What am I gonna do with you?"

Eddie could feel his knees go a little weak when he said, "What about Marisol and Nick?"

"What about them?" Gaspar said, narrowing his beady eyes to slits.

"Well, he took Marisol away from you. And when he broke up with her…well, word was you blamed Nick for her death, and you've hated him ever since. That right?"

Gaspar's face gave away nothing as he calmly replied, "It put a crimp in our relationship."

At that moment, Eddie's gut decoded Gaspar's unexpected and un-flappable reaction to the mention of the Nick-Marisol affair—and it convinced him that Gaspar had almost certainly stolen the statue.

"Crimp, huh?" Eddie said.

"Yeah, it means like a dent. You should know that, you're a writer. And you can forget any more questions on that score."

Gaspar lit another cigarette, and Eddie said, "You really should quit smoking."

Gaspar tapped his chest. "Too late," he said, the smoke mixing with his frigid breath as he exhaled into the night air. "My doctor's been after me to come in for X-rays on account of my coughing, and I been avoiding it. I know when I'm licked. I got lung cancer, you could make book on it."

Gaspar gave Eddie a shrug that punctuated his surrender to fate as the driver of the hearse opened the passenger-side door for his boss. "It is what it is," he said, and as soon as he settled into his seat, he rolled down the window. "Listen, what Nick did to me with Mary—hell, that was a lot of fucking years ago, before you were even born. Water under the bridge. And besides, I'm a superstitious person a lot of the time. No way I'd bring a curse on my head stealing something from a church. You got that?"

"Yeah, I do. And I want you to know that since you declared our conversation off the record, in your own inimitable way, I will honor that. I won't print any of it…until you're dead and gone."

"And then I won't give a flying fuck," Gaspar said, flicking his ciga-rette out the window and rolling it back up.

As Eddie watched the hearse disappear into the night, he wondered if Gaspar was imagining that one day soon, he'd be riding in the back of the hearse instead of up front.

Eddie believed he had managed to unearth another piece of the puzzle. He'd bet a year's rent that Gaspar's poor health had left him precious little time to exact his revenge on Arena. And after reading Eddie's account of Nick Arena and his statue, Gaspar figured he'd found the vehicle for his revenge, and had to act quickly.

Which left Eddie to ponder: Gaspar obviously didn't break into old Mrs. Bello's apartment with an accomplice and steal the statue with his own two hands. Neither did Stracci, whose size would've given him away. Hard to believe either Gaspar or Stracci would've trusted Buster with the job—so who did they use to do their dirty work for them?

CHAPTER 38

A SKELETON CREW WAS ON DUTY as Eddie walked through the newsroom a few minutes after ten o'clock. The first edition of Sunday's paper was on his desk. He skimmed his column before settling in front of his computer to tap out notes of his conversation with Gaspar while it was still fresh in his memory. A half-hour later, he had created a five-page file and stored it in a folder of column ideas on the desktop of his computer.

Eddie decided to pass up a nightcap at Pecky's and walk home. When he got to his apartment, Eddie hung his overcoat in the hall closet and threw his sports jacket on the couch in the living room. He went to the bathroom and plopped two Alka-Seltzer tablets into a cold glass of water, hoping it would douse the heartburn from the Tieri Tonga and wondering how in hell Gaspar could drink that shit.

He settled in for the night, sitting on his living room couch, feet up on the coffee table, and listening to a CD of mellow Coltrane. He was done drinking. As Coltrane eased into "It's Easy to Remember," infusing it with sublime elegance, he checked his watch and calculated he hadn't seen or spoken to Phyllis in more than twenty-four hours. And what the hell was he going to do about it? God, he was tired, too tired to even think about her with any sense of clarity.

Eddie turned off Coltrane and clicked on the TV, hoping that *Saturday Night Live* might be the ticket to a few laughs. Channel 4's local news was winding down when the anchor alerted the audience to a news flash.

Five minutes later, Eddie was in a cab, and in another eight minutes, he had reached his destination—205 Third Avenue. Four uniformed patrol cops were monitoring a crowd of curious onlookers, keeping them a respectful distance away from a white Toyota Land Cruiser parked in front of the building.

On the crushed roof of the car was the mangled body of Gaspar Tieri.

As he slip-slid through the crowd, Eddie could see CSU officers working over Tieri's nearly naked body, clothed only in baggy boxer shorts and a ripped-open bathrobe. They were taking photos, wielding tweezers and scissors and such, and bagging what they needed. He showed his NYPD-authorized press card to a solidly built cop with a dark, chiseled face and introduced himself. The cop's name was Nat Covington, who told Eddie that he and his partner were riding in their patrol car and happened upon the scene only a minute or so after Gaspar had fallen from the sky.

"That would be around eleven o'clock," Covington said.

"Where's your partner?" Eddie asked, pulling out his notepad.

Covington pointed him out. "That's him, over there. Harry Adcock."

Eddie saw Adcock talking to an Associated Press reporter he recognized. He then turned to face Covington again. "Tell me what happened when you got here?"

"First thing, the doorman of this building comes running up to us, said the guy's name was Gasper, um, uh…"

"Tieri."

"Yeah, that's him, and he tells us he's a big-shot mafia mobster. So I called the precinct right away—"

"What precinct?"

"The 13th," Covington said. "When I called it in, they told us to sit tight and do some crowd control until the troops arrived."

"What floor did he fall from?"

"The doorman said he lives on the twenty-second floor. I been thinking…you think it's a suicide, or was he pushed, being that he's a gangster?"

Eddie bent his head back and sighed, as though he were admiring the star-powdered sky. "Either way, it's a shitty way to die."

"True that," Covington said, looking skyward as well. "There's two detectives up there now."

As the CSU officers started removing Gaspar from the crushed roof of the car to bag his broken body—and knowing that he wouldn't get a crumb of information out of them—Eddie headed into the lobby of the building, where he identified himself to the doorman.

"And what's your name?"

"Mike Florio," he said.

"You were on duty when Tieri hit the car, right, Mike?"

"Right," he said, stroking his thick black mustache with a thumb and forefinger.

"What was your first reaction?"

"The sound. It was like a huge bang. You know, Mr. Tieri was a thin guy. I couldn't believe the sound he made."

"You let anyone up to his apartment before he died?"

When the doorman hesitated, Eddie said, "You did, didn't you, Mike?"

"I'll tell you what I told the detectives. Mr. Tieri had a visitor. I rang Mr. Tieri, and he said to send him up."

"The guy you sent up—he have a name?"

The doorman gave Eddie a sheepish look. "Al Capone."

"In the flesh, or his ghost?" Eddie said.

Irritated by the sarcasm in Eddie's voice, he said, "You think I didn't know it was bullshit? But that's the name he gave me, and Mr. Tieri said to send him up."

"What did he look like?"

"Hard to tell. He had a baseball cap pulled down very low on his forehead. You could hardly see his eyes and not much of his nose. Anyway, he never really looked me square in the face. But he was definitely taller than me. Six feet, I'd say, and kinda husky."

"You remember anything about the baseball cap? Mets? Yankees? Like that."

"It was black. Just black."

"What else was he wearing?"

"A black jacket. Thick. Puffy, like a ski jacket."

"Was he still up there when Tieri landed on the car?"

"I didn't see him leave," the doorman said, and swore he never left his post between the time Al Capone entered the building and when Tieri plunged to his death.

"Okay, that's it for now." Eddie started walking toward the bank of elevators, then turned back when the doorman called his name.

"It just came to me," the doorman said. "When the guy told me he was Al Capone, he sort of tilted his head up real quick, like for a second or two, and I remember thinking, *He's no George Clooney.* Weird, huh?"

"Had to be a reason why that popped into your mind. You telling me he was just plain ugly? Or was there something wrong with his face? Like scars? Bruises? Missing teeth? What?"

The doorman shrugged. "Like you said, maybe there was something wrong with his face. Otherwise, why would I think to myself that he's no George Clooney?"

Eddie thanked the doorman, then took an elevator to the twenty-second floor, where he identified himself to the detective in the hallway. His name was Sam Cahn. He was a six-foot slab of beef with a grayish crewcut. He wore a red, grease-stained tie, and in his left arm he cradled a black-and-white cat.

"We found him under the bed," Cahn said, stroking the cat's head. "My partner's still in there."

"What's his name?"

Cahn gazed at the cat. "I don't know."

"I mean your partner."

"Oh. James Rodgers."

"Any idea if Tieri was pushed or jumped?"

At that moment, when Rodgers emerged from Tieri's apartment, Cahn said, "Look who we got here, Jimmy. Eddie Sabella."

Rodgers was a little shorter and a lot thinner than his partner. He had a thick, neatly trimmed Afro that crowned a square-jawed face with sad eyes. "Shit, I guess this must be a really big death, huh?"

Eddie ignored the jibe and asked Rodgers, "You didn't by any chance see an old wooden statue in there? A religious statue is what I'm getting at."

"No," Rodgers said.

"Four feet tall or so? A statue of St. Joseph."

"Hey," Cahn said, "you talking about that statue you wrote about? That was stolen from the church?"

Eddie nodded. "That's the one."

"What the hell would Tieri have to do with that?" Cahn said.

"Just a hunch."

"That's a pretty strange hunch," Rodgers said. "Anyway, we searched the place top to bottom, and St. Joe wasn't anywhere in there."

Eddie decided to let the detectives know he'd talked with Tieri just a few hours ago. They tossed some questions at him, and he told them he was interested in the gangster's personal life for a future profile.

"Tieri was convinced he had lung cancer," Eddie said. "He had a cough that could scare the shit out of a surgeon at Sloan-Kettering, and when he coughed, he'd spit up blood into his handkerchief."

"That must've put a lull in the conversation," Rodgers said.

"If I didn't know he'd had a visitor, I'd think maybe it was a suicide. Was it?"

"He got tossed," Rodgers said. "Like I told the other reporter, the French doors that open to the terrace were busted. Glass all over the place. Looks like somebody crashed through them."

"You still haven't told us," Cahn said, "why you had this hunch that Tieri stole the statue."

"How much time you got?"

"Not much," Cahn snapped.

"Well, it's like this," he said, and then briefly told the detectives about the bad blood between Arena and Tieri.

Rodgers said, "This shit between them happened, like, thirty-five, forty years ago. What made you think Tieri still had a hard-on for Arena?"

Eddie shrugged. "He was Sicilian."

Rodgers laughed. "Even old-school *goombahs* aren't that demented."

"You know Arena well?" Cahn said.

"I've spent some time with him."

"You think he could be involved in something like this?" Cahn said.

"I seriously doubt it."

"I guess we'll find out," Rodgers said.

Back on the street, Eddie called the paper's night editor to make sure he had coverage of Tieri's death for the website. The night editor had just posted the AP's story and read it to Eddie. It was short and stuck to the same facts that Eddie had accumulated on the scene—except for the doorman's sudden recollection about Al Capone's face. He hadn't even shared that tasty tidbit with the two detectives.

"It's fine," Eddie said into his phone. "I can't add anything to what you've got. I'm calling it a night."

Eddie's suspicions about Gaspar still made him itch. By Eddie's reckoning, the gangster's untimely death added one more mystery to the story of the stolen statue.

CHAPTER 39

WEARING HIS BEST DARK SUIT, Eddie arrived at St. Joseph's Church just minutes before the start of the ten o'clock Mass, and was impressed by the size of the crowd of worshippers that had come to celebrate the Feast Day of St. Joseph. Many others were also there, he knew, to honor the memory of Giuseppe Arena, Nick's father.

Slowly walking up the center aisle as he scanned the pews for a seat, Eddie noticed a local TV news reporter—an attractive, pint-sized brunette he'd met a few weeks ago on another story—and her cameraman positioned along the right wall not far from the empty niche in which the stolen statue had resided. It was a slow news day, which meant that sound bites from a disappointed Father Keller and a few parishioners could fill a minute or two of precious airtime.

As Eddie took a seat to his left, several pews from the altar, it hit him. The empty niche was supposed to enshrine either a white marble or white limestone statue of St. Joseph in place of the old wooden one. He couldn't remember which, but he was certain that Father Keller had said he'd take the statue from the rectory and display it at today's Mass.

Eddie quit musing about the absent statue when he spotted Nick in the first pew on the right. At that precise moment, Phyllis leaned into her father, and after speaking a few quick words into his ear, turned her head. Her eyes laser-beamed into Eddie's. He took a quick breath and averted his eyes for a second, maybe two. When he looked toward her again, he got the back of her head, her dark hair partially covered by an elegant black-and-silver silk hat.

Eddie's mind wandered to the morning he saw Phyllis, the new girl in town, at a Sunday Mass. He had seen her for the first time at the pool a couple of days before, but didn't actually meet her until after that Mass. He could almost make himself believe that nothing had changed—she was still a beautiful stranger and seemingly beyond his reach, and he still had to catch his breath when he looked at her. He wondered if he could ever be as happy as when he walked her home that long-ago summer morning.

Eddie watched Phyllis stand and bow her head when Father Keller emerged from the sacristy to begin the Mass, and as the congregation sat back down, he could see her in profile, her eyes now on the man to her right. He had been so focused on Phyllis he hadn't noticed the man before. He was broad-shouldered with dark hair. Who was he, and what had he just whispered in Phyllis's ear that prompted her to brush her fingers down the side of his face?

Eddie felt like someone had kicked him in the gut when he saw her touch the dark-haired man like that.

Father Keller's sermon briefly transported Eddie out of his funk. It was short and spot-on, truly capturing the spirit of St. Joseph—a carpenter by trade, just and pious, devoted husband of the Virgin Mary and loving father of Jesus.

"No matter that St. Joseph, in our Roman Catholic tradition, is actually the foster father of Jesus—I like to think of today as a day when we celebrate the bonds between all fathers and all sons," Father Keller said. "And to mark this special occasion, I have great news."

Father Keller looked down from the pulpit at one of his altar boys, Johnny Bello, the same altar boy who'd stolen the statue and taken it home to his terminally ill grandmother.

As Johnny walked behind the altar to the sacristy, Floyd Walker, the church's long-time handyman, straddled the altar railing on the right side of the church and carefully pulled the metal bank of votive candles a few feet away from the wall, against which was propped a stepladder. Walker opened it, climbed three steps, and stood there, looking expectant.

A chorus of *ooohs* and *aaahs* greeted Johnny when he emerged from the sacristy cradling the old wooden statue of St. Joseph in his arms.

With an earnest expression that reflected the delicacy of his task, Walker held out his hands to receive the exquisitely carved statue. And when Walker gently placed the statue back in its niche, the congregation rose as one and applauded.

Eddie's head buzzed with so many questions, it was several long seconds before he stood with the rest of the crowd. When and where was the statue returned? Who returned it? Did Nick pay the ransom? And why the hell didn't Nick or Father Keller inform him instead of blindsiding him at the Mass?

Smiling proudly, Father Keller raised his hands to quiet the congregation and, pointing toward the statue, he said, "As you know, that beautiful, iconic image of St. Joseph was stolen from our church last week. Several days before that, it had seemed the statue was shedding tears, and that we may have had a miracle on our hands. It was no such thing, I'm afraid—a leak in the ceiling is not a miracle. It's simply another problem to bedevil your faithful old pastor." The worshippers laughed politely. "Well, as far as I'm concerned, the Good Lord decided to bless us with a miracle after all. What else can you call the return of our glorious statue of St. Joseph just in time for Mass this morning?"

The last few sentences of Father Keller's sermon barely registered in Eddie's head. He was still pissed about the statue. Some damn miracle. How could they do this to him? He'd played it straight with both Nick and Father Keller, and they didn't have the decency to give him the exclusive. It seemed that they'd tipped off that TV reporter, who'd now scored the kind of dramatic footage her local station would probably run several times during the day as a news flash and certainly as the lead story on the six and eleven o'clock newscasts—unless a particularly gruesome murder or a spectacular car crash happened to break in the meantime.

Gaspar Tieri was right: screw your friends first, they're the easiest.

As if he weren't already pissed off enough, when the Mass was over, Eddie watched Phyllis walk right by his pew without so much as a sideways glance in his direction. She had her arm linked with that of the man she was sitting next to. He was taller and sleeker than he'd appeared to Eddie when he was in his seat. He wore a black silk scarf with tiny orange dots wrapped around an open-necked white shirt and a fine gray overcoat draped over his shoulders. A lot of women would likely regard him as a dashingly handsome man, and Eddie had to admit that he was.

Nick walked a step behind them, his eyes straight ahead. As he passed Eddie's pew, Eddie couldn't be sure if Nick had deliberately avoided making eye contact with him, or simply didn't know he was there.

Eddie's attention then shifted from Nick and Phyllis to the local TV reporter. Approaching her, he held out his hand. "Justine, am I right?"

"Yes, Justine Arruda, *Eyewitness News*," she said, shaking his hand. "And you're Eddie Sabella, am *I* right?"

Eddie liked her smile. "Yes, I am. That was quite a show Father Keller just orchestrated, huh?"

"He turned the whole thing into a spectacle. It'll make great TV."

"If you don't mind my asking, did you know this was going to happen?"

"No, did you?"

"Not a clue."

"I called Father Keller yesterday and got his permission to film a few seconds of the Mass and what I assumed would be an empty space," she said, nodding toward St. Joseph. "Then I intended to get some reactions to the absence of the statue. We've got a different story on our hands now."

"That's for sure."

"Nice talking to you, Eddie," she said. "I have to catch up with some parishioners and get a few sound bites, and then I'll interview Father Keller. What about you?"

"I'll be right behind you," he said.

"Catch you later then," she said, hustling toward the back of the church with her cameraman in tow.

Eddie hustled in the opposite direction. He hopped the altar railing and went directly to the sacristy, where Father Keller was hanging up his vestments in a scarred mahogany wardrobe that looked like an antique.

"Eddie!" Father Keller bellowed. "How'd you like it?"

"To be honest, Father, I would've liked it a lot better if you had given me a heads-up it was going to happen."

"I did. I left you a message on your phone." Eddie's quizzical look prompted Father Keller to add, "At your office."

"Damn, I never got it. Did Nick know?"

"Of course. I called him, and I told him I'd call you."

"I wish you had called my cell phone."

"I don't have that number."

"Too late now. Did Nick pay the ransom?"

"No."

"Then how did you end up with the statue? Who returned it?"

"I have no earthly idea."

"Tell me what you can," Eddie said, notepad and pen in hand.

"It was about eleven forty-five last night. I couldn't sleep, so I was reading downstairs in our living room. The bell rang, and I answered the door, and there was this man…"

"What did he look like?"

"The outdoor light wasn't that bright, and he had on a baseball cap that was pulled down practically over his eyes."

At that, Eddie's right hand twitched as he wrote in his notepad. "Was there any kind of logo on the cap?"

"Not that I could see," Father Keller said, lighting a cigar. "It was black or dark blue."

"You must've been able to see what he was wearing. You were close enough to take the statue from him."

"A winter jacket that looked—"

Eddie anxiously cut the priest off. "Like a ski jacket?"

"Yes, that's what I was going to say. Why are you so jumpy?"

Eddie ignored the question. "What did he say when he handed it to you?"

"He just said, 'Here's your statue.' At first, I thought it was some kind of sick joke. But when I opened the garment bag—"

"Garment bag?"

"Like you hang a suit in, you know, for a trip. And there it was, and in good condition, except for the missing lily. But Nick's got it, and he graciously offered to pay for the cost of having it restored."

"Let's back up. The guy hands you the garment bag. Did you open it in front of him?"

"Didn't have a chance. The second he handed it to me, off he went into the night."

"You didn't go after him or try to stop him?"

"Look at me, Eddie. I'm an old priest, and I'd like to get older."

Father Keller placed his cigar in an ashtray, then secured his starched white collar and slipped into his black suit jacket. "Gotta look good for my TV interview," he said with a twinkling smile.

"Before you go out there and become a star—did you inform the police about the, uh, miracle?"

"Don't be disrespectful," Father Keller said, lifting his cigar from the ashtray. "In fact, I called the precinct when I got up this morning and asked for Detective O'Grady. He's off today, but he'll come by tomorrow and ask me the same questions you just did, I'm sure. They said there was no rush, since I have the statue back safe and sound."

"One more question: Why did you tell your parishioners that the statue's tears were caused by a leak in the ceiling? You told me it was, quote, 'bone dry' up there. You lied, Father. Why?"

The priest took a long puff of his cigar as he stared at Eddie. "Tell you what. Keep this to yourself for now, and we'll talk about it one day. On the record. Deal?"

"Deal. Guess I'll see you at Nonna's for lunch."

"You certainly shall," Father Keller said. "But first, I've got to get ready for my close-up."

CHAPTER 40

ON HIS OFFICE PHONE TO BASIC, who had the day off, Eddie said, "Here's my thinking. I'll bang out a straight news story, say four hundred words, on the return of the statue. As for Tieri's death, I'm gonna keep that George Clooney detail to myself for now. And tomorrow morning I'll hit the ground running and see what I can develop on that front."

"Makes sense," Basic said. "Now get the statue story online as fast as you can."

Eddie informed the Sunday city editor that he'd be delivering his story before lunch. He then quickly checked his voice mail. The message from Father Keller was brief and to the point: "The statue was returned. I've got it. Now I'm going to bed. Talk in the morning."

Something about the message bothered Eddie. He played it again, and then again. He rifled through his notebook, and there it was: he had clearly noted that Father Keller said the statue was returned about eleven forty-five, and then the thief walked away. But the voice mail pinned the time of the message at twelve twenty-five.

Father Keller was off by forty minutes. Okay, so maybe the priest took his sweet time calling him. He said he called Nick first. But how long could he have possibly talked to Nick at that hour of the night?

Eddie stared at the time he'd just jotted down: twelve twenty-five. There was a forty-minute gap that was unaccounted for, and he wanted an explanation.

———

Eddie got an email on his BlackBerry as he walked to Nonna's. It was from Liz Coyne, the attractive, green-eyed redhead in public relations whom he'd met in Pecky's the other night. *I don't have a single lunch date all this week,* she wrote. *How about you?*

He made a mental note to respond to her email later in the day, and he couldn't deny he was happy to get it. It was nice to be wanted, even if he was uncertain how he'd handle her request. Still, as he liked to tell himself in such circumstances, at least he had that going for him.

Eddie entered Nonna's just as Nick was toasting his father with a glass of red wine. "To my father, Giuseppe, on this, his name day. And to my mother, Filomena—I pray she is with my father in heaven."

Nick eyed Father Keller, who was seated at a table with Moe Vogel. "Since we are here celebrating the Feast Day of St. Joseph, Father, do you think it is appropriate that I toast him as well?"

"Why not?" Father Keller said. "The good man surely loved his wine."

"And how do you know?" Nick said.

"When Jesus changed water into wine at the wedding feast of Cana, you think that was the first time? He had a lot of practice doing it for his old man."

Nick laughed along with some seventy-five of his closest friends and loyal customers who had gathered for the lunch. "To St. Joseph," Nick said, "beloved among Sicilians for his devotion to family. He was, as we say, *omu di panza*, a man of stomach, one who had the guts to do the right thing."

As Nick raised his glass, Father Keller said out loud, "Finally."

From his seat at the bar, Eddie could see the priest taking a healthy swallow of red wine. And before Father Keller could place his glass on the table, Phyllis came into view, bending down to kiss him on his forehead. The priest grabbed her hand and gave her a celibate's smile, pure and joyful.

Gazing at Phyllis, Eddie didn't notice Nick approaching him until he called his name. "Eddie, I am so glad you could make it," he said with a big-hearted smile. "I have a seat for you with Father Keller and an old friend of mine." Nick leaned in close to Eddie and said, "Truth is, he was once my bookmaker. Morris Vogel—"

"Better known as Moe, right?"

"Yes, you know him?"

"In fact, we had lunch the other day."

"What a wonderful coincidence," Nick said happily. "Come with me."

"One sec, Nick. Have you heard about Gaspar Tieri?"

"Yes, I have. It seems he died as he had lived—violently."

"And you still believe he wasn't clever enough to steal the statue?"

"Is that so important now? From what I know of the news, he died before the statue was returned to Father Keller."

"One more question. Many years ago, were you in love with a young woman by the name of Marisol?"

A flicker of surprise swept across Nick's face, and with a blade-thin smile, he said, "Sometimes, Eddie, you ask too much of people. This is not the time or—"

"Yes or no, Nick? It's a simple question."

"Not so simple." Nick paused. "I was with her after she left Gaspar. I did not pursue her. We fell in with each other because that is what she wanted."

"And you didn't resist."

"She was a beautiful young woman. She had such fire. I was also young, and very human."

"And Gaspar blamed you for her death."

Nick paused, narrowing his eyes, as if he were focusing on his memory of Marisol, and then: "She was a dope addict. The hard stuff. Few people knew, and Gaspar preferred not to deal with it. I did. I sent her away to get clean. Twice. I took care of everything. But each time… well…" Nick sighed, slowly shaking his head. "It was hopeless. I broke up with her before I went to Bologna. When I met Filomena's mother, I stayed an extra week. During that week, she died. An overdose, as I am sure you know by now. Gaspar made the funeral arrangements and buried her, and in his mind, I killed her."

Eddie nodded. "You know what, Nick? I think it's time to eat."

Following Nick into the dining room, Eddie quickly set his gaze on Father Keller's table, where Phyllis had been standing, and found her gone. He felt disappointment one moment and relief the next, and before he could sort out exactly what the hell he was feeling, he found himself gently squeezing Moe's shoulder. "Cashmere, right?" Eddie said, referring to Moe's stylish, milk-chocolate-brown sports jacket.

"What else?" Moe said, patting Eddie's hand. "And look at you. Love the paisley tie with that suit."

Nick said, "Morris, I had no idea you and Eddie knew each other."

"Not only that, Nick, we happen to like each other," Moe said, drawing a smile from Father Keller, who shook Eddie's hand.

"Sit down, my young friend," the priest said, filling Eddie's glass with wine. "Nick has blessed us with some high-end grape for today's festivities. You must wrap your lips around this Brunello."

"Thanks, Father," Eddie said. "I see I have some catching up to do."

"Yes, you do, Eddie," Nick said. "Now, my friends, you must excuse me. Enjoy your lunch."

Eddie watched Nick as he crossed to the other side of the room and sat with Phyllis, the man she was with at Mass, and several others he couldn't identify. He thought Phyllis must have sensed his eyes upon her, for she suddenly turned away from one of the guests she was talking to and looked at him. And there it was again—that jolt he felt when he saw her face. She nodded almost imperceptibly at him, but he caught it. He didn't move a muscle, and she resumed her conversation. They had held each other's glance for maybe two seconds, tops, and he knew he'd have to talk to her soon, or he'd wind up in a padded room.

"What's on your mind, Eddie?" Father Keller said. "You seem distracted."

"Nothing, really," Eddie said, raising his glass to his table companions. "It's a treat to be here with two of the finest gentlemen in Gotham."

"I'll drink to that," Father Keller said, and then drained the wine in his glass.

"Slow down, Artie," Moe said. "We've got a long lunch ahead of us."

"That's right, Moe, and I'm just getting warmed up."

Moe rolled his eyes, and Father Keller cackled as he filled his glass again.

"Moe, you know about Tieri, right?"

"Nobody's shedding any tears. And what a coincidence, huh? You asking me about him just last night."

"Got anything you can tell me about what went down?"

"Not at this moment, but I can reach out to someone I know in his crew."

"He'll talk?"

"Like a yenta. He owes me twenty-two large."

"He must be betting on the Knicks," Father Keller said, "like another moron I know."

"Don't be so hard on yourself, Artie," Moe said.

After the three men had polished off a hefty plate of antipasto, a waiter came around to take their orders for the main course. Father Keller chose the *pasta chi sardi*, the most traditional of all Sicilian dishes for the Feast Day of St. Joseph. Moe pulled a face, as if he'd just gotten a whiff of a foul odor.

"What?" Eddie said, looking at Moe.

"It's what Artie ordered—the pasta with sardines," Moe said. "To be kind about it, it's an acquired taste."

"Maybe so, but it's a magnificent dish," Father Keller said. "The pasta is mixed with fresh sardines, fennel, pine nuts, and currants. Nick likes to have them throw some bread crumbs on top and then bake it. My mouth is watering just talking about it."

"I've never had it," Eddie said.

"You? That's heresy," Father Keller said, and told the waiter to bring Eddie a dish of the *pasta chi sardi*.

"You'll be sorry," Moe said to Eddie in a singsong voice.

One fishy forkful was all Eddie needed to realize he'd never acquire a taste for it.

When Father Keller finished his plate of pasta, he devoured Eddie's as well, while the others had their fill of veal and sausages and fried vegetables.

After the table was cleared, Father Keller rubbed his hands together in anticipation of the special dessert that was to follow: *sfinci di San Giuseppe*—puffy balls of dough filled with sweetened ricotta, chocolate chips, and candied fruits.

"It's maybe the greatest pastry of all time," the priest said.

"May I ask you a personal question, Father?" Eddie said.

"Yes, but I reserve the right to ignore it."

"You've been eating and drinking pretty good. Give up anything for Lent?"

"Bourbon. I love wine almost as much. But I drink it every time I say Mass, so there doesn't seem to be any point in giving it up."

"Ever consider giving up cigars?" Eddie said with smart-aleck smile.

"No, and I never considered wearing a hair shirt either. It's not my ambition to be a martyr for my faith. And what about you?"

"When I was a kid," Eddie said, "I used to give up ice cream."

Father Keller dismissed Eddie's answer with a tilt of his chin. "I could give up ice cream standing on my head."

"If anyone cares," Moe said, "I never give up anything. I'm Jewish."

"Yes, you are," Father said, laughing, and Moe and Eddie laughed along with him.

Eddie waited until Moe had left the table to make a phone call before asking Father Keller about the discrepancy he found in his notes. "I gotta ask you about something's been bothering me, Father..."

"Go right ahead," he said.

"You told me you got the statue back around eleven forty-five, but the voice mail you left me came in at twelve twenty-five. That's forty minutes later. I know you called Nick first..."

"That's correct."

"I'm sure the call was a lot shorter than forty minutes. Why the gap between the time you got the statue and the time you called me?"

"Simple. I was likely mistaken about the times. I must've received the statue a lot later than I thought."

Eddie wasn't buying Father Keller's explanation. "Hard to believe you were off by that much."

"What can I say? You reach a certain age, and...well, you know."

Eddie dropped his line of questioning when Moe returned to the table.

"Regarding Tieri, my guy tells me everything is quiet," Moe said to Eddie. "It wasn't a mob hit. They had no reason to get rid of him. He wasn't planting flags anywhere or stealing from the cookie jar."

"Thanks, Moe."

"And you can talk to him yourself. We're on for lunch tomorrow. Angelo's on Mulberry."

The trio started scarfing down the *sfinci di San Giuseppe* that had been deposited on the table, along with a pot of espresso and a bottle of Sambuca.

In between bites of the creamy pastry, Father Keller anointed his espresso with a splash of Sambuca, then did the same for Eddie and Moe. Less than half an hour later, having consumed his third spiked cup of espresso, the priest again reached for the bottle of Sambuca, but Moe got to it first.

"No more, Artie, I'm taking you home," Moe said, and got no argument.

As Father Keller and Moe stood to leave, Nick walked over and thanked them for sharing this special day with him once again. "And you, Eddie—I know you are a busy man. I am honored you chose to stay for lunch."

"He didn't have the *coglioni* to eat the *pasta chi sardi*," Father Keller said, the words slowly sliding off his tongue. "It was incredible, Nick, and so was the wine."

"*Grazie*, Father," Nick said. "And you, Morris, the next time you come, please bring your lovely wife."

"She'd love it, Nick."

Moe then slipped his arm into Father Keller's and escorted him to the coat check.

Eddie followed, retrieved his own coat, then hailed a cab for the bookie and the priest. He opened the door, and as Father Keller slid in first, Moe said, "See you at lunch tomorrow."

"Count on it," Eddie said.

When Eddie walked back inside the restaurant, he promptly spotted Phyllis as the dashingly handsome man was kissing her on both cheeks and sweetly reminding her, "Don't forget your glasses, you always forget your glasses."

"I won't, Henri," Phyllis said, enunciating his name with the proper inflective flourish and making it sound sexier than it should.

"*Au revoir*, Phyllis, and I hope you will be on time."

"Me too," she said, gifting him with a smile that almost made Eddie cringe.

Eddie had heard their conversation from a corner of the bar, where he had taken a seat, waiting to get Phyllis alone.

"Never figured you with a Frenchman," he said pleasantly.

Phyllis approached him, placing an elbow on the bar. "I don't know what you mean by 'with,'" she said coolly. "We're friends, and I guess you could say we're also colleagues. Henri owns a couple of bistros downtown."

"You going to a movie with him tonight or the theater?"

"It's an opera concert," she said. "A charity event that Henri's involved in."

"Don't forget your glasses."

"I won't."

"I didn't know you wore glasses."

"Only when I need to see things more clearly."

"Maybe you should be wearing them now," Eddie said, gently wrapping his fingers around her hand. "You walked into that one, Phyl."

She lowered her eyes. "Honestly, Eddie, I wonder how we'd end up if we met for the first time today, or tomorrow, or next week. Too bad we can't start out clean, isn't it? A clean slate…"

Phyllis had nothing more to say. She lifted her eyes and stared into Eddie's. Those eyes, he thought, they could radiate so many conflicting emotions so swiftly—joy and sadness, happiness and anger, boredom and astonishment. Exactly what they were expressing now, though, was hard to tell.

"Don't kid yourself, Phyl. There's no such thing as a clean slate," Eddie said. "Everybody's got some kind of baggage to drag around. I wish with all my heart we hadn't lost those fifteen years, and we'll carry that loss with us forever. But hell, Phyl, we can make it. I know we can."

Phyllis looked away from Eddie, somewhere above him, and when her eyes dipped down and fixed on him again, a brittle silence settled in the space between them. Eddie tried to blow it away with a jaunty pitch in his voice. "Think about it, Phyl. Do you really want to spend the rest of your life without me? What's the fun in that?"

When Phyllis gave him the warm smile he'd hoped for, Eddie said, "You've got to get it while it's hot."

"Is that your way of telling me you're in demand?"

"You always had first dibs, Phyl," Eddie said, theatrically pressing his hands to his chest. "Only you have the power to reclaim the desert that is my heart."

Phyllis's eyes glistened. "Please, Eddie, be serious. It doesn't matter how much two people may love each other. Love can fail. It failed us…"

She put two fingers to Eddie's lips as he was about to speak. "No, let me finish. I know you think that I failed us. I ran out on you—not once, but twice. And each time I did, I still loved you. I always loved you. And that's what scares me. Blame me all you want. I deserve it. But I loved you, Eddie, more than anyone else, and I couldn't make it stick. Don't ask me why. I've thought about it and thought about it, but I don't have an answer. I don't want to take that chance. For your sake, and for mine."

Seeming to end the conversation, Eddie pushed himself off the bar stool.

"Please say something, Eddie. Call me a coward. Tell me I'm mad, I don't make any sense, I—"

"You have to come to me," he said.

"What?"

Eddie reached into his jacket pocket for a pen. He wrote the address for Pecky's on a cocktail napkin and handed it to Phyllis. "I said you have to come to me. I'll be at that address tonight, having dinner with a friend. I'll stick around after we're done, and maybe, after the concert, you can—"

"Please, Eddie, not tonight."

"Then when?"

"I'm not sure."

Almost in a whisper, he said, "Always remember, Phyl, I'll be out there. I love you, and I want you. Always have. But next time, Phyl, you have to come running *to* me, and I'll catch you. I promise—I'll catch you and hold you and never let you go, never let you leave me again."

Eddie kissed her gently on the check and walked out of the restaurant.

CHAPTER 41

AFTER LEAVING PHYLLIS at the bar in Nonna's and fearing they were destined to move on without each other, Eddie walked aimlessly around the city before returning to his apartment. He had some time to kill before meeting Max at Pecky's. He poured himself a drink and reached for the three CDs that were still unopened on his coffee table. He chose to play the Diana Krall album, and as he struggled to unwrap its jewel case, he suddenly recalled a snippet of conversation from his dinner with Nick two nights ago.

He got up off the couch and knelt before the bookshelf where he kept his collection of CDs haphazardly arranged in rows on the bottom three shelves. He almost gave up finding it, but he was certain he'd kept it through all the years. He took another pass at the top row of CDs, and there it was: Nina Simone's *At the Village Gate*.

Eddie played the second song, the one Nick indicated had made Phyllis cry. He knew the song—"He Was Too Good to Me" by Richard Rodgers and Lorenz Hart, a classic ballad about the end of a love affair that could rip your heart out. Listening to the yearning and regret in Simone's voice, he slumped on his couch and felt his eyes sting. Like the discarded lover in the song, he'd have done anything for Phyllis, even brought her the sun. And if she were mean to him, he'd never tell her to go away and leave him be.

He recalled how Phyllis's eyes would shine whenever she heard the song. He'd always assumed they were shining with affection for him and for his devotion to her. Now, all these years later, he wondered if they were actually glazed with sadness, because she understood even then that they never would have a life together.

Eddie swallowed the last inch of Scotch in his glass as the song concluded with Simone longing for the man who was too good to be true. Those last words made Eddie feel like shit. Could he have been a bigger asshole? He and Phyllis hadn't laid eyes on each other for fifteen years, hadn't even spoken a word to each other in all that time, and how did he act when they finally came together again? He jumped down her throat at some stupid perceived slight, never gave her a chance to breathe. Why couldn't he ease up? What was the fucking rush? All she wanted from him was a little time to get her head straight, and her heart, after falling into bed with him. She hoped to find out if there was anything left between the two of them. Sure, it took her a while to let him know she'd returned home, but she overcame whatever was holding her back. She took a chance.

And what did he do? He took a powder.

So there he was, drinking alone again in his apartment, the glass not deep enough to wash away the hurt, while pretty soon she'd be looking as beautiful as always and stepping out with a dashingly handsome man.

Could he possibly feel much worse?

Oh yeah, he could.

He played the song again.

And then he got the hell out of there.

CHAPTER 42

STEPPING INTO PECKY'S at precisely eight thirty, Eddie inhaled the comforting aroma of spilled beer and broiling meat. Max hadn't arrived yet. Pecky was behind the bar, and he promptly brought Eddie a Dewar's the way he liked it.

"You at that Mass this morning when they brought out the statue?" Pecky asked.

"Quite a scene," Eddie said, raising his glass. "To us."

Pecky gave Eddie a thumps-up. "Saw it on the news at six. You write about it?"

"Online earlier this afternoon, and pretty soon you can read it in the paper when—" Eddie's cell phone rang. "'Scuse me, Pecky."

It was Max. "Sorry, Eddie, but I gotta cancel dinner. It's turning into a goat fuck with these ESPN folks."

"No problem, Max," Eddie said, concealing his disappointment. "All going well?"

"Yeah, they're a good bunch, except they're so damn young."

"Remember, Max, age before beauty. And I'd wager they won't be able to keep up with you, on or off the field."

Eddie hung up and ordered a hamburger to eat at the bar. The place seemed so quiet. He looked around the room and counted only eight customers. Okay, it *was* Sunday, and it was late, but he remembered more than a few Sunday nights at that same hour when a crowd of newspaper columnists and sportswriters and city beat reporters and magazine editors and local TV anchors—and sometimes even the ballplayers, politicians, and other boldface names they covered—would be standing two-deep at the bar and occupying every table in the back room.

A lot of Pecky's hardcore customers had opted to take severance packages and early retirement at the newspapers and magazines where they worked, and the younger generation that had admired them and hung out with them to shoot the shit about writing and reporting and story ideas had scattered to health clubs and dinners with the wife and kids and Internet jobs in other cities. They were Eddie's contemporaries, and he could count on one hand those who'd stick around after work to share a cocktail or two and maybe the illicit pleasure of a cigarette or a joint out on the street.

Eddie thought of Gaspar Tieri and made a scoffing sound as he realized that when he was in the company of the man, he had regarded Gaspar the chain-smoker with almost as much disdain as Gaspar the homicidal old mobster. What did that say about the world in which we now lived? Was that fucked up or what?

While he ate at the bar, Eddie read the "Book Review" section of Pecky's copy of the *New York Times*. It was almost nine thirty when the waiter cleared Eddie's plate. Pecky approached and tapped the bar. "Another?"

Eddie contemplated the empty glass that once was brimming with Dewar's and ice and said, "No thanks, Pecky. I'm gonna quit while I'm ahead."

"Hell, Eddie. It's early."

"Not tonight, it isn't," he said. "Tonight it feels late as hell."

Eddie paid his bill and grabbed his coat. Stepping outside, he spotted a woman several yards away taking quick steps directly toward him. She was wearing an overcoat belted at the waist, her dark hair blowing across her face. Then he saw her smile at him, and he felt that old feeling as she came to him.

Silently and forcefully, Phyllis gripped the lapels of Eddie's overcoat and pulled him to her, kissing him before he could say anything—a deep, lingering kiss that would've lasted a little longer had she not stopped to tell him, "There they go again, those damn blood cells colliding like crazy."

"The white ones or the red?" he said.

"It doesn't matter," she said.

"I know I'm not dreaming," he said, "but this is as close as you can get to déjà vu all over again."

Phyllis started to kiss him again, but Eddie tilted his head back. "Can you believe it?" he said. "Here I am, kissing the love of my life, and I'm quoting Yogi Berra."

After another long kiss, Phyllis dropped a deep sigh, then folded her arm into Eddie's, asking him to walk with her, walk anywhere.

They walked in silence for a while. Eddie supposed she'd ditched the Frenchman to be with him, and so he steered her toward his apartment, dismissing the risk he was about to take—that she'd check out in the morning and turn him inside out again. He didn't care. He needed her tonight.

"Did you remember to bring your glasses to the concert?"

"Yes, I did."

"If you don't mind my asking, what happened to the Frenchman?"

"He's still at the concert, but I had to leave early."

"You had to?"

"Yes. You see, there I was, swooning over a selection of Puccini arias, and I wasn't sitting next to the man I love. And I thought, what a damn shame."

Phyllis stopped, then said out loud, "I love you, Eddie Sabella."

He kissed her forehead and held her in a gently swaying embrace. "God, Phyl, how long has it been since the last time I heard you say that?"

"In my heart, Eddie, you were always my guy. It's just that...you had such an insane kind of love in you, and you loved so blindly and stubbornly and obsessively, and I was always afraid that I couldn't love you like you loved me, and that one day you'd end up hating me for it."

Eddie ran a finger down her cheek and across her lips. "All I ask is that you love me as much as you can. That's all I ever wanted."

"That's all?" she said, grazing his lips with her teeth and then kissing him. "Hell, I can do that."

"Something else you can do for me."

"Anything."

"Come up to my apartment."

"And then what?"

"Follow me to my bedroom."

"And then what?"

"A little bit of this, a little bit of that. And then in the morning I'll lock you in my bedroom, and I may never let you leave."

"If you play your cards right," she whispered in his ear, "I may never want to."

CHAPTER 43

EDDIE KISSED PHYLLIS on her cheek, her forehead, and her lips, and then was on the verge of moving his mouth a little lower when she opened her eyes and smiled up at him.

"Hey, sleepyhead. There's coffee for you in the kitchen," he said.

"Why are you dressed?" she said, throwing her arms around his neck, pulling him closer to her, and kissing him. "I thought you were going to lock us up in in here. Did I disappoint you?"

"If I stay another hour, I'm afraid my blood sugar will dip to dangerously low levels from physical exhaustion and—"

"I'll rush you to the hospital."

Eddie smothered her smile with a kiss. "It's almost ten o'clock," he said. "You've got a lunch crowd to deal with, and I'm off to see a priest."

"Father Keller?"

"Yeah, I think I'm onto something, and I need to talk to him. It's about the statue." He hesitated. "I'll tell you everything tonight— where I think this story's going. And if I'm right, Nick will figure into it. Nothing that will hurt him, though."

"Promise?' she said in a wary voice.

"Promise."

Phyllis got up out of bed. She straightened his tie, then wrapped her arms around his chest and pressed her naked body against him. "I won't let anything come between us again, Eddie, never. No matter what."

———————

"Come walk with me," Father Keller said when he opened the front door of the rectory to greet Eddie.

"Where we going?"

"I have to see one of my parishioners in hospice."

"Last rites?"

"I'll know soon enough."

Gazing at the topaz sky with hardly a cloud skidding above them, Eddie said, "Too nice a day to die."

"What did you want to talk about?" Father Keller said as they hurriedly crossed First Avenue.

"Did you talk to O'Grady?"

"An hour or so ago. He came over to the rectory."

"And?"

"And what? He doesn't know anything more than we do. Which is nada."

"Well, not exactly. I'd like to follow up on our conversation at the lunch yesterday. You know, about the guy who returned the statue, and the forty-minute gap between the time…"

"I told you," Father Keller said. "I was mistaken. That's all there is to it."

"Look, Father, you had a few glasses of wine, and I was hoping I'd be a little more successful jogging your memory this morning."

"I can handle the vino," Father Keller shot back.

"Of course you can. Just humor me, okay?"

When the priest didn't respond, Eddie continued, telling him about the gangster Tieri's death and his bitter past with Nick. "I think Tieri arranged to have the statue stolen out of revenge, and after he was pitched off his balcony, I think whoever did the pitching returned the statue to you."

"And why do you think that?"

"According to the doorman in Tieri's building, there was a guy wearing a ski jacket and a black baseball cap pulled down low over his forehead who was up in Tieri's apartment when he got tossed. Ring a bell?"

"Sounds like you're convinced it's the same guy."

"One more thing I didn't get to tell you yesterday. That same doorman told me he got a split-second look at the guy's face and he somehow came away with the impression that he was ugly, like there was something wrong with his face. He was no George Clooney, as he put it."

"I wouldn't know George Clooney if he walked up to me to receive Holy Communion."

"But you'd know an ugly man if you saw one, right?"

Just then, Father Keller stopped in front of a prewar apartment building with a circular driveway. "This is where I get off, Mr. Wiseass," the priest said, patting Eddie on the shoulder. "Nice talking with you."

"Wish you had said more, Father," Eddie said, and a few minutes later, he was on a subway to the paper.

CHAPTER 44

BEFORE EDDIE COULD TAKE OFF his coat, Basic called him to the city desk. "What do we got going this week?" Basic said.

"Dazzle us," Phoebe said. "I need to be dazzled."

"I've got one of those itches," Eddie said.

"That makes me feel glad all over," Phoebe said with a theatrical roll of her shoulders. "Tell me what you got, ace."

Eddie had already provided Basic with a few bullet points about the story he was after and the characters involved, and he repeated some of the more pertinent details for Phoebe's sake. When he was done, he said, "I'll need as much space as you can spare, if I crack it."

"What're you waiting for?" Blake said.

Eddie checked in with O'Grady, who couldn't care less about who returned the statue. Neither Father Keller nor Nick Arena had any intention of pressing charges anyway, and "for a very good reason," O'Grady said. "They don't have the slightest idea who took it from the Bellos' apartment. They've got the statue back, and that's all that really matters to them."

Eddie finished February's expense account, and then called Phyllis at Filomena's. "I just wanted to hear your voice," he said.

"I was hoping you'd want a lot more," she said.

"I love it when you talk dirty."

"You ain't heard nothing yet," she said, "but you will. Let's have a late dinner here, and then you can take me home."

"Whose home, mine or yours?"

"Mine."

"That include a sleepover?"

"Bring your toothbrush."

A soon as Eddie hung up, he checked in with Detective Cahn at the 13th Precinct to get an update on Tieri's death.

"We're treating it as a homicide," Cahn said. "No surprise there, huh? We checked out Tieri's office…"

"At the funeral home?"

"Yeah. Nothing there that could shed any light on anything. As for the whereabouts of Tieri's visitor, aka Al Capone, he's in the wind. That's all I can tell you so far. I got squat every which way I turned."

CHAPTER 45

Moe was sitting at a table in the rear of Angelo's, a landmark restaurant in Little Italy that had seen more years than Moe and Eddie combined. Sitting with him was a man Eddie made to be in his early forties and whose stomach strained the zippered maroon jacket of his velour tracksuit.

Moe rose to greet Eddie and introduced him to Robert Malzone, who remained seated.

"Nice to meet you, Robert," Eddie said, extending a hand.

"Call me Bobby," he said, shaking Eddie's hand.

Moe sat down and said, "He's being modest. He's known far and wide as Big Bobby."

Big Bobby gave Moe a goofy smile, then motioned to a white-jacketed waiter. "I'm hungry, Moe. Let's eat."

Eddie and Moe ordered fish, and Big Bobby had the waiter bring him a bottle of chianti and a plate of fried calamari with a side of eggplant parmigiana for starters.

"Moe tells me you're looking for some shit about Gaspar. We can talk, but I don't want to see my name in the papers. People I deal with, they don't like that."

"You've got my word."

"Good. First thing I can tell you, it wasn't business. The word is it had to be a personal thing. Gaspar was a cocksucker, which I'm sure you heard around. I been in his crew for God knows how long, and he never once said a nice thing to me. Like my mother used to say about my old man—the milk of human kindness wasn't in his veins.

"The only thing he cared about was his cats."

"Cats?" Eddie said. "He had more than one?"

"Not at the same time. He wasn't weird, just mean. When one cat died, he got another. What can I tell you? He had a thing for cats ever since he was a kid. And he named them all the same—Skoonj. That's short for *scungili*. Your name's Sabella, you probably know what *scungili* is."

"Snails," Eddie said.

"Crazy, huh? Who names a cat after a snail?"

"I think I can help you with that," Moe said. "Skoonj was the nickname for Carl Furillo. He played for the Brooklyn Dodgers in the fifties. Helluva player, but he was slow as a snail, and so they nicknamed him Skoonj. I sometimes took Gaspar's baseball action—a real fan, going way back. Furillo must've been Gaspar's favorite player."

"Yeah, figures. When he had a few drinks, he'd talk your ears off about baseball from when he was growing up in Brooklyn."

"That's great, Bobby," Eddie said. "You got anything else of a personal nature about Gaspar? I'm thinking of writing a story about him."

"Why? He's dead."

"But you gotta admit, he was a colorful character."

Big Bobby shrugged his big shoulders. "Besides the cats...oh yeah, almost forgot, he owned a pet store. I think it was more like an investment. He didn't run it hisself. He set up some guy to run it. Probably bleeded the poor bastard dry."

"You know the name of the store?"

"Sorry, but it was around here someplace," he said, shaking his head and then grabbing the arm of a passing waiter. "What's taking so long with the food?"

Eddie said, "The guy who runs it, maybe he can tell me some Gaspar stories like you did. Got a name?"

"Nah, Gaspar didn't discuss the pet store a lot with me or the crew," Big Bobby said, and then he coughed up a quick laugh.

"What's so funny?" Eddie said.

"A couple times I heard him call the guy Frankenstein, on account of his face being all fucked up."

Eddie cocked his eyebrows in surprise. "Fucked up? How?"

"You know, like Frankenstein. He didn't go into any details."

"Anything you can tell me about Willie Stracci?"

"I don't talk about anybody that's alive."

"Where do you think Willie—"

"I said don't ask me anymore about him, hear me? And don't bring up the Knicks either. I hate those fuckers."

After lunch, out on Mulberry Street, Eddie thanked Big Bobby and hugged Moe goodbye. He then called the Tieri & Sons Funeral Home.

CHAPTER 46

WITHIN FIFTEEN MINUTES, Eddie was greeted by Gaspar's strawberry-blonde executive assistant.

"Thanks for seeing me, Margaret."

"My pleasure."

Unbuttoning his coat, Eddie said, "I suppose Gaspar will be waked here, huh?"

"Tomorrow night. He's got a nephew who appeared out of the blue. A doctor. Can you believe it? He's paying for everything."

"Are you gonna be okay?"

"I honestly don't know what will happen to this place. Guess it's in his will, and I'll have to wait and find out." Margaret Mary huffed a sigh, then said, "Let's go to my office, and we can talk."

Margaret Mary's office was small and tidy, and as they sat facing each other across a spare oak desk, Eddie said, "You know Gaspar's death was ruled a homicide, right?"

"I never thought it was a suicide, not for one second," she said. "Woman's intuition."

Eddie told Margaret Mary he'd learned that Gaspar was fond of cats, and that he either owned or invested in a pet shop. "What can you tell me about it?"

"I knew he had a cat, but I don't know anything about a pet shop. You're sure about that?"

"Absolutely. A very good source."

"Well, it's news to me. And anyway, I stuck to my knitting. My only concern was this funeral home. I didn't poke my nose into any of his affairs, business or otherwise. And if I had, believe me, he would've bit my head off."

"That's too bad, I was hoping..." Eddie paused, his brow pleated in thought, and then: "I heard that this pet shop is somewhere in the area. Still doesn't ring a bell?"

"Nope."

"Let's say he wanted to check out his investment in this pet shop. How would he get there?"

"He'd take a cab, I guess."

"The other night, when he went to the tiki bar, he took a hearse out front. I remember he smiled at me and said it was a free ride. He do that often, have one of his drivers take him places in a hearse?"

"Now and then, yes. He would use Skip Vigorita, a distant cousin of his. He always drives the lead hearse. Gaspar trusted him."

"Can you give me a phone number for him?"

"Of course," she said, and punched it up on her desktop computer. "We don't have a burial today, so he might be playing the ponies at Aqueduct. Want me to give it a try and call him for you?"

"Sure. And put in a good word for me, will you?"

Margaret Mary made the call and got Vigorita at his home in Queens. "I thought you'd be at Aquaduct." Having heard his response, she cupped the receiver and half whispered to Eddie, "He said he didn't go to the track today out of respect for Gaspar."

And then: "Listen, Skip, I'm sitting here with Eddie Sabella. Yes, exactly, that's him. He's a stand-up guy, and he'd like to talk to you. Here he is..."

Margaret Mary handed the phone to Eddie, who said, "Thanks for this, Skip."

"Don't mention it."

"I'm just curious," Eddie said, pulling out his notepad and grabbing a pen off Margaret Mary's desk. "Did you ever drive Gaspar to a pet shop?"

"Yeah, a few times. He loved animals. Especially cats."

"Do you by any chance remember the name of the pet shop?"

"I do, because Gaspar was proud he invented the name for it. Kat's

Kradle, with two *k*s, since the guy who managed it was named Kat with a *k*. He could be very clever like that."

"Where is it?"

"Lafayette Street. You could look up the exact number in the Yellow Pages."

"Did you ever meet this guy Kat with a *k*?"

"No, I always stayed in the coach."

"Coach?"

"Yeah, that's what us old-timers call a hearse."

"Oh, didn't know that. By the way, did he ever call Kat by another name, like a nickname?"

"I think Kat *was* his nickname. His real name was longer, like a Polish name."

"So he didn't call him anything but Kat, huh?"

"Like what?"

"Frankenstein."

"Why the hell would he call him that?"

Eddie checked out the Kat's Kradle website on Margaret's computer and noted the address. The owner was listed as Arnold Katcavage, but there weren't any photos of him anywhere on the site.

When Eddie got up to leave, he thanked Margaret, extending his hand.

"That's it, a handshake?" she said, squeezing Eddie's hand and tossing him that smile of hers, this one with a seductive sheen to it. "I'm not going to let go until you promise to take me to dinner. I've been a good help to you, haven't I?"

"Better than good, Margaret. More like fantastic. But I've got to be honest with you."

Eddie told her about Phyllis and how she'd suddenly come back into his life, and he was afraid of screwing up the relationship if he allowed himself the pleasure of dining with such an exceptionally wonderful and attractive woman. He laid it on a bit thick, but he was seriously grateful for her help.

At the funeral home's front door, Eddie said, "I wish you all the best of love and luck, Margaret."

"Back at you," Margaret said, and kissed his cheek. "Goodbye, Eddie."

Eddie walked from the funeral home to Kat's Kradle in a little under twelve minutes. When he entered the pet shop, he was promptly greeted by a cacophony of pet sounds—puppies yelping, kittens meowing, parakeets tweeting. At the shop's counter, he introduced himself to an elderly man of medium height with wavy gray hair and a slight paunch. His name was Calvin Maxwell, and he was wearing a gray cardigan sweater.

Eddie told him he was doing a column on pet shops in the area, which pleased Calvin, though he wasn't curious enough to ask about the angle.

"You're not the owner, are you?"

"Oh, no. I'm a retired accountant. I just fill in when I'm needed, gives me something to do. The owner is Arnold Katcavage. That's with a *k*." Calvin's eyes lit up. "Get it? That's why he spells Kat's Kradle like he does."

"That's really clever," Eddie said as sincerely as he could. "Is he around, by any chance?"

"Sorry, but he left town for a few days, said he wanted to visit his sister. He asked me to run the place."

"When did he leave?"

"Yesterday."

"Oh, I talked to him on Saturday," Eddie lied, "and he said he'd be here."

"It was all of a sudden. He called me this morning and asked me to come in and feed the animals, and if I wouldn't mind taking over for the week."

"Do you have any publicity photos of him?"

"Oh, no, we don't, nothing like that," Calvin said, and it seemed to Eddie that he'd answered a little too quickly and nervously.

"That's too bad," Eddie said. "Well, anyway, I'm sure he'd like to be included in my story. Do you know his sister's name and where she lives?"

"Her name is Stephanie, but I'm afraid I don't know her married name. She's got two small children. All I can tell you is that she lives in Bucks County, you know, in Pennsylvania."

"What about a phone number? He must've given you his sister's number in case of an emergency, or his mobile phone number. A business owner like him, he has one of those, right?"

Leaving the shop, Eddie pulled out his BlackBerry, and within seconds, Katcavage answered the call. Eddie identified himself as a rep for a Florida spa resort, figuring he'd lull Katcavage into answering a few harmless questions and then see what kind of reaction he got when he suddenly threw Gaspar Tieri's name into the conversation.

Katcavage, however, was having none of it. At the mention of the words "Florida spa resort," he said, "Fuck you," and hung up.

Eddie was certain he'd get the same reaction if he called Katcavage back and revealed his true identity. What's more, he'd likely spook Katcavage into believing that the cops were onto him as well, and if he really was at his sister's in Bucks County, he'd be long gone before anyone could get near him.

Back at the newspaper, Eddie huddled with Basic and Phoebe. "I don't see what choice you have, Eddie," Phoebe said. "And you know they'll be pissed off that you didn't tell them what you had."

"I didn't think I'd get this far so fast," Eddie said.

"Did it ever occur to you that you could be wrong about this Katcavage person?" Basic said.

Eddie shook his head. "My gut tells me I'm right as rain."

"Next time it might not be a good idea to withhold information from the police about a homicide," Basic said.

"Though I probably would've done the same thing," Phoebe said.

"Me too," Basic said to Phoebe, "but we shouldn't encourage him. Plausible deniability and all that."

"It's your own ass you're worried about, huh?" Eddie said to Basic.

"Call the cops," Basic said. "Like Phoebe said, you have no choice in the matter. I don't picture you hunting for the guy in the wilds of Bucks County."

Sitting at his desk, Eddie phoned the 13th Precinct. He was told that Detectives Cahn and Rodgers had gone home, and that they were on the 8:00 a.m. to 4:00 p.m. rotation for another day. He left a message.

CHAPTER 47

THE DINNER CROWD WAS thinning when Eddie arrived at Filomena's. As he checked his coat, Phyllis came up behind him, grabbed him around the waist, and kissed the back of his neck.

"I hope this is who I think it is," Eddie said, and then he turned to face her. "As long as we're slipping into public displays of affection...

Eddie kissed her full on her mouth, until she gently pushed him away. "First things first, Romeo. Dinner's waiting."

Phyllis had the kitchen prepare a meal that included *spaghetti con pomodoro* and veal piccata, accompanied by a 2005 Sagrantino di Montefalco, a robust red wine from Umbria. They ate hungrily.

"This was a wonderful meal," Eddie said, "but the portions were... they were actually like half portions."

"I figured the quicker we ate," Phyllis said, a bewitching gleam working its way into her eyes, "the quicker we'd get to my place."

"I like the way you think, Phyllis Arena," Eddie said, rising from his chair and extending a hand. "Let's go, time's a-wasting."

Phyllis's place was a two-bedroom condo with stunning views near Lincoln Center. It featured high ceilings, oversized windows, and a wood-burning fireplace with an intricately carved walnut mantel. The walls were painted to look like white marble, and the dark herringbone floors were polished to a fine gloss.

Eddie couldn't identify the pedigree of the high-end furniture and the fashion photography that graced the living and dining rooms, but anyone who entered Phyllis's apartment would peg the owner as a person of elegance and good taste.

"Pretty fancy digs," Eddie said.

As Phyllis hung their coats in the foyer closet, Eddie walked from the living room through the dining room and into the kitchen, where he opened the refrigerator door.

"Still hungry?" she said.

"Just wanted to see what a hotshot restaurateur has in her refrigerator."

Phyllis tugged at Eddie's sports jacket. "Follow me," she said.

The spacious master bedroom was decorated in muted tones of lilac and laurel green, which Eddie admired with a soft whistle moments before he and Phyllis tumbled onto a thickly upholstered chaise lounge. She landed on top of him. He kissed her, and with his fingertips, softly played her back like a piano.

"You still have that easy touch," she said.

"And you always liked it."

"But not tonight," she said, scraping her lips against his ear.

"Guess I'll have to up my game," he said, and then he lifted her off him and tangoed her to the king-size bed. He quickly started undressing while she watched with a smile that stopped him. "You smile like that at any man but me, and I'll—"

"Shut up and help me out of this, will you?" she said, unbuttoning her blouse.

————

The ringing of Eddie's cell phone woke him up at 9:10. The phone was on the carpeted floor near his side of the bed, and he couldn't answer the call before it went to voice mail. He guessed it must've fallen out of his jacket pocket when he took it off in a lust-crazed frenzy to get at Phyllis. Where was she?

The thought had barely escaped his brain when Phyllis appeared with a tray that held two mugs of coffee, along with a creamer and a bowl of sugar. She was wearing gym shorts and a tank top, and Eddie couldn't take his eyes off of her.

"Stop ogling me," she said. "I look like a mess."

"A fine mess I'd like to get into," Eddie said.

"Slow down, cowboy. I've got a meeting at the restaurant in another hour. But I'd like to know if you've got a plan for tonight."

"I certainly do," Eddie said, reaching out and slipping his hand halfway down the front of her shorts. "But why wait?"

Phyllis's loud laugh had a bawdy pitch to it. "You can knock, but you can't come in," she said, and pulled Eddie's hand away.

While she was taking a shower, Eddie checked the message on his phone. It was Detective Cahn, returning Eddie's call from yesterday. Eddie called him back, and he arranged to meet Cahn and his partner, Rodgers, for lunch at a coffee shop within a couple blocks of the precinct.

———

"One more time, Sabella," Cahn said, putting down his turkey sandwich. "You think Tieri stole the statue—"

"Not personally."

"Yeah, I get that," Cahn said. "And the guy who pitched him off his balcony is the same guy who returned the statue to the church."

"Look, both guys were around six feet, husky, and wore a ski jacket and a black baseball cap pulled down over their foreheads."

"And we had a couple of people who saw somebody like that leaving the building right after Tieri got tossed," Rodgers said. "Apparently he was carrying what looked like a large package."

"You think Sabella's onto something here?" Cahn asked Rodgers.

"Yes," Rodgers said, digging into his omelet.

"Guess we'll have to talk to the priest too," Cahn said. "Like I said, he insists he didn't get a good look at the guy."

Rodgers pointed a fork at Eddie's plate. "You haven't touched your sandwich."

"I will, but first I gotta come clean about something."

Both detectives stopped eating and stared at Eddie, who said, "I think I know where the guy is, the guy who killed Tieri. Can we make a deal for the information?"

"Just one minute," Cahn said. "What makes you think you know who the guy is, and what makes you think you know where he is?"

"I'll tell you, and you can decide for yourself. But first, do we have a deal?"

WHERE HAVE YOU GONE WITHOUT ME?

"Depends on what you got," Cahn said, and then looked at his partner.

"Okay by me," Rodgers said. "What do you want?"

"You catch this guy, and if he's the guy I think he is, you tell me first. I get the exclusive. And I get an interview, if you can arrange it."

"We can't promise to deliver an interview," Cahn said, "but we have no problem handing you the story if things pan out."

Eddie told them about the doorman's tip and how he'd caught a break with information from a reliable source that eventually led him to a disfigured man named Arnold Katcavage. Tieri had bankrolled Katcavage in a pet shop called Kat's Kradle on Lafayette Street. "That's with two *k*s," Eddie said.

"What's with two *k*s?" Rodgers said.

"Kat's Kradle. The pet shop. I checked it out, and I was told Katcavage suddenly decided to visit his sister in Bucks County. Maybe he did, maybe not. But I got his cell number, and you're welcome to it."

"This is fucking rich, Sabella," Cahn said in an agitated voice. "The doorman gives you a vital piece of information, and what? You don't tell us? Didn't your mother ever teach you to share, especially with cops?"

"I thought the doorman would tell you," Eddie lied.

"Oh, sure," Rodgers said, "and could be you told him to keep it to himself."

Eddie held up his right hand. "No, not true, hand to God."

"But I bet you were praying he'd forget to tell us," Rodgers said.

"I'll cop to that," Eddie said with a cocky grin. "No pun intended."

CHAPTER 48

THE DETECTIVES HAD DEVISED a simple scheme to lure Katcavage into returning to New York. They instructed the Kat's Kradle's temporary proprietor, the grandfatherly ex-accountant Calvin Maxwell, to call Katcavage on his cell phone and tell him he had an emergency on his hands: he needed to leave the shop for several days to attend the funeral of a dear friend in Boston, and he didn't have anyone to fill in for him and feed the animals while he was away. No, Maxwell assured him, nobody had come around asking questions and looking for him.

Katcavage, it turned out, was indeed at his sister's home in Pennsylvania, and when he walked into his store the next day, Cahn and Rodgers were there to question him. He was arrested and booked, and the detectives told Eddie that Katcavage never asked for a lawyer as he calmly coughed up a confession. Less than twenty-four hours later, with a court-appointed lawyer at his side, Katcavage was arraigned and charged with second-degree murder. Thanks to Cahn and Rodgers having kept their part of the bargain, Eddie got a jump on every other reporter in town and scored an exclusive. He then contacted Katcavage's lawyer the day after the arraignment, and two days after that, secured an interview with Katcavage at the Riker's Island Correctional Center.

The interview done before noon, Eddie took a cab back to the paper, calling Father Keller on the way.

"Now I know why there was that forty-minute gap between the time Katcavage returned the statue and you left me a message at my office. You were hearing his confession."

Father Keller paused before saying, "No comment."

"That's what Katcavage just told me, that you heard his confession. Was he blowing smoke up my ass?"

"No, nothing like that. He asked me to hear his confession, and I obliged. And that's all I intend to say on the matter."

"You could've told me, Father. I didn't ask you to violate the Seal of Confession and tell me what he confessed."

"According to canon law, my young friend, I can't even acknowledge that someone had made a confession, let alone reveal what was said. But since Katcavage told you I heard his confession, I won't deny it."

Over the next hour or so, Eddie transcribed Katcavage's interview off the digital voice recorder he'd used. He wrote the last sentence of his story around five o'clock, and a few minutes later was sitting next to Basic, who was poised over the keyboard of his computer, ready to edit.

The two men pored over the story line by line. Basic got Eddie's approval for almost every edit and trim he made. Meanwhile, Phoebe had tapped out the front-page headline, and Basic approved it. All three were elated by the story:

EXCLUSIVE: PET SHOP OWNER TELLS WHY HE MURDERED MOBSTER
Thief Who Stole St. Joe Statue Tossed Mafioso Off Condo Terrace Over Personal Insult

Arnold (Kat) Katcavage isn't easy on the eyes.

As a teenager, he lost most of the cartilage in his nose in a vicious street fight with a Latino gangbanger who had accused him of disrespecting his mother at the Food Emporium in Hell's Kitchen, where he bagged groceries after school. The next day, the same gangbanger wanted another piece of Katcavage and attacked him with a wood-handled steak knife. He took a chunk out of Katcavage's chin and his left earlobe, tattooing him with an angry, three-inch scar along his brow, just beneath a crown of close-cropped, blondish hair.

His mother told him to quit, that no job was worth losing your face piece by piece. She didn't have to tell him twice.

"My mother was the best, the all-time best," Katcavage said. "I'm glad she isn't alive to see me like this."

He was referring to the gray jumpsuit he wore as an inmate in the Riker's Island Correctional Center, having been charged with second-degree murder for tossing Gaspar Tieri, 75, a wise guy of some repute in the Vitale crime family, off the terrace of his Second Avenue condo.

Katcavage sat at a table opposite me in a cold and drab interview room. His young, court-appointed lawyer, Nathaniel Mason, sat next to his client.

Mason had strenuously objected to the interview, as his client had not yet been formally indicted. He may have graduated from Yale Law School, but he was no match for this pit bull of a pet shop owner.

"It's my ass, not yours," Katcavage snarled in a succinct explanation to Mason regarding his decision to talk to me.

Mason was able to get in a few shots of his own, though. He would have to be present when the interview was conducted, of course, and the interview could last no more than twenty minutes. Why Mason had settled on twenty minutes, he wouldn't say, but the interview spilled over a few minutes longer than that.

The moment I turned on my small digital voice recorder, Katcavage said, "Look, one thing you should know right off the bat. I didn't want to kill Gaspar. I just snapped. I'm a thief, not a murderer. Gaspar used to say that if someone paid me enough, I'd try to steal a steak off the devil's plate."

Now 38, Katcavage says he was Tieri's go-to guy when the gangster wanted to outsource a job for purely personal gain, a job that didn't compromise the Vitale family's more vital business interests. Jobs like heisting furs, rugs, silverware, copper pipes.

"You name it, I took it. I even stole a rare book once—the one about Scrooge. Sometimes I had help, most times I worked alone. Gaspar always had people that were looking for a bargain, and I was always looking for some extra pocket money. We got along good for almost ten years. I was efficient, and a clean deal. No arrests on record. He liked that."

Katcavage paused, taking a deep breath. "A friggin' shame this happened. Gaspar was better to me than my old man. When I told him about the time he slapped me when I was a kid because I kept asking him for a dog, Gaspar felt bad for me. He loved animals too, especially cats.

"Always had one, from the time he was a kid. We shared that in common, loving animals. So he bankrolled me in my pet shop, even came up with the name—Kat's Kradle. He was one smart dude."

Nick Arena would disagree with Katcavage. He didn't think Tieri was so smart. He thought Tieri was a vicious thug who needed to hurt people "like you and I need to breathe."

Arena is the owner of two popular restaurants in Manhattan—Nonna's and Filomena's. (Full disclosure: His daughter, Phyllis, and I are best friends.) Back in the day, Arena crossed paths with Tieri when both worked for the eye-patched mafia kingpin Giovanni "Long John" Vitale. Arena managed bakeries for the Don, while Tieri made his bones in much riskier enterprises, like murder and armed robbery.

When they were young men, the two had a falling out of a very personal nature. A woman was involved. She had dumped Tieri and hooked up with Arena. Then Arena split from her, and she ended up dying of a drug overdose. Tieri blamed Arena for her death.

Tieri's hatred of Arena deepened when Vitale rewarded Arena by bankrolling him in Nonna's. This did not sit well with Tieri, mainly because Vitale later ordered him to operate a funeral parlor on Sullivan Street that the Don had acquired in an extremely hostile takeover. After all, Tieri had been a loyal soldier, and he quietly considered the funereal assignment a betrayal.

"Screw your friends first," a still-bitter Tieri told me, "they're the easiest."

And so, many, many years later, a statue of St. Joseph was stolen from St. Joseph's Church on the Upper East Side of Manhattan. It was an ancient statue of painted wood that Arena had brought to America for his mother and in remembrance of his father, Giuseppe, as St. Joseph was the old man's patron saint.

If you're a reader of this column, you know that the statue was originally taken from the church by a teenager, who brought it home for his grandmother to pray to. She is dying of cancer. (No charges were brought against them.)

We know now that the man who stole the statue from the grandmother's apartment was Katcavage—and the man who set the theft in motion was Tieri.

I believe Tieri wanted to hurt Arena for the personal reasons noted above. He was convinced he was dying of lung cancer, and time was running out to exact his revenge. He had come to know how much the statue meant to Arena, and he wanted to hurt Arena by destroying the statue piece by piece. Sound crazy? Yes, but it also sounds very Sicilian. As Arena once told me, "Revenge is not always achieved with piles of corpses and rivers of blood."

(The police are also looking to question Willie Stracci, a reputed mobster in the Vitale crime family and Tieri pal, and a Stracci employee named Buster Bustamante, in connection with the theft.)

"For the record, do you know either Willie Stracci or Buster Bustamante?"

"Like I told the cops, never heard of them."

"And you've refused to name the person who helped you steal the statue."

"I'm no rat."

"But you're spilling what you know about Tieri."

"He's dead. It don't matter."

"How much did Gaspar pay you to get him the statue?"

"Fifteen hundred."

"Did he tell you why he wanted you to steal it?"

"No, I never asked him why he wanted me to do something."

"The big question now, Arnold. Why did you kill Tieri?"

The lawyer Mason cut in. "I'd prefer you didn't answer that."

Katcavage gave Mason a hard stare for a few fat seconds, and then he said, "I want to."

He turned to me again and rotated his head like he had a stiff neck. He seemed to be gathering his thoughts as he rubbed his mutilated chin, his eyes darting this way and that.

Finally: "When I read your story in the paper about that restaurant guy offering a $25,000 reward…well, I figured Gaspar had shortchanged me. Taking that statue was a bigger deal than he let on, paying me only $1,500 and all. It really started to bother me, you know. So I go to see Gaspar. I told him I thought he suckered me, and he should maybe throw in a little more cash."

"I guess Tieri didn't agree with you."

"He was insulting. He said a deal was a deal, and then he called me a lot of disgusting names you can't even print in your newspaper. But that wasn't the worst of it, far as I was concerned."

Katcavage went silent, and Mason chimed in, "I think we're done here."

I pressed Katcavage. "What was worse, Arnold? Come on, get it off your chest."

"He...he...Jesus Christ, it was...I say to him, 'Okay, then, you don't want to give me any more money. I accept that. But how's about you use your juice and get me into the family. I'd be a good earner, and you know I'm reliable.'

"Gaspar just laughs at me. Laughs right in my face and keeps laughing. I say, 'Stop laughing, Gaspar. What's so funny?' And he says, 'You friggin' moron. First of all, you're not Italian, and second, you're too friggin' ugly. We don't allow people in who look like friggin' Frankenstein.'"

"That must've hurt."

"What the hell do you think? When he dissed me like...well, like I said, I snapped."

"Then what happened?"

"I punched him in the face. He went down, and then he got up and came after me. A tough old bird. I don't remember much after that, except I picked him up and threw him off his balcony."

"He must've put up a hell of a fight."

"From what I remember, he was squirming and screaming, but I was a lot bigger and stronger than him."

"What about the statue? Where'd you find it?"

"It was right there in his living room, standing in a corner. I didn't see it until I was leaving."

"Why'd you take it, and why'd you return it to the church?"

"It was a spur-of-the-moment kind of thing," Katcavage said, shaking his head and twisting his lips together. "Maybe I was thinking I'd get the reward for myself. I don't know. Anyway, I found a suit bag in Gaspar's closet near the door, and I put the statue in it."

"And you went down to the lobby and walked out the front door without any problem, because everybody was looking at Gaspar on top of the car. Am I right?"

"That's right," Katcavage said. "And I was able to flag a cab, no problem. So I go to my apartment—"

"Where's that?"

"Over on East Thirty-Eighth. It's a walkup. I put the thing on the table in my living room, and take the statue out. And the face is wet—"

"What? What do you mean, it's wet?"

"It's wet. The face is wet, like it was crying, and it freaked me out."

"Was it still crying?"

"I don't think so, but so what? It was a sign from God—you know what I'm saying? Right away I put the statue back in the bag, and I hightail it to the priest's house."

"Did you tell Father Keller that you thought the statue had cried?"

"Sure, but when he took the statue from the bag, the face was dry. He said, 'I guess you were mistaken.' Well, I wasn't gonna argue with him. Doesn't get you anywhere arguing with a priest."

Mason stood up and knocked twice on the table. "That's it, Sabella. We're over the time limit we agreed to, and I'm sure you've got more than enough."

Katcavage wasn't so sure. He had something more he wanted to say.

"Your readers should know I'm not a bad person. When I returned the statue, I told the priest I was raised a Catholic, being Polish and all, and asked him if he could hear my confession. He said sure, and I told him about killing Gaspar. I said I didn't mean to do it, told him I was real sorry, and he forgave me."

"Where did he hear your confession? In the rectory?"

Katcavage nodded. "Yeah, right there, in his office, and he told me I should give myself up. I said I'd think about it, and I asked him if I didn't, would I still be forgiven. He said yes, as long as I was truly sorry for my sins. Which made me feel good, because I hadn't been to confession in a long time, and I needed to get that mortal sin off my soul. It was the biggest sin I ever committed. If I died without confessing what I did to Gaspar…oh, man, not good. It's watch out, fire down below!"

Father Arthur Keller, the pastor of St. Joseph's Church, confirmed Katcavage's account of the night he returned the statue. "He asked me to hear his confession, and I obliged. And that's all I intend to say on the matter."

Katcavage will be indicted in a few more days, and then plans to plead guilty at his first court appearance after the indictment. Veteran court observers tell me he's looking at a long sentence—"double digits," is how they put it.

As for Gaspar Tieri, he was waked at his own funeral home and then buried in Calvary Cemetery in Queens, next to his wife and a daughter who died young of leukemia.

"He once told me that when she died," Katcavage said, "he didn't give much of a damn about anything anymore."

"This makes me very happy," Basic said, leaning back in his chair. "But may I remind you this is a newspaper, not a magazine. I know how you are—don't start busting my chops about writing another two thousand-word epic anytime soon."

"What's a few thousand words between friends?" Eddie said cheerily. "Come on, cocktails are on me, and I'll tell you about the Gaspar Tieri epic I'd like to write. A terrific story, I promise. You'll be proud as hell when I get the Pulitzer."

Basic stood to face Eddie. He placed his hands on his columnist's shoulders, and in a voice dripping with faux concern, said, "Eddie, sounds to me like you need a vacation."

CHAPTER 49

EDDIE WAS SIPPING A SCOTCH on the rocks as he waited for Phyllis to finish dressing when his BlackBerry rang. "Hey, Eddie, it's me."

"What's up, Basic?"

"I thought you should know we're doing a story about the statue up at St. Joe's. It cried for about four minutes late this morning."

"This is a joke, right?"

"No joke. The handyman saw it first, and there were a few other people in the church at the time, and they saw it too. I had Murphy cover it."

"What did Father Keller have to say about it?"

"He couldn't explain it. He called here looking for you..."

"You know, Basic, Father Keller once indicated to me he wasn't absolutely positive there *was* a leak in the ceiling the last time this happened. He said it was bone-dry when his handyman checked it out."

"Same thing this morning. Murphy said the area above the statue was dry to the touch when the handyman got up there to see for himself."

"You said it stopped crying, right?"

"Yes, it did. Damnedest thing, though, huh? We'll have to keep on top of it. But listen, Eddie, I've got no problem handing off the story to you if you can get your ass in gear."

"Not funny, Basic. You're the one who insisted I needed some time off."

"I know, I know. What're you up to, anyway?"

"Taking my best girl out to dinner," Eddie said, catching sight of Phyllis out of the corner of his eye. "Gotta run, Basic. And I wouldn't mind some updated reports about the statue."

"I figured you would," Basic said, chuckling.

Phyllis leaned down and kissed Eddie on his forehead. "Who was on the phone?"

"Basic…I'll tell you about it at dinner. Ready to roll?"

"I didn't come here to quit eating."

"Then let's not waste another second," Eddie said, standing and grabbing Phyllis's hand, then guiding her through the Raphael's lobby door. "We're gonna walk the length of the Piazza Navona and head toward the Campo de' Fiori. When we get there, we make a left at the Via dei Giubbonari, and down the block is a trattoria my father recommended, called Roscioli. And after dinner, we'll…"

THE END

ACKNOWLEDGMENTS

Like the countless winners I've seen at shows where Oscars and Emmys and Grammys are awarded, I fear I may forget someone who deserves at least some measure of thanks for cheering me on to the finish line. But here goes:

It is very likely that my great good fortune in teaming up with Turner Publishing would never have happened without the unflagging encouragement of Joseph Olshan, a critically acclaimed novelist and the Executive Editor of Delphinium Books. Full disclosure: I'm married to Joe's sister Donna, but I am firm in the conviction that he believed in my novel on its own terms. Right, Joe?

I must also give a shout-out to Raffaela Belizaire, my brilliant niece who is an Assistant District Attorney in Manhattan, New York. Time and again she patiently answered my many questions about police and criminal court procedures in clear and elegantly composed emails.

As you embark on writing your first novel, it's a marvelous advantage to have generous friends who will read your work-in-progress when you ask and lend their support. Friends like Jim Gaines, Betsy Carter, Neil Leifer, Maggie Murphy, Joe Basirico, Pam Sztybel, Jim Calio, Diane Shah and Jim Murphy. Bless them all.

And kudos to the talented people at Turner Publishing who gave me and my novel such gracious help: Executive Editor Stephanie Beard, Managing Editor Heather Howell, Cover Designer M.S. Corley, Marketing Manager Lauren Ash, Editor? Lauren Smulski, etc, etc, etcOne more hurrah: A raised glass to two late, great city columnists, Jimmy Breslin and Pete Hamill. New York is not the same without them.